WINNER AND LOSER

I looked back in the ring. The judge was making her cut. The Bulldog was on top, followed by Tar, then a Shiba Inu. When Mrs. Koenig pointed to Tar for second place, Davey and I whooped and hollered like tourists who'd never been to a dog show before. Surprised by all the commotion, Sam cast a startled glance our way and grinned.

Clutching the big ribbon, he headed for the gate. Davey and I made our way through the crowd to meet him. Unexpectedly, Brian Endicott was standing beside him.

Even from a dozen feet away, I knew something was wrong. Sam had gone absolutely still; his face was white. Brian looked as though he might be sick. Tar's leash dangled limply from Sam's hand. The puppy, sensing his owner's distress, stopped playing and looked up questioningly.

Dropping Davey's hand, I ran on ahead. "What?" I demanded. "What's happened?"

Brian swallowed heavily. Words seemed beyond him. I looked at Sam.

"Brian just heard," he said, "Sheila is dead. She was murdered last night. . . ."

Books by Laurien Berenson

A PEDIGREE TO DIE FOR

UNDERDOG

DOG EAT DOG

HAIR OF THE DOG

WATCHDOG

HUSH PUPPY

UNLEASHED

ONCE BITTEN

HOT DOG

BEST IN SHOW

JINGLE BELL BARK

RAINING CATS AND DOGS

CHOW DOWN

HOUNDED TO DEATH

DOGGIE DAY CARE MURDER

GONE WITH THE WOOF

DEATH OF A DOG WHISPERER

THE BARK BEFORE CHRISTMAS

LIVE AND LET GROWL

MURDER AT THE PUPPY FEST

Published by Kensington Publishing Corporation

UNLEASHED

A MELANIE TRAVIS MYSTERY

Laurien Berenson

KENSINGTON BOOKS
KENSINGTON PUBLISHING CORP.
http://www.kensingtonbooks.com

KENSINGTON BOOKS are published by

Kensington Publishing Corp.
119 West 40th Street
New York, NY 10018

All Kensington titles, imprints, and distributed lines are available at special quantity discounts for bulk purchases for sales promotion, premiums, fund-raising, educational, or institutional use. Special book excerpts or customized printings can also be created to fit specific needs. For details, write or phone the office of the Kensington Special Sales Manager: Attn. Special Sales Department. Kensington Publishing Corp., 119 West 40th Street, New York, NY 10018. Phone: 1-800-221-2647.

Kensington and the K logo Reg. U.S. Pat. & TM Off.

ISBN-13: 978-1-4967-1512-8
ISBN-10: 1-4967-1512-8
First Kensington Hardcover Edition: September 2000
First Kensington Mass Market Edition: August 2001

eISBN-13: 978-0-7582-8447-1
eISBN-10: 0-7582-8447-0

10 9 8 7 6 5 4

Printed in the United States of America

ACKNOWLEDGMENTS

Many people, far more expert in their fields than I, have helped with the creation of this book, and I am deeply grateful for their assistance. I would like to thank:

Patrick and Pippi Guilfoyle, for all the great stories,

Peggy Jay, who knows more about real estate than anyone else I know,

Vicki Ivar, DVM, who supplied just the right fact at just the right time,

Skip Chard and Bruce Emond, who made sure I didn't make up the insurance parts.

And, as always, thank you to my husband, Bruce. I couldn't do any of it without you.

One

Run, I thought. Run like the wind.

Instead I heard myself say, "Sure, Sheila, that sounds like fun."

About as much fun as knee surgery.

"Wonderful." Sheila's low, husky voice flowed through the phone line. "I'm so glad you can come. Brian and I will look forward to it."

"Sam and I will, too."

Liar, I thought as I hung up the phone. Idiot.

I don't often call myself names, but in this case it was justified. Though Sam Driver is my fiancé, I don't usually accept social engagements on his behalf without checking with him first. Especially not when they've been extended by his ex-wife.

Sheila Vaughn is a relatively new wrinkle in my otherwise placid life. Not that there haven't been other wrinkles, mind you, just that this one tended to be more annoying than most. I was supposed to be planning a wedding—mine—but both Sam and I had been so busy, we hadn't exactly gotten around to setting a date yet.

Meanwhile, Sheila had shown up in March for what was supposed to be a three-month stint in the Northeast. Now it was mid-July. That made four months and counting, by my calendar.

On the other hand, just the fact that it was summer meant that I had cause for celebration. I'm a teacher, so June, July, and August are, hands down, my favorite months. I'd spent the last year working as a special needs tutor at Howard Academy, a private school in Greenwich, Connecticut. The transition from the public school system to the private sector had been rocky at times, and I was delighted to have two successful semesters behind me.

Also thrilled by the fact that it was summer, was my six-year-old son Davey. He was enrolled in soccer camp, a move recommended by my ex-husband, who lived halfway across the country with his new wife. Since I'd been a single parent for most of Davey's life, I resent it like crazy when Bob comes up with good ideas like that.

I wasn't about to tell him, but Davey was thriving at camp. Not only that, but he and his best friend, Joey Brickman, had convinced half the kids in the neighborhood to sign up, too, which meant I only had to drive the car pool twice a week. For once, it was looking like I mostly had things under control.

If you didn't count that fact that our Standard Poodle, Faith, was seven weeks pregnant with her first litter of puppies.

Or that Sheila Vaughn seemed determined to remain a part of Sam's and my lives. I hadn't heard a word from her or about her in more than a month, until that unexpected phone call. With warning, I might have come up with a good excuse. Or even a bad one. Anything would have been better than what I'd done: mutter and mumble, then blurt out, "Sure."

Just a casual dinner at her house in North Salem, Sheila had said. Don't dress up. No need to bring a thing.

It all sounded so simple. There had to be a catch. In my life, there was always a catch.

I wondered what it would be this time.

"Tell me again who the other guy is," Sam said.

He'd arrived at my house, looking casually gorgeous in a faded polo shirt, pressed khakis, and sockless topsiders. Judging by the warm glow of his skin, the white-blond highlights in his tousled hair, or the way the squint lines framed his deep blue eyes, one might have guessed he'd spent the warm, summer day sailing on Long Island Sound.

Looks can be deceiving though. Not only did Sam not own a boat, but as far as I knew, he was a pretty inept sailor. What he was good at was designing software systems for the legion of clients who hired him to make their networks user-friendly. No doubt he'd actually spent the day squinting at his computer screen and raking his fingers impatiently through that rumpled hair.

By the time he arrived to pick me up at six o'clock, I'd already delivered Davey to Joey Brickman's house, where my son was going to be spending the night. Faith was home, though. As always, she greeted Sam like a member of the family, planting her front paws on his chest and dancing delightedly around him on her toes.

Faith is a Standard Poodle, the largest of the three varieties. She has thick, black hair which, since she's taking some time off from the show ring, is currently in a modified continental trim. Her dark, expressive eyes reveal volumes about her intelligence and empathy; and her tail, which she carries straight up in the air, is always wagging.

When I was seven months pregnant, I'd looked like I was wearing a barrel. Impending motherhood hadn't cramped Faith's style, however. With two weeks left to go in the nine-week gestation, she looked thicker through the middle but was otherwise unchanged. Certainly her love of life hadn't diminished one bit.

And right now, she had her legs wrapped around the sexiest man I knew. Lucky dog.

"Sheila mentioned his name," I said in answer to Sam's question. Frowning, I tried to remember. "Ryan, maybe? She said he's her new business partner. Kind of implied he's her new boyfriend, too."

"If they're in business together, she must be working with him on the magazine."

"What magazine?"

"It's called *Woof!*, and it's a new start-up. The first issue should be out any day now. I'm surprised you didn't get a flyer asking you to subscribe. I got one about a month ago."

"I may have," I admitted. "Things get so hectic at the end of the school year that I tend to throw out anything that even resembles junk mail. I probably tossed it."

While we were talking, I'd gathered up my cotton cardigan and the bottle of chilled Pouilly-Fuisse I had waiting by the door. Faith got a large Milk-Bone, a scratch under the chin, and the reassurance that we would be back before it was too late, then we were on our way.

Sam's Blazer was sitting behind my station wagon in the driveway. The skirt I'd worn was teal linen, short enough and tight enough that in order to get into the SUV,

I was going to have to turn my back to the seat and hop up into place.

Sam opened the car door, saw my dilemma, and reached around to help. He fitted his hands to either side of my waist and lifted. Easily, I landed on the seat.

"Thanks," I said, sliding my bare calf up the side of his leg. "I'm glad you noticed."

"With that much leg exposed?" His fingers drifted down onto my thigh, and I heard the smile in his voice. "Only a blind man wouldn't notice. You don't have to compete with her, you know."

"Her, who? Sheila?" I sat up straight and spun around to face forward.

Looking thoughtful, Sam closed the car door. He waited until he was behind the wheel and the car was moving before speaking again. "You're the one who accepted this invitation. I thought you wanted to go."

"She caught me by surprise," I admitted grumpily. "Saying all sorts of things about how we should let bygones be bygones. That now that she understands how things are between you and me, she just wants us all to be friends."

"Friends." The word seemed to stick in Sam's throat.

Four months earlier, I'd have felt a pinch of jealousy, but I'm getting much better about things like that. Plus, recently I'd had my Aunt Peg running interference and keeping Sheila, for the most part, out of Sam's and my way. Which was a huge relief considering that the woman had spent the first part of her East Coast sojourn trying to entice Sam back to her side.

It was only one dinner, I told myself. One evening out of my life. So how bad could it be?

It never hurts to be forewarned, however, and I decided

to catch up on what Sheila had been doing since the last time Sam and I had spoken about her.

"Tell me about the new magazine," I said, as Sam pulled out onto High Ridge Road and headed north toward New York. "I thought Sheila worked in marketing. Didn't she come to New York on a temporary assignment for her job?"

"That was the original plan. But once she got here and began going to dog shows, she met a whole different crowd of exhibitors than she'd known in the Midwest."

Dogs are the one thing we all have in common. Thanks to my Aunt Peg, whose line of Cedar Crest Standard Poodles is renowned throughout the dog show world for their beauty and fine temperament, I'd been introduced two years earlier to the sport of dogs. Faith was one of Peg's Poodles, of course—a gift whose presence had enhanced every facet of Davey's and my lives.

Sam was a Standard Poodle breeder as well, though on a smaller scale than Aunt Peg. His ex-wife, Sheila, bred Pugs; and five of them had accompanied her East.

If this evening ran true to form, we'd probably spend the majority of our time discussing nothing but our canine companions. Considering the other options, it wasn't an all-bad prospect.

"I'm somewhat sketchy on the details of how it all came about," said Sam.

He slid a glance my way. When Sheila'd first arrived I'd been a little sensitive about the amount of time he'd spent talking to her on the phone, or running to make repairs every time a faucet leaked or a fence broke in the older home she'd rented. All right, a lot sensitive.

But at the time, the fact that Sheila existed at all had just come as a rude shock. On top of that, she hadn't made any secret of her intentions. Sheila wanted Sam back, and didn't care who she had to push out of the way to get him.

You can see why she might have taken some getting used to.

Eventually Sheila had gotten the point and things had finally begun to settle down. Supposedly, this dinner was her way of making amends. Call me a cynic, but I was still reserving judgment.

"All I know is that Sheila got hooked up with someone who was looking to start up another dog show magazine. She looked at the prospectus and thought they could make it fly."

"There are already plenty of show magazines out there," I said, ticking off a few on my fingers. "*Dogs in Review, Canine Chronicle, Dog News.* Why would anyone think there's a need, or a market, for another?"

"Apparently, *Woof!* is going to be different." Sam grimaced slightly. "Most of what I know about it, I read in the flyer. It looks like it's aiming to be pretty sensational. The pitch promises subscribers 'all the news, all the gossip, all the dirt, you won't find anywhere else.'"

"Kind of like the *National Enquirer?*" I asked, grinning. Sheila the muckraker. What a copacetic arrangement.

"Something like that."

"And she quit her other job to get involved with this?"

"Apparently so. Sheila seemed to think it was an excellent opportunity."

"What do you think?"

"That the whole thing is none of my business," Sam said firmly. "Sheila's an intelligent woman who's more than capable of making her own decisions. It's probably not the path I would have chosen, but I'm in no position to say what might be right or wrong for her."

Well, I thought, he could talk the talk. It remained to be seen whether or not he would hold to that resolve.

The drive through North Stamford and up into lower Westchester County wound through a succession of narrow country roads flanked on either side by beautiful older homes and lavishly maintained estates. Part of me enjoyed the view. The other part—that small, petty, portion of my personality that I obviously hadn't worked hard enough to quash—noted that Sam navigated the tricky course with the total assurance of someone who'd driven it plenty of times before.

When we got to Sheila's house, it wasn't what I'd expected. Sam had described the home as somewhat dilapidated, hence the need for his frequent repairs; a rental that Sheila had taken, in large part, because the owner had not objected to her five dogs. What Sam had neglected to mention, however, was that the property was truly charming.

The small house was set back off the road, at the end of a rutted dirt driveway. A large lawn wrapped around three sides of the house. Thick woods beyond it obscured the neighbors. Birds were singing in a lush maple tree that grew by the front door. As we parked at the end of the driveway, a cherry red male cardinal swooped down and landed on a bird feeder beside the porch.

"It's lovely," I said, opening my door and breathing in the moist, evening air.

"It needs paint," Sam said absently. He was staring at a car that was parked by the small shed that served as a detached garage.

It was a black Porsche Boxster; a car designed, as far

as I could tell, for the express purpose of making grown men drool. In an instant, the rest of the evening flashed before my eyes: the two men out here, beers in hand, heads poked under the hood, comparing notes on such endlessly fascinating topics as wind resistance and turbo-charged engines, while Sheila and I hovered in the background and chatted like a pair of sorority sisters. Yuck.

I walked around the Blazer and linked my arm through Sam's. He was still staring.

"Maybe he'll let you drive it, if you ask nicely enough."

"It's not that."

"What then?"

"Probably nothing." Sam shook his head slightly. "For a moment, I thought—"

As we stepped up onto the porch, a chorus of canine voices sounded from within the house. The Pugs were heralding our arrival. Before we could knock, the door opened.

Sheila had a glass of red wine in one hand and a dazzling smile on her perfectly outlined lips. Her filmy sundress looked more like a slip than outerwear, and her ivory skin glowed in the light of a dozen candles that flickered in her front hall.

"Sam, Melanie, I'm so glad you could make it. Come on in. Let me introduce everyone. Brian, where are you?"

"Right behind you." He walked through the archway from the living room and placed his palms on Sheila's naked shoulders.

He looked tall standing behind her, but then, Sheila was tiny. Still, it was hard not to notice the possessiveness implicit in his gesture. Both of them had dark hair, Sheila's, straight and shiny, swinging in a long fringe to just above her collarbone. Brian's hair grew in thick, tight curls and was complemented by a thick mustache that obscured his upper lip.

His eyes were dark, too. Piercingly so, I noted as they flickered past me and came to rest on Sam. His brow lowered slightly as he smiled, showing white, even teeth. The expression looked more like a feral grin than a welcoming gesture.

"Melanie, I'd like you to meet Brian Endicott."

Automatically, I stuck out a hand. Brian followed suit.

"Sam?" Sheila paused. For just the briefest moment, she looked uncertain, then her smile returned. "You remember Brian, don't you?"

"Yes," said Sam. It sounded as though he was speaking through clenched teeth.

"Driver." Brian nodded tersely.

I guessed this meant I didn't have to worry about them bonding over the Boxster.

"Won't this be fun?" Sheila said brightly. "Just like old times; well, except for Melanie, of course. But don't worry, dear, we'll get you caught up in no time."

For a fleeting moment, I wondered if I should just make my life easier and run right then. Unfortunately, good manners, drummed in since birth, asserted themselves. I plastered a smile on my face, took Sam's cold hand in mine, and followed Sheila inside.

⌐◦❋ *Two* ❋ ◦⌐

"What's going on?" I whispered, crowding close to Sam as we found seats on a chintz-slipcovered love seat.

Sheila had gone to the kitchen to fetch drinks. Brian was gazing out a picture window that overlooked the backyard. I wondered why both men seemed to feel the need to place the length of a room between them.

"Nothing good," Sam muttered, as Brian turned to face us.

"You're not afraid of big dogs, are you, Melanie?" he asked.

"No, of course not." I wondered what that had to do with anything. "I have a Standard Poodle at home."

"I should have guessed. One of Sam's?"

"No, I got Faith from my Aunt Peg. Margaret Turnbull, Cedar Crest Standard Poodles?"

"You're related to Margaret Turnbull?" Brian sounded impressed. "Sheila didn't mention that."

"Didn't mention what?"

Sheila reentered the room carrying a small tray with drinks and a platter of cheese and crackers. Quickly both men moved to help her. Sam was closer. Was I imagining things or did he look vaguely triumphant as he lifted the platter from her tray and set it on the coffee table?

"That Melanie's aunt was dog show royalty."

Despite, or perhaps because of, the tension building in the room, I found myself laughing. "I'm sure Aunt Peg would be mortified to hear herself described that way."

"Nevertheless it's true," Brian insisted. "Margaret Turnbull has been a fixture in Standard Poodles for what, thirty years?"

I nodded.

"She's also one of very few breeder, owner-handlers ever to win the group at Westminster. That alone is enough to make some people stand up and salute." He paused, gazing at me thoughtfully. "I seem to recall she was the subject of some gossip a couple of years ago, around the time her husband died. Something about one of her stud dogs. . . ?"

Brian wasn't just another dinner guest, I remembered suddenly. He was also Sheila's new partner in journalism. Yellow journalism. This was one bit of innuendo I could nip in the bud.

"I imagine you mean Beau," I said evenly. "Champion Cedar Crest Chantain. He was stolen—"

"And then recovered," Sheila chimed in. "I read all about it in *Dog Scene.* Sam had just moved here, hadn't you?"

"Right. I appeared just in time to be considered a suspect. That's how Melanie and I met."

"How very romantic." Sheila cut off a sliver of cheese, slid it on a cracker, and offered it to Sam.

"But there was something else," Brian persisted. Though the rest of us were seated, he remained on his feet. Not quite pacing, but not standing still either; as if he had more energy than he could contain. "Something about the dog himself . . ."

It wasn't hard to figure out what he was getting at. "Beau has SA," I said. "Sebaceous adenitis. He failed a punch skin biopsy and, in fact, had been removed from active stud duty right before he disappeared."

"Right!" said Brian. "That was it." Now it was his turn to look triumphant. Also speculative. "Considering the amount of winning that dog had done, the news must have come as quite a shock to the Poodle community."

"It did," Sam agreed. Like me, he obviously meant to disarm Brian's suspicions with honesty. "Many people felt blindsided, myself included. There was a lot of admiration for Peg as well, though. Considering all the problems we're currently battling in purebred dogs, she was one of the first big breeders to come right out and say that despite all our efforts, despite the testing, there are still affected dogs and she had one."

"Of course, there was a backlash, too," I added. When this had all happened, I'd been too new to dogs to understand what was happening. But now I knew what Peg had been through. There were plenty of people in the dog show world who had too much money, effort, and ego invested in their dogs to ever consider admitting that something might be wrong. "Other breeders whose dogs shared common ancestors with Beau were horrified, afraid that Aunt Peg's disclosure would taint their lines, too."

"As well it should have," Sheila said firmly. "I'm always amazed by how many breeders are willing to bury their heads in the sand over issues like this. They do no testing and then assert that such-and-such a problem has never been found in *their* dogs. Well, of course it hasn't, if they've never looked for it."

"Hear! Hear!" said Brian. "That's exactly the sort of story that's going to make *Woof!* fly off the presses." He glanced in Sheila's direction. "Right, partner?"

"Right." She lifted her glass in salute.

Outside, the dogs began to bark. Five higher-pitched, little-dog voices were joined by one deep-throated bass.

"Good Lord." I laughed. "It sounds like your Pugs have cornered a bear."

"That's Boris, my Saint Bernard," said Brian, heading for the kitchen. "I was about to bring him inside. That's why I asked if you minded big dogs."

The minute he disappeared, Sheila leapt up. She opened a cabinet in a sideboard and withdrew a small stack of towels, keeping two for herself and tossing the rest so they landed on the couch between me and Sam. "Trust me," she said. "You'll need them."

Then she picked up the platter of cheese and moved it to a higher spot. "Brian insists that dog is trained, but you'd be amazed how much food just happens to fall into his mouth. Boris seems to have developed a fondness for brie, and a half-pound wedge is barely a morsel to a dog that size."

Precautions complete, Sheila was seated sedately in her chair when Brian returned. The Pugs preceded him. We heard them gallop through the kitchen, then all five appeared, in a flurry of scrambling legs and eager noses.

"Hi, guys." Sheila leaned down from her chair and held her arms wide, making snuffling noises under her breath. The Pugs reciprocated, while Sam and I both grinned, just as pleased that they weren't our dogs, so we weren't the ones making fools of ourselves.

"This is Boris," Brian announced from the doorway. From the solemnity of his tone, I wondered if we were meant to stand up as the Saint Bernard entered the room.

I had to admit, though, the dog was beautiful. Huge, with a sparkling red-and-white coat, massive bones, and large, soulful eyes. Everything about him exuded quiet authority, and I could well imagine that his forebears had been superb rescue dogs.

"Hey, boy," Sam said. Boris's ears lifted slightly as he looked in our direction. He ambled toward the couch.

Like most big dogs, Boris seemed to have a sense of his size, relative to the room. While the Pugs gamboled and rolled on the rug, the Saint's movements were calm and measured. Even his tail seemed to move in slow motion as it wagged from side to side.

"Nice dog," I said admiringly, as Boris edged between Sam and the coffee table and came to greet me.

Just in time, I managed to snag a towel and slide it across my knees. A moment later, a head the size of Davey's backpack was resting in my lap. A long string of drool dripped from his flews.

"Must be hell fitting him in that car," Sam mentioned.

"Tell me about it." Brian laughed. He sat down in an armchair by the couch, and Boris went to lie down at his side. "But we manage, don't we, boy? If you want something badly enough, you can always find a way to make it happen. I imagine you'd agree with me about that, wouldn't you, Sam?"

There it was again, that undercurrent to the conversation that was about as subtle as a Rottweiler with bad breath. Obviously something had come between these three in the past. I wondered how long it would take me to find out what it was.

The Pugs began to disperse and lie down; one of them flopped across my feet. I reached down to rub the round head with its velvety button ears, and asked, "How did you all meet?"

The three of them glanced at one another, each waiting to see if someone else was going to answer.

"In business school," Sam said finally, when no one else volunteered. He reached for his beer and took a long swallow, then set the glass down on the table with a finality that seemed to declare the subject closed.

"Now, Sam," Sheila chided gently. "Melanie wants to know more than that." Her eyes shifted my way, declaring herself my sister, my ally. "She's looking for details."

"Don't hold back on my account," Brian said. "In fact, maybe I should just tell the story myself and get it over with."

Beside me, Sam tensed, ever so slightly. Sheila, meanwhile, was smiling. No doubt whatever was about to be revealed showed her in a good light.

"Go ahead," I said.

Brian leaned forward in his chair. "Sam and I were buddies, I guess you might even have said best friends. We met the first year, had a lot of the same classes, hung out together on the weekends."

"I was a year behind," Sheila interjected. "By the time I arrived, these two were upperclassmen."

"I noticed Sheila right away," Brian continued. "Hard not to, even though in those days her hair was all wild and frizzy, sticking out like some giant, dark dandelion all around her head."

"A bad perm." Sheila sighed. "The hairdresser told me it would add body. Two years later, I was still growing it out."

"Anyway, Sheila and I began seeing each other. It got pretty serious, pretty fast. We were looking into getting an apartment together. Then I made the mistake of introducing her to my good friend, Sam." Brian paused, ceding the others a chance to continue.

For a minute, no one did. Sam was staring straight ahead, looking as if he could have gone the rest of his life quite happily without having this particular episode from his past rehashed. Even Sheila finally had the grace to look uncomfortable.

"You have to understand," she said softly. "When Sam and I met, I felt as though I'd been struck by a speeding train. I know it sounds corny to talk about love at first sight, but that's what it was. I knew I'd met the man that I was destined to marry. Neither of us wanted to hurt you, Brian."

Brian shook his head curtly, warding off any sympathy she tried to offer. "It all happened a long time ago. And it wasn't that big a deal. I got over it fast enough."

"And took up with Miss Cheerleader from Alabama," Sheila prompted, trying to lighten the mood. "What was her name again? The one with the lacquered hair and big pompons?"

"Honey Sue Beaudine." Slowly Brian smiled. "Now there was a woman who knew how to take a man's mind off his troubles."

Even Sam seemed amused by the memory. "As I recall, taking things off was a specialty of hers."

"So you see," Sheila said, "the three of us go way back. And now that Sam and I have split up, and Brian and I are working together on the magazine, I guess you might say things have come full circle."

Indeed, I mused, as Sheila got up and went into the

kitchen. In my experience, life never revolved quite that neatly. It was hard not to suspect that Sheila might have given fate a nudge.

In March, she'd come to the East Coast hoping to reclaim the attentions of her ex-husband. Failing in that, she was now involved, professionally and otherwise, with a man from both their pasts. From what I'd seen of Sheila, she was much too savvy to make a stupid career move for the sake of a man. Still, I had to wonder whether the new job at the start-up magazine was the golden opportunity she'd claimed it to be.

Excusing myself I got up and followed her into the kitchen. A lamb roast, spiked with fat cloves of garlic and sprinkled with rosemary had just come out of the oven. Sheila was applying the finishing touches to a homemade salad dressing.

"Can I help?" I asked.

"Dress and toss?" she said, indicating a wooden salad bowl on the counter. She opened a drawer and pulled out a long fork and spoon.

"Nice kitchen," I said, as we worked side by side.

"It's getting there. You should have seen what this place looked like when I first moved in."

"I heard about it," I said, trying to keep the edge from my tone.

For the first month Sheila had been in residence, her calls to Sam for aid had been constant. She'd never struck me as the helpless type, and after a while, I'd begun to wonder just how many things could possibly go wrong in one small house.

"This place was really in bad shape," Sheila said, as

though reading my thoughts. "The woman that owns the house is quite old, probably in her late eighties. It's at least a decade since she'd had any serious maintenance work done. Finally, I guess she realized it was just too much for her to keep up. After she leased the place to me, she went into managed care."

I could see how a property that size would be hard for an older woman to keep up by herself. "Didn't she have any relatives nearby who could have helped?"

Sheila sliced the lamb on a cutting board, transferred it to a platter, and arranged roasted new potatoes around the border. "One, a son named Chuck, who apparently didn't realize how much of a burden the place had become. I gather his mother had always been the independent type, so maybe they hadn't seen each other much.

"Anyway, after she checked into Southbury Oaks, he dropped by. Frankly, he seemed pretty appalled by the shape the place was in. Sam had been helping me out some, but there was still plenty to be done. So, for the last couple months, Chuck's been stopping by and fixing things up—you know, painting, small repairs, general handyman stuff. If you ask me, he feels kind of guilty that he never got around to doing those things when his mother was here. How's that salad coming?"

"All set."

"Great. Then we're ready to eat. Go get the guys, would you, while I carry this to the table?" Sheila frowned prettily, an expression of concern she didn't quite manage to pull off. "I hope they're not at each other's throats in there."

If they were, I decided, I wouldn't give her the satisfaction of letting on.

They weren't. In the living room, Sam and Brian were drinking beer, petting dogs, and swapping stories about Honey Sue Beaudine and other classmates they hadn't heard from in years. Maybe what Brian said was true, and the trouble between them had ended a long time ago.

For all our sakes, I hoped he was right.

᏶❖ Three ❖᏶

Sheila had opened most of the windows in the small house and a gentle, evening breeze floated through the dining room. Once again, there were candles, flickering on the table and the sideboard. The lamb was delicious; the merlot, a better vintage than I could afford. In short, the ambiance was all one could have wished for.

And the company? Once everyone settled down, that wasn't half-bad either.

Over dinner, Brian told us all about the plans he and Sheila had made for their new magazine. Gesturing with his fork, toasting their venture with his wine, laughing heartily to punctuate his own stories, he made his enthusiasm for the venture abundantly, and infectiously, clear.

By the time dessert and coffee were served, Brian had me sold. Thank God he wasn't soliciting backers, or I probably would have signed on. As it was, *Woof!*'s upcoming launch was beginning to sound less like a gamble and more like a sure thing. Maybe I'd been wrong in thinking that Sheila's career path had taken a precipitous detour.

Sam, however, wasn't as easily convinced. Though he joined in the conversation and the laughter, his eyes never entirely lost their slightly wary look. Even after downing several glasses of wine, it was clear to me, if not the others, that he was far from relaxed.

"You know," Brian said to his old friend, "if this project is a success, I'll have you to thank."

Sam looked up sharply. "How do you figure?"

"You were the one who got me started in dogs in the first place. Without your guidance, I would never have known the dog show world even existed."

"Don't you mean my interference?" Sam permitted himself a small smile. "As I recall, that's what you called it at the time."

Brian waved away the interruption. "I wanted a dog," he explained for my benefit. "A big dog. I'd seen a Saint Bernard in a movie and thought it would be just the thing. I figured any pet store would have one."

"Thank goodness Sam was there to set you straight," Sheila said, voicing the antipathy that any informed dog lover feels toward pet shops.

"Sam told me I had to find a breeder. Someone who did genetic testing and had healthy puppies with good temperaments. Before he started all his lecturing, I figured I was just looking for something cute with floppy ears and big feet."

"I dragged him to a dog show," Sam said. "*Drag* being the operative word."

"I couldn't believe he wanted me to waste a whole Saturday watching pampered canines prance around a show ring."

"You couldn't believe they didn't have a beer stand." Sam laughed.

"Hey, you sold the thing to me as a sporting event, okay? Let's just say I had certain expectations. And then this big guy steers me to the Poodle ring. The Poodle ring! Where I discover that otherwise sane-looking people are putting hair spray on their dogs."

Been there, done that, I thought, enjoying the teasing banter, and the glimpse of what the two men must have been like when they were young and still friends.

"I got him out of there just in time," Sam said, grinning. "Luckily the Saint Bernards were coming up two rings over."

"Once I saw them, I was hooked." Brian smiled with pleasure at the memory. "They were massive, majestic. I'd never seen anything so beautiful. I got on a waiting list for a litter that afternoon and bought Boris's great-grandmother six months later."

"Did you show her?" I asked.

"Of course. I got lucky for a first-timer and she was a good one. Even with a rank beginner on the end of the lead, she still managed to pick up half a dozen points. That first purple ribbon sealed my fate; there was no turning back after that. Her breeder stepped in when it was time for the majors and finished the job. Boris is the third generation of my own breeding, and there have been half a dozen champions along the way."

"Is Boris finished?" I asked, exhibitor's shorthand for "has he accumulated enough points to be awarded the title of champion?"

The big dog knew we were talking about him. Lying along the edge of the rug, he lifted up his head and stared at us balefully. Brian picked up an oatmeal cookie that had been resting on the edge of his saucer and tossed it. Boris's mouth opened, then snapped shut. I never even saw him swallow, but his tail thumped up and down happily on the floor.

Sheila rolled her eyes. The Pugs looked annoyed. It wasn't hard to figure out that they wanted a treat, too. "Now look what you've started," she said.

Brian was unrepentant. "Live a little," he said. "Cookies for everyone."

"Feed them from the table even once, and they'll expect it every time. Besides, training issues aside, my guys have to watch their weight." Looking as disgruntled as her Pugs, Sheila got up, whistled the dogs to her, and went to the back door to put them all outside.

Brian shook his head slightly as he watched her go, then turned back to me. "In answer to your question, no, Boris isn't finished. I'm taking a break from the show ring until after the magazine is launched. I wouldn't want anyone to think I have a conflict of interest."

"What Brian really means," Sheila said, returning to the table, "is that he's lying low until we see how people take things—how many judges, exhibitors, and officials we manage to tick off with the first issue."

"Do you expect it to be that controversial?" I asked.

"We're starting out with a bang," said Brian. "And we'll know how it goes over soon enough. The debut issue is already in the mail, and we'll be handing out freebies at the show this weekend."

"I'll be disappointed if our audience doesn't think *Woof!* is controversial," Sheila said earnestly. "But I hope people make an effort to understand what we're trying to do. The dog show world is a fascinating subculture. Some people, even some who've been exhibiting for years, still see mostly the surface.

"It's like a Poodle's show coat, and believe me, I

watched Sam put together enough of those. From ring-side, that great mass of mane hair looks incredibly thick, almost solid, like it stands up by itself. Then you go back to the grooming tent and watch someone break down a topknot and see all the layers underneath. The half dozen rubber bands, the hair spray, sometimes there's even fake hair.

"That's what we're going to do with *Woof!*. Go beyond the pretty surface and expose some of the stories that nobody wants talked about. Like that terrier breeder in Delaware a couple of years ago The one whose top stud dog died, but he kept taking stud fees anyway, and breed-ing bitches to the dog's sons? It took years for the AKC to nail him, even though other breeders had been suspicious forever. All those pedigrees are compromised now. That stud book may never recover."

"And lots of people are still very angry about it," said Sam. "If that's the kind of story you're planning to cover, you'd better realize that you're not going to be very pop-ular."

"We're not looking to make friends," Brian declared. "We're performing a necessary service. Besides, people love to know all the latest dirt. The response rate to our subscription offer has been incredible. In a couple years, we're going to be bigger than the *Gazette*. Maybe nobody wants to admit they're going to read *Woof!*, but it's obvi-ous that no one wants to be left out either."

He pushed back his chair and rose. "I'm going to go outside and grab a smoke. Be back in a few."

Sam's foot nudged mine under the table. "Why don't you keep Brian company? Sheila and I will get things cleaned up in here."

"All right," I said, though I wasn't pleased by the

prospect. Clearly Sam wanted a few minutes alone with his ex-wife.

I was trying very hard not to play the role of the disgruntled fiancée. Sam could have made the whole stupid charade a lot easier if he hadn't kept doing things for me to be disgruntled about.

"I left my cigarettes in the car," said Brian. "Let's go out the front. Then we can walk around back and check on the dogs."

In the ten minutes the dogs had been outside, we hadn't heard a sound. Faith, left to her own devices in my yard would have long since been clamoring to come in. Then again, that was probably the difference between having one dog and a houseful. Faith looked to me as her chief source of entertainment and companionship.

In less than two weeks, however, that would change. Much as I was looking forward to having puppies, I hated the thought that the Poodle and I might lose, even temporarily, the special bond that we'd built.

Which probably indicated something about one of those rules I should have learned in kindergarten. Obviously, I'm not very good at sharing.

Brian retrieved his cigarettes and lighter from the front seat of the Boxster with a sigh. "It's a miserable habit. Too bad it's so damned enjoyable." He lit up and inhaled deeply. "Did you ever smoke?"

"No. I never saw any reason to start."

"You're one of the lucky ones, then. You don't know what you're missing."

We strolled around the side of the house, where a wire-mesh fence stretched between the porch and the garage, then continued across the yard and into the woods. We headed for the gate.

"I always figured I'd stop when I had children." The tip of Brian's cigarette glowed red in the gathering darkness. "It seemed like a good plan when I was young."

"You're still young."

He shrugged slightly. "I've always been an overachiever. Had a lot of success, financially, very early. I guess I always thought that the rest of my life would fall into place just as easily."

I unlatched the gate and swung it open. "Maybe you and Sheila . . . ?"

"Maybe." Brian didn't match my hopeful tone. "I gather that would make your life easier."

"Sheila had Sam, and she left him. Now I just want her to leave him alone."

"Maybe Sam doesn't want to be left alone, have you considered that?"

More times than I'd ever admit, I thought. Especially to someone like Brian. I had no intention of letting him see me react.

He and Sam might have been friends once, but they hadn't seen each other for a decade. Maybe Brian still thought he had a score to settle. Maybe he thought he could get to Sam by going through me.

"Let's go find the dogs," I said.

"Sure." He dropped the butt and ground it out beneath his foot. Then he lifted his fingers to his lips and whistled. There was no response.

In the time we'd been outside, night had fallen. A curved sliver of moon barely illuminated the enclosed acreage. I squinted into the darkness, but didn't see any dogs.

"Come on." Brian shut the gate behind us. "They must have gone over the hill. This paddock is pretty big. I think Sheila said it used to hold a llama once upon a time. They probably chased a squirrel out to the back fence."

We trudged to the top of the small rise in silence. Still no dogs. Whoever had installed the fence had had a capricious streak. The mesh snaked in and out of the woods that bordered the lawn, so there were parts of the enclosed area we couldn't see.

"Damn."

"What?" I looked where Brian was gazing.

Tucked in along a thick row of bushes was another gate. It was standing open.

"The wild bunch is out. They've probably gone to terrorize the neighborhood."

"The dogs know you," I said. "Why don't you start after them? I'll go back for leashes and reinforcements."

"Good idea."

Brian took off down the slope at a steady jog. Loose dogs, even in a quiet neighborhood, were cause for concern. And since these dogs were used to being contained, they weren't car-savvy.

I turned back and went the other way at the same pace. The flats I'd worn with my skirt weren't made for running. Maybe Sheila would have a pair of sneakers I could borrow.

An outside light above the kitchen door guided me quickly back to the house. Sam and Sheila weren't in the kitchen, however. As I drew near, I heard the sound of their raised voices through the open living-room window. It wasn't until I'd opened the back door and gone inside, however, that I could make out what they were saying.

Someone with more scruples might have immediately announced her presence.

I entertained the thought for a moment or two. Then I closed the door quietly behind me and crept across the room.

"You're crazy!" Sheila was saying vehemently. "I don't want to talk about it anymore."

"We have to talk about it," Sam's tone was firm. "I know you don't want to hear this, She, but I can't just stand by and watch you screw up your whole life."

"It's *my* life," Sheila shot back. "Isn't that what you've spent the last four months telling me? We're divorced, Sam. You have no right to an opinion anymore."

"The fact that we're not married doesn't mean that I don't still care about you . . ."

There was a pause, then a muttered curse from Sheila. I had to strain to hear her words. "Don't touch me!"

I didn't realize I'd begun to move. I had no idea I was backing away until my legs hit a kitchen chair and I nearly tripped. I didn't want to hear any more; I'd heard too much already.

I wished I could go back in time five minutes and make an entirely different decision. Irrationally, I found myself pretending that if I ignored what I'd heard, it would all just go away.

I reached for the door, opened it and slammed it shut. "We need help," I called out.

As I glanced around the kitchen for leashes, Sam and Sheila appeared in the doorway. "The back gate's open, and the dogs are loose," I said. "Brian's already gone after them. I came back for you guys."

Sheila opened the door to a pantry and scooped several leashes off their hooks. "Let's go."

I hadn't looked at Sam. I hadn't even glanced his way. But somehow I knew he was staring at me, weighing

my expression, wondering about my tone. He knew me
entirely too well.

As Sheila opened the door, he held out his hand. Part
of me was just angry enough to ignore him. The other
part won out. I reached out my hand and folded it in
his.

I felt like I was holding on for my life.

☙❖ *Four* ❖☙

As it turned out, rounding up the missing dogs was almost anticlimactic. Think about it. How far would five Pugs and a Saint Bernard be likely to run? It's not like we were chasing Afghans, after all.

As we herded the unrepentant crew back through the gate and shut it securely behind us, Sheila stopped to check the latch. Closed, it held firm.

"This gate shouldn't have been open. I'm positive I didn't leave it like that."

"Maybe neighborhood kids?" Sam suggested.

Brian only shrugged. Now that he knew Boris was fine, the matter had ceased to interest him.

"Look around." Sheila's flamboyant hand gesture revealed her annoyance. "I don't live in a subdivision. This house sits on eight acres of land."

"Mistakes happen," I said.

"Not to me." She turned her back and started up the slope.

Sam looked like he was going to go after her, then thought better of it. Brian grimaced slightly and shook his head. As for me, I'd had enough of the whole bunch of them. I just wanted to go home.

Sam must have been reading my thoughts. Back at the house, he cocked a brow in my direction, and I nodded. Our silent communication system was still intact. We thanked our hostess for a lovely evening and made our escape.

Neither of us said a word until we were back on the road. I opened my window and let the wind ruffle through my hair and cool my cheeks. I wondered if Sam realized I'd overheard part of his conversation with Sheila. I wondered if he cared. And I wondered, even more, about the part I hadn't heard.

Finally, I couldn't stand it any longer. "So?" I said. "What's Sheila up to this time?"

Sam's eyes left the road briefly to glance my way. "I guess that means you didn't buy the innocent act of hers either. I wish she'd told me sooner that Brian was her new partner."

"Obviously she wanted to spring it on you in person."

"Right." Sam frowned. "I'm sure my reaction didn't disappoint her. While you and Brian were outside, I tried to talk her into giving up the magazine."

Now we were getting somewhere. "You and he used to be best friends," I pointed out.

"I was young then," Sam said shortly. "Now I'd know better."

"He seemed like a nice enough guy to me. Very enthusiastic about his magazine and its prospects. Didn't you tell me once that Sheila was a terrific marketer? Maybe between them, they can make this thing take off."

"It's not the magazine I'm worried about. People will either want to wallow in that kind of dirt, or they won't.

Sheila's got a terrific head for business, but emotionally, well . . . sometimes she gets carried away. I'm afraid that the only reason she got mixed up with Brian is to get back at me."

So at least I wasn't imagining things. On the other hand, Sam had just confirmed my fears. Sheila still had no intention of letting go. And for whatever reason, Sam couldn't seem to bring himself to make the break either.

I wondered where that left us, and I didn't like the answers I came up with. I sat and watched the trees slide by outside my window. All at once, my life felt as though it was rushing by in just the same manner, heading irrevocably toward some conclusion over which I had no control.

"Sheila must have realized that would only work if you still had feelings for her," I said finally.

I heard Sam sigh. I waited, sitting absolutely still, for him to deny what I'd just said. His eyes remained trained on the road. My fingers twined together in my lap.

"We've discussed this before."

He sounded tired. I wanted reassurance, and he sounded like a man who figured he could use a little consoling himself. Too bad Sheila wasn't here to rub his shoulders for him.

"Before I met you," Sam said, "Sheila was a very large part of my life. In many ways, she and I grew up together. I'm not in love with Sheila anymore, but that doesn't mean I don't care about what happens to her. Sometimes Sheila could use someone to look out for her—"

"And you think you should be that person?" I tried hard not to sound as incredulous as I felt.

"Well, it sure as hell won't be Endicott."

Was it jealousy I heard in his tone? Or maybe resentment? It certainly wasn't detachment.

"What's with the two of you anyway? From the moment you saw him walk into that hallway, you've been prickly as a bear."

"I just know him too damn well."

"Meaning what?"

"It's a long story," Sam said as he put on his blinker and turned in my driveway. "It's an *old* story. Nothing I want to go into tonight. Suffice it to say that Brian Endicott is about the last person I would choose to go into business with. Sheila needs to be very careful. I only hope she realizes that."

"You told her."

"I tried. She didn't listen. She said it was too late. The partnership's already been formed. The magazine's about to be launched."

"Maybe it will be a huge success," I said as I got out of the car. Personally, I was hoping for a thriving business that would give Sheila better things to think about than my fiancé. "Listening to Brian earlier, I got the impression that pretty much everything he touches turns to gold."

"He's had his share of luck. Some might even say more than his share." Sam walked around the car and wrapped his hands around my waist. "Can we stop talking about this now?"

I would have answered, but his mouth covered mine. After a moment, he lifted his head, and said, "One last thing?"

"Mmm?"

"The next time Sheila invites us over, figure out a way to say no, okay?"

His fingers found the ticklish spot just below my ribs. I yelped, twisted away, and ran for the steps.

We'd left some lights on in the house, and I could see Faith, watching us through the living-room window. Her nose was pressed against the glass, and her tail was wagging like mad. There's something about the sight of a happy dog that always makes me smile.

I felt my heart lifting as I set my worries aside. For the moment, Sam and I were back in sync. It was only a minor victory, but for now it was enough.

On Saturday, there was a dog show. Like that was news.

There's a dog show every Saturday, and every Sunday, too. That's the beauty of living in the Northeast. There are so many show-giving kennel clubs in a relatively concentrated area that dog fanciers can exhibit every week of the year, if they choose.

Faith, of course, wasn't entered. Aside from the fact that her puppies were due soon, she was also missing some much-needed hair on the back of her neck. According to the breed standard, adult Poodles must be shown in either one of two elaborate trims. Both mandate that the dog possess a substantial amount of hair on the front half of the body.

Consequently, once the decision has been made to exhibit a Poodle, incredible care must be taken to protect that hair at all costs. Faith had an excellent, correctly textured, coat—thick, and harsh, and very black—but an accident in the spring had created a hole just where it would be the most obvious. She'd been sitting out of the show ring for three months already. As long as the

puppies didn't cost her too much more hair, I'd probably
have her ready to show again by fall.

Resisting the tendency to "cluster" together with the
other clubs holding shows that weekend, the Durham
Valley Kennel Club event was to be held at a beautiful,
outdoor location. Such venues are becoming increasingly
rare in Connecticut, and Davey and I planned to make
a day of it. My son was in high spirits after having spent
a week learning how to dribble with his feet and bounce
a ball off his head.

As I worked in the kitchen, packing a cooler with sandwiches and drinks, he demonstrated his new skills for
me in the backyard. "Watch!" Davey crowed, as he kicked
the ball around the trunk of a big old oak tree with Faith
trotting in pursuit. Seeing he had my attention, he turned
and fired a shot toward the fence.

The soccer ball hit the post and ricocheted back. Nim-
bly, Faith jumped out of the way. "Score!" yelled Davey,
arms upraised. "The mighty dog defender cannot stop
the march to victory by our hero, Captain David!"

Captain David? I wondered if this was his way of
telling me that he felt he was outgrowing his diminutive
nickname. Davey would be seven in September, when
he started second grade. He'd shot up two inches in the
last year and was beginning to have an opinion about
the clothes I picked out for him to wear to school. Though
it seemed like hardly any time at all had passed since I'd
held him in my arms, I was reminded daily that my son
no longer thought of himself as a little boy.

"Come on in and bring Faith with you," I called.
"We're just about ready to go."

I'd already loaded Faith's crate in the back of the station
wagon, and I carried the cooler out to join it. In theory,

unentered dogs aren't supposed to be brought onto the grounds of a show, but considering Faith's delicate condition, I wanted to keep an eye on her. Sam would be showing his puppy, Tar, so I knew he'd have a spot staked out beneath the grooming tent where I could set up Faith's crate. That way, she could enjoy the day with us, while remaining cool and not unduly stressed.

The drive took just about an hour. By dog show standards, that meant the show was just around the corner. Aunt Peg thinks nothing of packing up her van and traveling all up and down the East Coast. I've tried to set a more sensible schedule for Faith's show career, but already she's picked up points in Connecticut, New York, New Jersey, Rhode Island, and Massachusetts.

At the gate to the fairground, I paid our admission and bought a catalogue. Usually when we're at a show, I'm rushing to get Faith ready for the ring. Having an entire day to devote to merely enjoying the spectacle seemed like an incredible luxury.

Two long rows of rings, each half-covered by a huge, green-and-white-striped tent filled most of a large field. Sometimes there's a separate tent for the handlers and exhibitors to groom under; other times, extra space for grooming has been left beside the rings. Today's club had chosen the second option. I looked up the number of the Poodle ring in the catalogue and drove slowly across the grass to the back of the tent.

As I'd hoped, Sam had saved me some room. Not only that, but Aunt Peg was already there, too. Though Sam owns and shows Tar, Aunt Peg is the puppy's breeder. She had high hopes that today's judge would award Tar the last two points he needed to finish his championship.

"Good morning," Aunt Peg sang out cheerfully as I

pulled into the unloading spot, and Davey and Faith tumbled out of the car. She had a pastry in one hand and a catalogue in the other. "How's my darling girl?"

The question was directed at Faith, not me. Don't worry, I'm used to that.

Nearly six feet tall, Aunt Peg had to bend way down to check out the expectant bitch's condition. She had to put down her pastry, too. For my aunt, whose sweet tooth is legendary, that constitutes a hardship.

She ran a knowledgeable hand over Faith's midsection and nodded approvingly. "You've got her in good weight. How's she feeling?"

"Wonderful. Exuberant." I unloaded Faith's crate and dragged it over beside Tar's portable grooming table. Sam leaned around and gave me a kiss as I pushed it into position. "She played soccer with Davey this morning."

"Gently, I hope." Peg's tone was stern.

She takes this breeding business seriously. Before I'd even been allowed to consider letting Faith have a litter, I'd had to have her genetic testing done—hips x-rayed so she could be certified clear of hip dysplasia by OFA; a punch skin biopsy to rule out sebaceous adenitis; eyes examined by a canine opthamologist for progressive retinal atrophy. In three decades of breeding, Aunt Peg had managed to steer her Cedar Crest Standard Poodles free of two other maladies that can affect Standard Poodles— seizures and bloat. Since there are no tests to predict an inherited tendency toward either one of those conditions, we were both keeping our fingers crossed.

"Of course, gently." I patted the top of Faith's crate. She jumped up and placed her front paws on the rubber-matted surface. Carefully, I hoisted her heavier than usual hindquarter up into place. The Poodle turned once in a tight circle and lay down.

"Gently," Davey echoed solemnly. "She's going to have babies." His small hand reached up to pat his dog's thigh. Then he turned to his great-aunt. "Got any more doughnuts?"

"Plenty. I brought some chocolate-covered ones, just for you."

"There's fruit in the cooler," I offered, wasting my breath. "And Cheerios . . ." Davey was already digging through the supplies beneath the table. "When the sugar high hits, he's all yours," I said to Peg.

"Pish. Little boys are meant to have lots of energy." Aunt Peg grasped Davey's hand, pulled him to his feet, and led him in an impromptu jig around Sam's grooming table. "We'll dance in the aisles together, won't we, Davey?"

Aunt Peg's next birthday would be her sixty-first. In defiance of the passing years, she seemed to be growing younger with each one. Davey giggled his reply, kicked up his feet, and stuffed the first bite of pastry into his mouth.

"I'm pretending I'm not with them," I said to Sam. Here by the ring, tables and crates were stacked in cozy proximity. Ours wasn't the only attention the dancing duo had managed to attract. "Are you sure you really want to marry into this family?"

"Positive." Sam grinned, seemingly unfazed by the potential for embarrassment offered by his relatives-to-be. "Go park your car. I'll try to keep them in line until you get back."

The parking lot was at the other end of the field. Predictably, most of the spaces were already full. Finally, in the last row I found some openings. As I parked and got out, another car came flying down the row and pulled in beside me. A black Boxster.

I glanced inside the car. Brian didn't have Boris with him. Instead the passenger seat was filled with a large box.

"*Woof!*'s first issue. Hot off the presses," Brian announced proudly as he hopped out and locked up. "Want one? Or did you already get a copy from Sheila?"

"I haven't seen Sheila yet. I just got here."

"You're not showing then?" Brian looked at his watch. It was nearing eleven.

I shook my head.

"I'm running late myself. Sheila was supposed to get here around nine and start handing them out. With any luck, by now there should already be some buzz."

Brian's expression was calculated. Running late, my foot, I thought. He'd shown up late on purpose in order to make an entrance.

Brian opened the Boxster's trunk. More magazines were stacked inside. He gathered up an armful.

"Off to the trenches," he said cheerfully.

I hoped it wasn't an apt metaphor.

➳❀ *Five* ❀➳

Unfortunately for Brian, his grand entrance was a bust. Sheila hadn't arrived yet, which meant that the first issues of *Woof!* to reach the show ground were the ones he held in his hands.

I had taken a copy with me when we'd parted and was still thumbing through it an hour later, reading various tidbits aloud to Sam and Peg. From our vantage point next to the rings, we could see Brian working the show— shaking hands, giving away freebies, and generally building goodwill. I didn't see a single person who received a magazine set it aside. Even exhibitors who were busy with their dogs opened it right up and began to read.

If today's response was any indication, Sheila's marketing expertise wasn't overrated. Brian was obviously delivering his magazine to an audience that was salivating to get their hands on it.

As he worked his way over to our setup, I filled Aunt Peg in on Brian's background and his connection to Sam and Sheila. She'd heard of *Woof!*, of course, having received her flyer like everyone else. Though she claimed she hadn't planned to subscribe, I could see she was curious. If I didn't keep an eye on my copy, it would probably go home in her purse.

Sam, who knew all the players better than I did and might have contributed a great deal to the conversation, was uncharacteristically silent. Aunt Peg is one of his favorite people. Usually when the two of them get together, it's all I can do to keep up.

Today, however, Sam concentrated on getting Tar ready for the ring and trading jokes with Davey. I might have chalked his reticence up to show day jitters, except that unlike me, Sam doesn't get nervous when he's showing a dog. He's just that good, and he knows it.

By the time Brian came strolling down our aisle, Tar was standing on his grooming table as Sam applied the finish to his trim. Though Sam's attention was ostensibly on the puppy, he'd clearly been keeping track of Brian's progress because he knew the moment the other man approached.

"Looks like you're making quite a splash," he said, putting down his scissors.

"Trying to." Brian held out a copy of the magazine to Aunt Peg as I made the introductions.

"So you're the man who thinks he can expose the sordid underbelly of the dog show world," she said, eyes twinkling. There's nothing Peg enjoys more than provoking an argument. "You may be disappointed. I'm afraid we're not nearly so scandalous as you may hope."

"So far, there's been no shortage of news." Brian held her gaze. "Read the first issue before you form an opinion. And speaking of opinions, I'd love to know what you think."

Aunt Peg has enough of a name in the dog community

that she meets flatterers every day of the week. I wouldn't say she's immune to sweet talk, but she's certainly been inoculated.

"What I think is that you're going to have a hard time finding advertisers. Magazines don't live by subscription alone."

"True," Brian agreed. "Sheila and I have considered that, and we're aware that things may be slow in the beginning. But we're confident they'll pick up. After all, exhibitors want to showcase their dogs in the magazine that offers the widest exposure for their advertising dollar. Based on the response we're getting already, we think that's going to be *Woof!*."

Gazing around at the crowds of spectators and exhibitors, many of whom were clutching copies of his first issue, it was hard to refute Brian's claim.

"Speaking of Sheila," he said, turning to Sam. "You haven't heard from her, have you? She was supposed to be here first thing this morning to help me get the word out."

Sam shrugged. He seemed amused by Brian's annoyance. "You know Sheila. She's never been known for her punctuality."

"But this was important!"

"So was our wedding," Sam said mildly. "The organist went through his entire repertoire twice before she finally put in an appearance. Don't worry, she's probably on her way."

"I should hope so," Brian growled. "There's no answer at her house, and her cell phone directed me to voice mail. In the meantime, I had to call a couple of staffers and tell them to swing by the office for more copies, then get up here on the double."

Still grumbling under his breath, Brian moved on.

"Is that the new magazine?" I heard a woman in the next setup squeal. "Can I have a copy? And one for my friend who's in the ring?" Sunny smile restored, back in salesman mode, Brian handed out the copies.

"You'd love to see him fail, wouldn't you?" I said to Sam as Brian walked away.

He grimaced slightly. "Do I really seem that petty?"

"Not usually, no. But don't forget, if Brian goes down, he'll drag Sheila with him."

"Sheila can take care of herself," Peg said firmly. "Nobody forced her to get involved in this business to begin with. That was her choice. But since you're asking, I, for one, wouldn't mind seeing *Woof!* fail."

That didn't surprise me. Where dog shows are concerned, Peg tends to see the bright side. It's not that she doesn't know about the underhanded things that go on, just that she's positive that the good outweighs the bad. Curious though she might be, *Woof!* was not the kind of endeavor to which she would lend her support.

"Hey!" said Davey, standing up on the top of Tar's crate. "Why is that lady waving at us?"

We all turned to look. The lady in question was the steward for the Poodle ring. While we'd been occupied with Brian, the breeds before ours had finished being judged. Now Standard the Poodle Puppy Dog class was in the ring.

Not only that, but the judge was handing out their ribbons, so the class was almost over. Though Tar was still a puppy, Sam had entered him in Open. With no entries in the intervening classes, his turn would come momentarily.

"Thank goodness for Marjorie," Aunt Peg said, as Sam

swept Tar down off the grooming table and headed toward the gate, where the rest of the entrants had already gathered. The steward had Sam's numbered armband out and ready for him to slip on.

I put Faith in her crate, helped Davey down off his high perch, and followed Peg and Sam to ringside. When we got there, Sam and Tar were already in the ring, standing at the end of a long line of Open dogs. Peg waved her thanks to Marjorie, the steward, who smiled a reply as she checked off the exhibitors' numbers in her catalogue.

The essence of the ring steward's job is to assist a judge in the efficient running of his ring. They mark off absentees, lay out the colored ribbons appropriate for the class being judged, answer numerous questions for harried exhibitors, and generally try to make the judge's life as easy as possible.

Apart from announcing each class, it is not their job to call individual exhibitors to the ring. As it happens, however, stewards are usually members of the show-giving club, or local volunteers. Members of the dog show community themselves, they often know many of the entrants. And since they're also holding a catalogue which spells out who belongs where, they can often be counted on to give a nudge when needed. Luckily for us, today's steward had been more on the ball than we were.

Holding Davey's hand, I stepped in close beside Aunt Peg, who was busy consulting her catalogue. Normally she'd have scoped out the competition ahead of time, but today she'd been too busy with *Woof!*. Now she ran a knowledgeable eye down the line, much like the judge who was taking her own first look from inside the ring.

There were six dogs in the class: four blacks, two whites, all adults except for Tar. I could tell that at a glance because he was the only one still wearing the puppy trim, which allows for a scissored blanket of hair all over the Poodle's body. Traditionally, the Open class is the one with the most competition, and consequently, the hardest to win. Entering Tar here was Sam's way of letting the judge know that he felt his puppy had the maturity and the quality to take on all comers.

"Who's going to win?" I asked Peg in a low tone.

"You are," said a voice behind us. "More's the pity."

"Terry!" I turned and slipped my arms around him for a gentle hug, careful not to muss the beautifully coifed Standard Poodle puppy he held at his side. "How have you been?"

"Better on days when Crawford thinks he has a shot." Terry sighed theatrically. He's young, and gay, and impossibly handsome, and he never makes a small gesture when a large one will do.

Crawford Langley was a busy and successful professional dog handler, and Terry's boss. He'd already won the Puppy Dog class with the Poodle Terry was holding at ringside, and he had another entry in Open to show against Sam.

"Shhh!" Peg snapped. "You'll jinx us."

"I doubt it," Terry said, but he looked hopeful. "That puppy's been beating the tar out of us for the last six weeks."

Davey giggled at the bad pun. We adults politely ignored it.

"If he wins today, that's it," said Peg, meaning that Tar would have accumulated the fifteen points required to finish his championship. "He'll be out of your hair forever."

"In the classes, maybe." Terry pulled a comb out of his jacket pocket and began to comb through the puppy's silky ears. "What about the specials ring?"

"We'll worry about that when the time comes," Peg said firmly, but her crafty look gave the game away.

Specials dogs are those rare animals that possess the quality to be given a career in group and best in show competition. Tar was young yet to be making such predictions, but I knew Aunt Peg had high hopes for his future.

"Oooh." She drew in a breath.

The judge had completed her individual examinations and was going back for a second look at the dogs she planned to use. A flick of her finger moved Tar to the head of the line. Crawford was too much of a pro to let his expression betray his feelings when he was pulled out behind Sam's puppy, but I knew he couldn't have been pleased. Rather than concede defeat, however, he began to work even harder.

"Tail," Terry whispered as the judge glanced Crawford's way. "Hair!"

I used my elbow to nudge him, none too politely, in the ribs. Terry winced, but didn't retreat.

Each dog, no matter how beautiful, has his faults. And every handler knows that it's his job to ferret out the competition's weaknesses and exploit them. Though he carried his tail correctly, Tar's tail set could have been higher; and as he was still a puppy, his coat lacked the harshness it would naturally attain in a year or two.

Standing second, it was Crawford's duty not only to showcase his own dog's assets, but also remind the judge of Tar's deficiencies. He tried, but his efforts didn't succeed. When the judge pointed to her placings, Tar was still in the number one spot.

Peg and I clapped our appreciation, but we weren't ready to celebrate yet. Championship points are won not by taking an individual class, but by beating all the other class winners within the same sex. Today, only two dog classes—Puppy and Open—had had entries, but that still meant that Crawford's puppy had a chance to beat Tar for the title of Winners Dog and the points that went with it.

Terry hustled the Puppy class winner over to the gate, where he and Crawford switched dogs. After that, it was all over in a moment. The judge compared the two puppies briefly, then motioned Tar to the winner's spot.

Beside me, Davey whooped with delight. Even Aunt Peg, who likes to think she's discreet, was cheering. "A puppy champion," she said proudly. "That doesn't happen every day."

Sam floated out of the ring, wearing a goofy smile. He didn't even seem to notice that Tar, reacting to our excitement, was dancing beside him on his hind legs.

"Well done," I said.

Sam was beaming. "What a puppy! Wasn't he great?"

"Perfect," Peg agreed. Ever practical, she added, "Now don't let him get messed up. He still has to go back in for Best of Variety."

"Don't remind me," said Crawford, coming out of the ring with the Reserve ribbon. "Thank God you're not showing any bitches. I'd like to think I'm going to get one turn today."

None of us wasted a moment's pity on Crawford. With his skills and his reputation, he was usually the man to beat. As if to reinforce that thought, he promptly handled his class bitch to Winners Bitch.

Two specials had been entered for Best of Variety. Crawford was handling one, a brown bitch with whom he'd done a fair amount of winning; another pro had the other. Terry was back in the ring with the Winners Bitch and Sam had Tar.

"This should be fun," Aunt Peg murmured. "This judge is the kind who loves to discover new talent. Let's see how much she thinks of our puppy."

Tar had shown well in the Open class but now, sensing Sam's delight and the excitement from ringside, he was positively electric. Head and tail high, he strutted around the ring as though he owned it. And though he was attuned to Sam, he never took his eyes off the judge.

The very best show dogs seem to have an inner sense of who the game is being played for. Tar cavorted for the judge; he flirted with her. By the end of the class, he'd all but captivated her. Clearly she was delighted with her choice when she awarded him the big purple-and-gold ribbon for Best of Variety. The ringside, realizing they'd witnessed the emergence of a new star, roared its approval.

"Who's judging the Non-Sporting Group?" I asked, reaching for the catalogue. Since Tar had begun the day as an unfinished puppy, it hadn't occurred to me earlier that this was information I might need to know.

As usual when it came to dogs, however, Aunt Peg was one step ahead of me. She nodded toward the ring, where Sam and Tar were waiting with the judge for the arrival of the show photographer. "Sylvia Koenig, again. I trust Sam is making good use of his time."

He was. Edging closer, I heard him tell the judge that

she'd just finished Tar's championship, and that he'd accomplished the title with three major wins. Oh, and by the way, Tar had also recently won Best Puppy in Show at the Poodle Club of America specialty, under renowned breeder-judge, Helen Sokopp.

Sam's usually more modest about his accomplishments, but there's nothing judges like more than hearing that the decisions they've made in the ring are validated by those of their peers. You're not the only one who saw merit in this puppy, Sam was telling her. And I hope you'll give him some more consideration in the group.

Like Brian with his magazine, Sam was just creating a little buzz. Later, we'd find out how well his efforts would pay off.

Speaking of which, I thought, I'd meant to ask Crawford and Terry what they thought of *Woof!*. Getting Crawford to gossip was about as easy as teaching a Whippet to retrieve, but Terry loved to talk. Together, they were a great combination. Crawford had all the right connections, and Terry had a big mouth.

My kind of people.

❧❋ Six ❋❧

"Hey, doll, what's up?" Terry had the brown Standard Poodle bitch up on a grooming table and was taking apart her topknot. Crawford was already gone again, probably off showing another dog. "Come to gloat?"

"Why Terry, I never thought of you as a sore loser."

"Just the fact that you think of me at all warms my heart. Where's your *petit enfant?* Don't tell me you're letting Sam practice his parenting skills?"

"No, Sam's taking care of Tar. Davey's with Aunt Peg."

Terry's raised brow spoke volumes. "Feeling brave in the face of victory, are we?"

"Not at all. Aunt Peg's great with kids."

There went that eyebrow again. Darn it.

"All right," I conceded, "she'll probably feed him sweets for lunch. And buy him a toy at the concession stands. But at least I don't think she'll lose him."

He popped a rubber band with the tip of his comb. "Nothing I like more than a woman who throws caution to the wind . . . unless, of course, it's a man—"

"Enough!" I laughed. "I came to see what you and Crawford think of Brian Endicott's magazine."

"Ah, *Woof!*" Terry nodded toward a copy on top of their tackbox. "Be there, or be square."

"For now." I hiked myself up on an empty table, announcing my intention to stay a while. "Because it's new and it's provocative. But do you think it will catch on?"

"Brian certainly thinks so. He was over here earlier, telling us all about it. The grapevine says he's put up plenty of money and now that he's taken on a new partner ..." Terry's voice trailed away as comprehension dawned. "So that's why you're interested. Gathering ammunition for a catfight?"

"You wish. I'm just curious. Sam thinks Sheila is crazy to get mixed up in something like this. Brian seems to think he's going to save the dog show world from itself. I can't decide whether this magazine is going to turn into a legitimate defender of breeders' rights or just a sleazy dog show tabloid."

"Probably some of both. Have you looked at the first issue yet?"

"Briefly. Most of the headlines seem designed to titillate, not educate." I reached for the issue and flipped through it. "Best in Show Judge Implicated in Puppy Mill Sting. Prominent Exhibitor Flies to Sweden For Sex Change. At this rate, Brian and Sheila will be lucky not to get themselves sued."

"But won't we have fun in the meantime?" Terry grinned. "Besides, considering how deep Brian's pockets are, a little thing like a lawsuit is hardly going to cramp his style."

"Brian is rich?" Nobody had mentioned that before.

"Loaded. Made his fortune in the eighties by inventing a computer game. You've probably heard of it, Island of Mutant Terror?"

He glanced up from his work, and I shrugged.

"When I was a teenager, it was the biggest thing around. It sold millions."

Terry was in his twenties. If Brian had invented a game Terry had enjoyed as a teen, he must have done so right out of business school.

"Not only that, but you should see his car. It's TO DIE FOR."

I grinned at the naked longing in his tone. "Funny thing, Terry, I wouldn't have figured you for a car envy kind of guy."

"Hey, I may be gay, but I'm not blind."

"You're also not working. Why am I not surprised?" Crawford came hurrying down the aisle. He was leading a Dalmatian and carrying a red-and-white ribbon. "Hi, Melanie. Bye, Melanie. You two can chat later, okay?"

"Sure," I said quickly, as Crawford ushered the liver-spotted dog into his crate. "I was just wondering what you and Terry thought of the new magazine."

Crawford tossed the Best Opposite Sex ribbon into his tackbox and pulled off his sports coat. "I think I just got beat for the breed in Poodles and Dalmatians, so if my Lhasa doesn't go up, I can pretty much pack it in for the day. That's about the only opinion I can afford to have at the moment."

"Got it," I said, and made my retreat.

Back at Sam's setup, Faith and Tar were both resting quietly in their crates. Sam had disappeared, but Davey and Aunt Peg were back. Both were slurping on Popsicles, blue for Davey, red for Aunt Peg. One look at those colors, and you didn't have to be a mother to know that the drips would stain.

"Did you have a sandwich from the cooler?" I asked. "And a carton of milk?"

"No. Aunt Peg said it was too hot to eat real food."

She would.

"You didn't happen to run across Sheila in your travels, did you?" asked Peg. "We saw Brian again. He's doing his best to hide it, but I think he's livid that she hasn't shown up."

"I wonder if she chickened out," I said. "It's one thing to publish all the dirt that's fit to print, it's another to walk around and hand it to people personally."

Aunt Peg shook her head. "If that's the reason she's not here, I imagine she'll live to regret it. Brian seems quite pleased with himself, and most of the response I've heard so far has been pretty favorable. Even without Sheila's help, Brian's managed to blanket the show ground with copies."

"Where'd Sam go?" I asked.

"He said he wanted to have a word with Brian." Peg glanced at her watch. "Saint Bernards were due to start in ring ten at one-thirty. I think he headed that way."

"Let's go look," I said to Davey. "Want to watch the Saint Bernards?"

Davey scrambled eagerly to his feet. Though he adores Faith, he's fascinated by the giant breeds, like Great Danes, Irish Wolfhounds, Great Pyrenees, and Saint Bernards. Far from finding their size overwhelming, he responds instinctively to the big dogs' inherent gentleness. Besides, when you're six, the fact that they drool is an added bonus.

The entry in Saints must have been big. Ring ten was

on the end of the row, and, as we approached, I could see at least twenty of the large dogs sitting with their owners at ringside.

In deference to the sunny day, most were either being held under the tent or shaded by large umbrellas. Stainless-steel water bowls, bobbing with ice cubes, were everywhere; and a number of the dogs wore bibs made of towels, tied around their necks to catch the drool before it could mar their sparkling-clean coats.

I saw Sam on the far side of the ring and turned to go that way, but Davey had other plans. Eyes round as pennies, he pulled me toward the nearest Saint Bernard, a shorthaired female lying on a towel next to her owner's chair. Obviously unimpressed by the judging in the ring behind her, the brown-and-white bitch watched our approach with equanimity.

"Can I pet her?" Davey asked, already reaching toward the soft coat.

I hauled him back. "We have to ask permission first."

Judging by the kind look in her soft brown eyes, the Saint's temperament wasn't a problem. But being largely unfamiliar with the breed, I had no idea what kind of preparations her owner might have gone through before bringing the dog to the ring. I knew from my experience with Faith that there was nothing more frustrating than spending hours getting a Poodle ready to be shown, only to have someone stick a hand into its hair at ringside.

"Don't worry about Julie," said the Saint's owner, who'd heard our exchange. "She loves kids."

As Davey sank to his knees on the ground beside her, the bitch's large pink tongue licked the length of his arm. Clearly this was a dog who liked the taste of blueberry Popsicles.

On the other side of the ring, Sam and Brian were now engaged in a heated discussion. If Sam had noticed our approach, it hadn't been enough to distract him from the conversation.

I wondered if they were talking about Sheila. I wondered if asking him about that later would make me sound paranoid. And I wondered how a woman, whose existence I'd been completely unaware of four months earlier, had come to be such an insidious presence in our lives.

"Davey, I'm going to go around the ring and talk to Sam. Do you want to stay here and pet the nice dog or come with me?"

"Stay here," Davey said firmly.

I pointed to Sam and Brian. "That's where I'll be. Don't go anywhere else but here or there, okay?"

"Okay."

Acquiescence that comes that easily doesn't always mean much, but since I'd be able to see Davey from the other side of the ring, I doubted he'd be able to give me the slip.

As I rounded the corner of the ring, Sam and Brian stopped talking. For a moment, I thought it was because of me, then I realized I wasn't the only one heading their way. A man and woman were approaching from the other side too. Each was carrying a stack of magazines. The office staff, no doubt.

"You're the talk of the show ground," I told Brian as I joined the small group.

His answering grin was dazzling. "Tell me about it. We can't give these out fast enough." He gestured toward the two staffers. "Melanie Travis, meet Aubrey Jones and Tim Golonka. They came to help out with distribution."

Aubrey looked to be about my age, early thirties, with delicate features and pale, lightly freckled skin. Given the strength of the late-June sun, I hoped she was wearing plenty of sunblock.

Tim was short, slight, and eager-looking. The Jimmy Olsen of *Woof!*. While Aubrey gave me a cool nod and an appraising glance, Tim stuck out his hand, grabbed mine, and pumped it vigorously.

"What's your breed?" he asked, the ever-popular first question among dedicated showgoers.

"Poodles."

"Little or big?"

"Standards."

"Man, I love those dogs! Had one when I was a kid. Best dog in the world." Tim's chatter was fast and exuberant. If he expended any more energy, he'd be dancing in place.

"Melanie is Sam's fiancée," Brian explained. I assumed Sam had been introduced earlier. "Her aunt is Margaret Turnbull—"

"Cedar Crest," Aubrey broke in before Brian could finish. She looked like a student sitting in the front row and hoping to impress the teacher.

"Wow!" cried Tim. "Great dogs. Cool lady. I read an article about her in *Dogs in Review*."

"She is a cool lady," I agreed. "And I'm sure she'd like you, too." I looked at Brian. "I don't know why I'm surprised. Maybe I shouldn't be. Are all your staffers so familiar with the dog show world?"

"All my staff?" Brian laughed. "You make it sound so grand. We're a small outfit, you've pretty much met everybody. Sheila and I are copublishers. Aubrey is managing editor. Tim, here, is her assistant."

"Assistant editor on my business cards," Tim confided. "But you can call me gofer. And don't forget Carrie."

"She answers the phones," said Aubrey. "We hired her from an ad in the paper. She lives with two cats and I think she thinks the rest of us are seriously nuts."

"She makes good coffee," Brian said in Carrie's defense. "And she's already been to her first dog show. We'll win her over eventually."

"If you'll excuse me," said Sam, "I have to go get ready for the group."

"Of course." Brian nodded. "Don't forget what I told you."

"You have a dog in the group? Cool! Non-Sporting?"

"A Standard Poodle puppy," I said, wishing Tim hadn't chosen that moment to ask more questions. Sam was already walking away. "Come and cheer for us, okay?"

"Will do!"

I hurried to catch up to Sam. "What was that all about?" I steered him toward the other side of the ring where I had to pick up Davey.

"What?"

"What did Brian tell you?"

"It was nothing."

"It looked like he thought it was important."

"Brian thinks everything that relates to him is important." Sam turned away, took two quick strides, and reached down to scoop Davey up into his arms. "Hey, champ! Looks like you've been taking pretty good care of that Saint Bernard. Or is she taking care of you?"

"Her name is Julie," Davey said happily. "And she likes cookies. I got to feed her one. She has the biggest mouth in the whole world."

"Bigger than the sharks at the Maritime Center?"

"Much bigger!"

"Thanks," I said to Julie's owner. "You've made his day."

"No problem. He was charming."

Davey? My son was adorable, precocious, maddeningly opinionated, and slippery as an eel when he wanted to be. But charming? That was a new concept.

I let it roll around in my head as we walked back to the setup. By the time we got there, I'd decided I was rather pleased. Maybe some of those manners I'd been trying to teach him were finally taking hold.

"Hey, Aunt Peg!" Davey yelled, sliding down out of Sam's arms. "What have you got to eat?"

Then again, maybe not.

"There's fruit in the cooler," I said. "And those sandwiches you never had for lunch."

"Spoilsport." Peg sniffed. She was sitting in a canvas chair and had a copy of *Woof!* open in her lap.

"Precisely." I reached past her to open the cooler. "I'm the mother. That's part of the job description." I took out an apple and a tuna sandwich and handed them to Davey. "Having fun with that magazine?"

"I don't know if fun is the right word, but it certainly is interesting. Did you know that Kenny Boyle's been busted for overbilling his clients?"

"Busted?" I laughed. "That doesn't sound like your kind of word."

"It didn't used to be. But with all the trouble you manage to get yourself into, I've had to develop a whole new vocabulary."

"I was under the impression that most handlers padded their bills," Sam mentioned. He'd gotten Tar out of his crate and put the puppy up on the table. "How come Kenny was singled out?"

Kenny Boyle specialized in the working breeds. His client list comprised some of the most influential, and well-heeled, members of the dog community. We all knew who he was.

"Apparently his padding bought him a new van and sent his son to private school." Peg's finger stabbed the page. "It says so right here."

I looked at Sam and grinned. "She's hooked."

"It's my duty to stay informed," Peg said primly. "Now that I've seen an issue, I think I may subscribe after all."

"Hooked," I repeated.

Peg harrumphed and went back to her reading. Davey settled down beside her and ate a belated lunch. While Sam worked on getting Tar's topknot back up, I got Faith out of her crate and took her for a walk. With a litter of puppies all jockeying for space, her bladder isn't as big as it used to be.

The group judging started at two o'clock; and the Non-Sporting Group was the third to be judged. Groups that start early entice spectators to stay and watch, and the gallery was sizable when Sam walked Tar into the ring.

Some handlers see a benefit in heading up the line, and the Dalmatian and Standard Poodle, the two big dogs of the Non-Sporting Group, often vie for that first position. Since this was Tar's first group appearance, however, Sam was content to let the puppy take his time and look around. They settled in behind the Dal, where Tar would have a lead to follow.

"He really looks good," I said to Peg. She, Davey, and I had found a place right up front.

"He should. That puppy is the culmination of thirty

years of hard work. Pity they don't all turn out so well. Now let's see if Sylvia Koenig remembers how much she liked him earlier."

If she didn't, the crowd at ringside seemed more than ready to remind her. Since Poodle puppies show in a different trim than the adults do, it was immediately apparent to all who were watching that Tar was a young dog who'd already triumphed over his elders in winning Best of Variety. That alone was enough to get their attention.

Then they saw him move.

By the time Tar's turn came to be individually examined, he already had a following. Peg and Davey and I were clapping, of course, but our applause was merely a small part of the acclaim that followed the puppy's performance. As Tar finished gaiting down and back and did a flawless free-stack in front of the judge, someone whooped loudly. Looking across the ring, I saw Brian, Aubrey, and Tim all standing together. Tim grinned and flashed a thumbs-up.

Seeing the sensation her puppy was causing, Aunt Peg turned pink with pleasure. Even the judge permitted herself a small smile as Sam spun Tar around and raced with him to the end of the line. Everyone knew they were watching something special. When the show was rehashed during the week, Sam's puppy would be the dog they all talked about.

"Told you so," said Terry, wiggling in beside us. Though Crawford had lost with his Standard Poodle, and his Dalmatian, he was in the ring with a Lhasa Apso. "You're going to beat us again, too."

"Maybe," Aunt Peg said under her breath. "But the Bulldog's going to win."

She spoke with certainty as she always did. There was no use trying to figure out how she knew these things. Questioned, she'd tell you it was a combination of experience, knowing the dogs' records and the judges' preferences, and intuition. Or maybe it was just luck. But whatever contributed to them, her predictions were seldom wrong.

"Not Tar?" I asked, disappointed already, though the judge hadn't even made her cut.

"It's not his time yet," Aunt Peg said complacently. "He'll win his shares of groups, but not this one. That Bulldog's owned the East Coast all spring, and rightly so. Not only that, but there are some other very good dogs in there. I'd be very pleased if Tar managed a ribbon in this company."

As the judge examined the other entrants, I let my gaze drift. On the other side of the ring, Brian was talking on his cell phone. I saw him frown, then reach up to cover his other ear with his hand.

Obviously it still wasn't enough to block out the noise, because he turned abruptly and shoved his way back through the crowd. Aubrey watched him go but made no attempt to follow. Tim's gaze was focused on the dogs in the ring.

Aunt Peg's elbow jabbed me in the ribs. "She's pulled him."

I looked back in the ring. The judge was making her cut. The Bulldog was on top, followed by Tar, then a Shiba Inu. Crawford's Lhasa was in fourth place.

"I think that's it," said Peg, hands poised to clap as the judge sent the dogs around.

When Mrs. Koenig pointed to Tar for second place, Davey and I whooped and hollered like tourists who'd never been to a dog show before. Terry smirked at our undignified behavior, then joined in the fun by whistling through his fingers. Surprised by all the commotion, Sam cast a startled glance our way, and grinned.

Clutching the big red ribbon, he headed for the gate. Peg, Davey, and I made our way through the crowd to meet him. Our progress was hampered by the hordes of spectators, and Sam had already come through the gate when we got there. Unexpectedly, Brian Endicott was standing beside him.

Even from a dozen feet away I knew something was wrong. Sam had gone absolutely still; his face was white. Brian looked as though he might be sick. Tar's leash dangled limply from Sam's hand. The puppy, sensing his owner's distress, stopped playing and looked up questioningly.

Another exhibitor, passing by on the way out of the ring, congratulated Sam. He didn't answer. He didn't even seem to hear.

Dropping Davey's hand, I ran on ahead. "What?" I demanded. "What's happened?"

Brian swallowed heavily. Words seemed beyond him. I looked at Sam.

"Brian just heard," he said. "Sheila is dead. She was murdered last night."

❧❀ *Seven* ❀❧

"No," I said. My voice was firm, as if denying the news could change it. "You must be wrong."

"Wrong about what?" asked Peg, coming up beside us.

I glanced down at Davey and shook my head. "Why don't you two go get some ice cream?" The cheery words seemed to stick in my throat. "I'll catch up in a minute."

Aunt Peg's gaze ricocheted between us, trying to discern the problem. After a moment, she reached out and took Tar's leash and ribbon from Sam. "That sounds like a good idea. Maybe we'll put the puppy in his crate, too. Okay, Davey?"

"Okay," my son agreed, oblivious to the strained silence of the other adults. "I want chocolate!"

"And so you shall have it," Peg said, leading boy and dog away.

"What happened?" I said as soon as they had gone.

"I don't know." Brian's hand trembled slightly as he shook a cigarette out of his pack and lit up. "Maybe there's been some kind of mistake. Do you think that's possible?"

"Who gave you the news?" asked Sam. "Who did you talk to?"

"Some guy from the state police in Somers. You know how Sheila was supposed to meet me here? I've been calling around all day, trying to figure out where she was. A few minutes ago, there was an answer at her house. A detective picked up, asked who I was, and then told me that Sheila was dead."

That didn't sound like the kind of thing someone would have been mistaken about to me.

"I've got to get over there," said Brian. "I want to see for myself what's going on."

The news seemed to have energized him. He seemed agitated, almost frantic. Sam, on the other hand, was withdrawing into himself. His features looked blank. His eyes were stunned, void of all emotion.

"I'm coming with you," he told Brian. As an afterthought, he turned to me. "Can you take Tar home?"

I nodded.

"I'll call you later."

He started to walk away, but I caught up, grabbed his hand and gave it a strong squeeze. Sam stopped and looked in my direction. Even so, he seemed far away. Whatever he was seeing, it wasn't me.

"It'll be okay," I said softly.

"How?" For just the briefest moment, feeling broke through, and his voice was anguished. "How can things possibly be okay?"

Then he was gone.

I stood and watched him go. Watched the two men—once friends, then adversaries, now reunited by tragedy—stride away together.

Sam had been right, I thought. My reassurances were

as empty as they'd sounded. Things weren't going to be okay. Something, maybe everything, was going to change. I just hoped we'd be able to put our lives back together when it was over.

I found Aunt Peg and Davey back at the setup. Peg was undoing Tar's tight, show ring topknot. Davey was industriously working his way through a hot fudge sundae.

I sighed. Loudly.

"I wanted something that would keep him occupied," Aunt Peg said.

Right. In light of what had just transpired, it didn't seem worth arguing about. I stopped beside my son's chair. "It's such a nice warm day. Why don't we move you out from under the tent so you can sit in the sun?"

"Okay." Davey hopped up. "Look what Aunt Peg got me. It had three scoops of ice cream and two cherries!"

"That's an awfully big sundae. Want some help finishing it?"

"No!"

No surprise there. I took his chair and placed it out beside an exercise pen, holding three Norwich Terrier puppies. Davey was watching their antics and spooning up hot fudge at a rate guaranteed to overload his circuits when I went back in to rejoin Aunt Peg.

"Well?" she demanded.

"Sheila Vaughn has been murdered."

"Oh Lord. Did Brian have any details?"

"None that he mentioned. He and Sam are on their way over to Sheila's house now. I'll take Tar home with me, and Sam's going to call me later."

"What are you two whispering about?"

I'd been so intent on the bad news, I hadn't even noticed Terry's approach. Now I shut my mouth, wondering how much we should say.

But while I hesitated, Peg jumped right in. "Sheila Vaughn's been murdered."

Talk about letting the cat out of the bag.

Terry's eyes grew large. He immediately looked at me. "Good thing you have an alibi. You've been here all day. I can vouch for that myself."

"That's not funny!" I snapped.

Terry wasn't chastened.

Even Peg looked faintly amused. "You have to admit, it does remove one problem from your life."

"And substitutes another," I said irritably. "You should have seen Sam's face when he heard. He was devastated."

"As well he would be," Peg said. "Sam's not the sort of man to turn his back on someone he once loved. On some level, I imagine he still cared for her deeply."

"He did," I grumbled. "Which will make this that much worse for him."

"Gotta go." Terry looked like a man with a secret he was dying to share. Within minutes, the news would be all over the show ground. "Keep me posted, okay?"

Terry didn't wait for an answer. He skipped away down the narrow aisle, dodging around Tim and Aubrey, Brian's two assistants, who were heading our way.

"Oh dear," said Aunt Peg. "Do you suppose they know what happened?"

I didn't even have to speculate. The first words out of Aubrey's mouth provided the answer.

"Have you seen Brian?" she asked. "We were watching

the groups together, then all of a sudden he just disappeared."

"Brian had to leave." I was unsure how much I wanted to divulge. Although with Terry on the loose, the news was probably already spreading like parvo.

"Oh? Any idea where he went?"

"To North Salem," said Aunt Peg. "To Sheila's house."

"What's with her, anyway?" Tim asked. "She was supposed to be here."

"I'm afraid there's been some bad news."

"About Sheila?" Aubrey prompted. She didn't seem upset by the prospect.

"Is she okay?" asked Tim.

"Not exactly," I hedged.

"She's dead," Peg added helpfully.

"Dead?" Tim grinned. "This is a joke, right?"

"No," I said. "No joke. According to the police, Sheila was murdered."

"By whom?" Aubrey demanded, as if she thought this was the sort of information we ought to have.

"I don't know. The state police were at her house when Brian spoke to them a little while ago. He and Sam both left to go over there. I don't know any more than that."

"Sam ..." Aubrey mused aloud. Her lips pursed as she thought. "He was Sheila's ex, right? I wonder if there were any hard feelings there."

"There weren't," I said firmly, feeling a small tremor of shock. It hadn't occurred to me until that moment that Sam might be a suspect. "He and Sheila hadn't seen each other in years until recently."

"That's what I mean," Aubrey persisted. "The timing seems pretty suspicious, doesn't it?"

In other circumstances, I might have appreciated her curiosity. Now, it was really getting on my nerves.

Beside her, Tim was fidgeting like a Jack Russell with a bone in its throat. He coughed loudly. "Aubrey, shut up. Now."

"Why?" Her shocked look clearly indicated that she wasn't used to being addressed in such a manner by her assistant. "I'm sorry about what happened, but it's not like we were friends or anything. I mean, you can't help but speculate—"

"About Melanie's fiancé?" he finished for her.

"Oh!" Aubrey gasped and cast a startled glance my way. A dark flush started beneath her collarbone and worked its way up her neck. "Oh God! Don't pay any attention to me! I was just saying stupid things off the top of my head. It's not like I think Sam could do something horrible like that . . . Well, how would I know if he could or not? I mean, we just met . . ."

Aubrey was so flustered she could barely speak, much less form coherent thoughts. Now Tim was rolling his eyes. If Sam were there, he would have laughed. That thought made me smile.

"Don't worry about it," I said. "I've speculated about a few mysteries myself."

"Hopefully with more tact," said Aunt Peg, who didn't look appeased.

"Sorry about that," said Tim, steering Aubrey away.

She was digging through her purse. "Do you have Sheila's home address?" I heard her ask Tim, her voice fading as they walked. "I'm sure Brian needs me . . ."

"Interesting pair," said Aunt Peg. "I wonder where they were when Sheila was killed."

Good question.

Unless I missed my guess, it would be the first of many.

I waited all evening to hear from Sam. Resisting the urge to call him. Knowing that he had to be busy; otherwise, he'd surely have gotten in touch.

I told Davey only that Sam had been called away on business, but that we'd be hearing from him soon. By nine o'clock, when I put my son to bed, there'd still been no word.

What could possibly be going on in North Salem that would take this long? I wondered. Sam had left the dog show five and a half hours earlier.

When I finally did hear from Sam, it wasn't by phone. At nine-thirty, headlights swept through my living room as his Blazer turned in my driveway. I had the front door open before he'd even gotten out of the car.

Faith and Tar ran past me to greet him, the two Poodles nudging each other aside playfully in their attempt to get there first. Sam stopped and braced for the canine onslaught. He bent low over both dogs, talking to them, ruffling his hands through their hair. It seemed to take forever before he straightened and looked at me.

As he stepped into the pool of light by the door, I saw that his face was haggard. Somewhere, he'd shed the sports coat and tie he'd been wearing at the show. His shirt was open at the throat, the cuffs were rolled back. There was dirt on the knees of his khakis and a grass stain on his shirt.

I met him on the bottom step and realized that he smelled of Scotch. Sam wasn't a drinker. Beer, sure; and the occasional glass of wine. But until that moment I wouldn't have been able to tell you what kind of hard liquor he preferred.

His gait was steady, but his eyes were bloodshot. I wondered how much Scotch you had to consume for the scent to linger.

I didn't kiss him. Maybe I should have. I thought about that later.

But his expression was so forbidding that it seemed like a better idea to wrap my arm around his and lead him up the steps. Subdued, the two Poodles followed us inside.

"You okay?" I asked.

"Hell no," Sam growled. He walked into the living room and sank down on the couch. "Do I look okay?"

All evening, I'd been concerned. But now, seeing the shape Sam had gotten himself into, I was suddenly all out of pity. "Frankly, you look like shit."

"Perfect." His head lolled back on the cushion. His eyes closed. "No reason the outside shouldn't match the inside."

"How about some coffee?"

One eye opened. Sam brushed a hand over it as if the lighting in the room was too bright. "I'm not drunk."

"I didn't say you were."

"And if I was drunk, I don't think I'd be ready to get sober just yet."

"Fine," I said, sitting down opposite him. "What about your dogs?"

Aside from Tar, Sam had three other Standard Poodles, who lived with him in Redding. When he knew in advance that he was going to be away overnight, he had a pet-sitter come and stay with them.

"They're covered." Sam exhaled loudly. "I called Holly

this afternoon. Luckily she wasn't busy and was able to go right over. She'll stay 'til after breakfast tomorrow."

One problem solved. At least I didn't have to worry about Sam getting back on the road tonight.

"So," I said, "where have you been?" I tried hard not to sound reproachful. I didn't add the words "all this time" though they did seem to dangle in the air. I certainly didn't go so far as to ask if his cell phone battery was charged.

"Drinking," Sam said succinctly. "Can't you tell?"

Even Tar and Faith could tell that. Rather than continuing to vie for his attention, the two Poodles were now lying on the floor, watching Sam curiously. They knew something was different about him; they just weren't sure what it was.

"I thought you and Brian were going to Sheila's house."

"We were. We did. We met the police there. They seemed delighted to see us, suspects arriving on the scene and all. Made their job a little easier." His words were measured, spoken with care, as if he was trying to distance himself from the memory.

"So Sheila is dead."

"Yup." His nod only went halfway. His head dropped, but it didn't come back up.

"Do the police really think you're a suspect?"

"Hard to tell. So far, they're just not ruling anything out. They questioned both Brian and me. Separately. Ex-husband and current lover. I think they were surprised to see us show up together."

I know I would have been.

"You both have an alibi, though. You were at the show all day."

"Doesn't help. There'll be an autopsy, but the medical

examiner on the scene was sure Sheila was killed some-time last night. At least twelve hours earlier, probably more."

Friday night. Sam had been home bathing Tar, getting him ready for the show. I'd been here with Davey. We'd spoken on the phone briefly, and made plans for today.

Maybe Sam didn't have an alibi, I thought. But he didn't have a motive either.

"What about Brian? He and Sheila have been seeing each other. Were they together last night?"

"Brian said no. He was working late at the office by himself. He said he wanted to make sure everything was perfect for today's launch." Sam grimaced. "The detective seemed skeptical, but I thought that sounded just like Brian. He'd choose financial success over a personal rela-tionship any day."

Sam looked like he was speaking from experience. I wondered if that was why Sheila had left Brian a decade earlier. Aside from that love-at-first-sight thing.

Sam's eyes were closed again. Though it wasn't late, he was fighting to stay awake. Effects of the alcohol, or of the day? Maybe he just needed the oblivion that sleep would bring.

I walked to the closet in the front hall and got out a blanket. Sam rallied enough to see me coming. He shook his head. "Don't take care of me."

"Why not?" I pulled his legs up onto the couch and spread the blanket over him. "Would you rather stay here or do you want me to help you upstairs?"

"No, I don't . . ." His voice faded away.

"You don't need my help?"

His next words were soft. I had to lean closer to hear them.

"I don't deserve it."

"Oh, Sam." A tear hovered in the edge of my eye. Annoyed, I blinked it away. Sam didn't notice. He was already snoring.

I let the dogs out and back in, turned off the lights, and left him to sleep it off.

ᴄ❀ Eight ❀ᴄ

Sunday morning I awoke to the aroma of fresh coffee and the sound of Nintendo. Faith and Tar had both been in my bedroom when I'd gone to bed. Now they were gone, downstairs with the game players, no doubt.

Checking my clock, I saw that it was just past seven. I hoped Davey hadn't awakened Sam too early. Throwing on a robe, I ventured down to find out.

"Hey, Mom!" Davey yelled when he saw me. Just in case I couldn't hear him across the expanse of our small living room. "Look who's here!"

Considering the shape I'd left him in, Sam looked remarkably well. His clothes were rumpled, his blond hair, damp from a shower. But the blue eyes were clear, and the day's growth of beard looked pretty sexy.

Immediately, he levered himself up off the couch. "Let me get you some coffee."

"But it's almost your turn," Davey complained.

"Let Tar play for me," Sam said. "If you can beat the puppy, we'll let you try your hand against the grown-up dog."

We walked to the kitchen together, Sam trailing a somewhat hesitant halfstep behind. "I'm sorry about last night," he said. "I probably should have gone home."

I let the gap close between us and wound my arms around his waist. "You did come home."

I felt him relax just a bit and hugged him to me harder. After all the time we'd been together, how could he still have any doubts about where he belonged?

Sam squeezed me back for a moment, then stepped away and went to the cupboard for a mug. I almost followed, wanting to keep him close, but something about the way his gaze evaded mine held me back. Instead, I pulled out a chair at the kitchen table and sat down.

"Did we have a chance to talk last night?" he asked. "Or did I fall asleep right away?"

"We talked some. I still have plenty of questions."

"I figured you would. Shoot."

"Who found Sheila and called the police? What happened to all her Pugs? And at what point did you manage to get yourself pickled in alcohol?"

Sam added milk to the mug of hot coffee and set it down in front of me, then pulled out a chair and sat, too. "Sheila was found by her next-door neighbor, Nancy Benning. Apparently the Pugs had been barking for much of Friday night, and they kept it up on Saturday. According to what Mrs. Benning told the police, that was very unusual.

"She knew that Sheila had a number of dogs, but she'd never been bothered by them before. It wasn't clear whether she went to Sheila's to complain about the noise or investigate, but she found the front door open, walked in, and immediately called 911."

Sam's fingers drummed lightly on the tabletop, keeping

time as he spoke. "Judging by what they told us yesterday, the police seem to think Sheila was the victim of a burglary gone bad. A secluded home, a woman alone. They figure she looked like an easy target.

"There doesn't seem to have been much stuff stolen, but then, being a furnished rental, Sheila didn't have much in the house. Brian had a better idea about that than I did. The TV and a CD player were gone. He thought maybe some silver candlesticks were missing. The police were guessing that she might have come upon the burglars unexpectedly. They panicked and killed her."

I blew across the top of my steaming mug and ran through the scenario in my mind. It didn't make sense. "What about Sheila's Pugs? If someone was casing the neighborhood looking for a place to rob, I'd think that all those dogs would serve as a pretty strong deterrent."

"I agree," said Sam. "When the police arrived, the Pugs were outside in the back. My guess is they'd been out all night; that's why Mrs. Benning was able to hear them barking. The guy in charge, Detective Holloway, told me that's why the burglars weren't worried about the dogs. Because they knew Sheila kept them outside."

"But she didn't," I protested. "They were house dogs, just like yours and mine. I bet Sheila never left them out when she wasn't there."

Sam nodded. His thoughts on the matter had clearly mirrored mine. "She didn't. Aside from the fact that they were her pets, those Pugs were champion show dogs, and irreplaceable building blocks in Sheila's breeding program. She never would have treated them so carelessly.

"I told Holloway that, but you know how it is when someone isn't a dog person. He probably has neighbors who keep their dog chained to a tree in the backyard, and he thinks that's the way everyone does it. He didn't think that the fact that the Pugs were outside was important."

"Dope," I muttered. "It makes a huge difference. If Sheila wasn't home when the burglars got there, then the Pugs would have been locked in the house. So if the Pugs *were* outside, that means Sheila was home. It also probably means that she let her murderer into the house."

Sam was silent, digesting what I'd said. "There weren't any signs of forced entry," he said, after a moment. "Several windows in the house were open. The police surmise that's how the burglars gained entry. They were grumbling about how lax people get with security in the summer. Warm night, older home, no air-conditioning. Especially living out in the middle of nowhere like that, everyone leaves their windows open."

I nodded in agreement. The part of Stamford Davey and I lived in was more suburban than North Salem, but we'd both slept with the windows in our bedrooms open the night before.

"They found Sheila's body in the kitchen," Sam said quietly. "You remember those leashes she had hanging on a hook in the pantry? That's how she was killed. The murderer strangled her."

I glanced at Faith's leash, hanging over the knob to the back door. A six-foot strip of sturdy leather, it was meant to form a subtle line of communication between dog and owner. I'd never thought of it a weapon before; now I wondered how long it would be before I could see it as anything else.

"I guess that supports the detective's theory that Sheila

surprised an intruder. It sounds like the killer just grabbed whatever was handy."

"Or knew she kept the leads there."

Stranger or friend? I wondered. Who was the last person Sheila had seen? Neither thought held the slightest bit of comfort.

The coffee Sam had poured me was hot and dark. I took a large swallow and felt it burn its way down my throat. "What happened to the Pugs? You didn't leave them at Sheila's house?"

"No, of course not. Brian has them at his place in Purchase. Big house, couple acres of land, kennel out back. Built for the Saints, but the Pugs seemed to find it pretty comfortable. That's where I ended up going last night. Brian volunteered to take care of the dogs, and it seemed like a good solution. Except of course, they didn't all fit in Brian's car."

Whereas Sam's Blazer would hold five Pugs quite handily.

"So you drove the Pugs to Purchase . . ." I prompted.

Sam looked sheepish. "When we got there, Brian said I should come on in for a drink. You know, just something to settle our nerves? Next thing I knew we were doing shots of Chivas. A toast to Sheila. Another to the good old days."

He shook his head. Judging by the way his eyes narrowed to a squint, the small movement hurt. "God, what was I thinking?"

I reached across the table and covered Sam's hand with mine. "That you'd just been through a terrible experience and wanted to forget about it for a while?"

"I guess. But that doesn't make it right. And to drown

my sorrows with Brian, of all people. I must have been out of my mind."

Sam shoved back his chair and stood. My hand fell away. He walked over to the sink and stared out the window.

"Grief does funny things to people," I said quietly. My fingers stung from having smacked against the tabletop. Sam didn't seem to have noticed. "Everyone handles it differently."

"Well so far, I guess I haven't been doing a very good job. It's not like Sheila was still part of my life. The only thing we really had between us was the past. And yet somehow, I can't believe that she's really gone."

He strode out the arched doorway and into the narrow hall that led to the front of the house. A minute later, I heard the front door open and close.

My first impulse was to go after him. My second, more rational thought, was that I was still wearing pajamas and a robe. Instead I walked into the living room and looked out the window.

Sam's Blazer was still in the driveway. He was on foot, which meant he'd have to come back eventually. Besides, I still had his puppy.

"Where did Sam go?" Davey asked, briefly distracted from his video game.

"For a walk." I let the curtain fall. "Let me just get dressed and we'll take the dogs and go find him, okay?"

"Okay. You can hold Faith, and I'll hold Tar."

On leashes, I thought, and my stomach plummeted.

During the past couple years, I'd been involved in the investigation of several murders. Usually the victims had been people I barely knew; occasionally, they'd been someone I'd despised. But Sheila's death was different.

I could see the effect her loss had had on Sam; now I was beginning to realize how much it would affect me, too. The discovery that he still cared so much made me feel all hollow inside. I'd had a hard enough time with Sam's ex-wife when she was alive. I couldn't compete with a memory; I wasn't even sure I wanted to try.

Twenty minutes later, I was back downstairs and ready to go. I'd gotten Faith's lead and was looking for something to use on Tar when the phone began to ring. I reached across the counter and picked up.

"Melanie? It's Brian. I've been trying to find Sam. Is he there?"

"He is, but he went out for a walk. Do you want me to give him a message?"

"Sure. Tell him I need a favor. Did he tell you I've got Sheila's Pugs?"

"Yes."

"I should have thought of this at the time . . . I guess I had other things on my mind. The old bitch, Blossom, has a thyroid deficiency and needs her medicine. Sheila had tablets she gave her every day. On Sunday, there's no way I'm going to be able to get them replaced by a vet. Do you think Sam would mind going up to Sheila's place and picking them up?"

"No . . ." I said slowly. We were about half an hour from North Salem. Brian, in Purchase, was probably a few minutes closer. "Of course, then he'll have to bring them down to you. Wouldn't it be easier if you just went and got them yourself?"

"Can't," said Brian. "I don't have a key."

I opened my mouth to state that Sam would have the same problem, then stopped, wondering. "Does Sam?"

"He said he did last night."

Funny, I thought. He'd never mentioned that to me.

Or maybe, depending on your outlook, it wasn't funny at all. Giving someone a key suggested a certain level of intimacy. Sheila had been seeing Brian, yet she hadn't given him a key. So why had Sam needed such easy access?

Silence on the line attested to the fact that Brian was waiting. "Sure," I heard myself blurt. "We'll be happy to pick up the pills. Do you know where Sheila kept them?"

"On a shelf in the bathroom. It's one of those little orange vials. I'm sure it's marked. You shouldn't have any trouble finding it."

"Will you be home later this morning?"

"I'll stay here 'til you get here. And thanks."

I hung up the phone and immediately dialed again. Davey's best friend, Joey Brickman, lived down the street. His mother, Alice, was also one of my best friends, and she'd had Davey dumped on her more times than I could count.

Of course, Joey makes plenty of unexpected visits to our house, too. We tend to think of the system as a series of last-minute play dates. Otherwise known as covering each other's butts.

Alice, her husband Joe, and their two children, Carly and Joey, were on their way to church, but Alice said they'd be back in an hour. I offered a sketchy scenario of how I'd be spending my day, and she told me to drop Davey off on our way to North Salem.

As I hung up the phone, I heard a commotion in the front hall. Poodles barking, Davey laughing. I was guessing Sam was back.

"Hey," he said, walking into the kitchen, with my son

hanging from one leg and the two Poodles acting as an honor guard. "What's up?"

I was pleased to see he looked much better than he had half an hour earlier. But not thrilled to realize that time alone had helped, whereas time with me had not.

"Breakfast is up," I said, hoping I sounded more cheery than I felt. "I'm making French toast. Then Davey is going over to Joey's house and you and I are going to North Salem. Brian called. One of the Pugs needs her meds, and I told him we'd pick them up."

I didn't mention the house key. Neither did Sam. Instead, he was quiet through much of breakfast, and I wondered what he was thinking. Davey ate three pieces of French toast and got caught trying to slip Faith a bite under the table. It took me ten minutes to wash the maple syrup out of her hair.

By ten o'clock, we were on our way. Davey chattered nonstop as we drove up the street. Sam and I watched him dribble his soccer ball up the Brickmans' walk and in the front door. I could only hope that Alice was nearby, keeping an eye on the fragile stuff.

Once Davey was gone, the silence in the car was palpable. Sam turned on the radio, flipped through the buttons, turned up the volume.

I stared out the window and sighed.

It was going to be a very long day.

❧❦ *Nine* ❦❧

Sheila's place looked different in daylight than it had days earlier in the forgiving light of dusk. More a cottage than a house, the structure that had seemed charming then, now looked shabby. The paint was faded and peeling in spots; the yard out front was overgrown.

Standing beside Sam's car, I studied the small home dispassionately, as a burglar might have. The out-of-control vegetation offered plenty of cover. On the other hand, the home's state of disrepair didn't seem to promise much in the way of valuables.

"No crime-scene tape," I remarked as we walked to the front door. "Are the police finished here?"

"I think they've cordoned off the kitchen." Sam pulled a key out of his pocket and fitted it to the lock. "We won't need to disturb that."

Since I hadn't mentioned it, I guessed that meant Sam knew Sheila had kept her dogs' medicine in the bathroom. What else did he know? I wondered. How many times had he been here over the last several months?

"I didn't realize you had a key until Brian told me," I mentioned, following him inside.

"Sheila made a copy and gave it to me. She figured I knew better than anyone how forgetful she could be. She thought people who stuck their spare under the mat or above the doorsill were crazy."

Sam stopped and sucked in a breath. "I guess you could say that's ironic, considering how things turned out."

I started toward the living room and found myself hesitating in the doorway. With its faded hooked rug and stone fireplace, the room looked peaceful and cozy, the last kind of place where something sinister might take place. A ribbon of bright yellow tape crossed the kitchen door. Deliberately, I looked the other way.

"Did you ever have to come and let her in?"

"Once." Sam smiled faintly. "Right after she got here."

Back in the days when Sheila'd still believed that all she'd have to do to win Sam back was ask.

"Don't tell me, it was after dark, right?"

"After work," Sam corrected.

"Candles lit?"

"Um, yeah."

Sheila had loved candles. Several fat, ivory wax globes sat, even now, on the mantelpiece and the sideboard.

"Was she wearing a negligee?"

Sam slanted me a look. "She was outside when I got here. That was the point, remember?"

I shrugged. "Just trying to set the scene."

"She was wearing a suit. Navy blue jacket and skirt. No blouse. No stockings. High heels."

This from a man who took a week to notice when I

got my hair cut. Obviously what had stuck in his mind was what she hadn't had on.

I watched him glance toward the open door to Sheila's bedroom. The double bed hadn't been made. Pale yellow sheets lay tangled around a burgundy patterned quilt.

Sam must have felt my gaze. "She never made the bed," he said. His voice sounded thick. "It used to drive me crazy."

Then you got over it, I thought. Then you got over *her.* Right?

I knew it was normal for him to grieve. And that it was petty and selfish of me to resent the feelings he'd had for his ex-wife—especially under the circumstances. But the worst thing was, deep down inside, I knew I wasn't sorry Sheila was dead. In some ways, I was even relieved. So how awful a person did that make me?

"The pills should be in the bathroom," Sam said. "Do you mind having a look? I'll be along in a minute."

"Okay." I wondered where he was going. And why he was trying to send me in the other direction.

It took only a minute to find the Pug's medicine. The vial was right where Sam and Brian had said it would be. Synthyroid, the label read. Prescribed for Blossom by Thaddeus Read, DVM.

I walked back out into the living room. Sam had disappeared, but it wasn't hard to figure out where he'd gone. The bedroom door was farther ajar than it had been a minute earlier and I could hear the sound of his footsteps on the hardwood floor.

"Sam?" I crossed the hall and stopped in the doorway. He was standing on the other side of the small room, between the bed and a window. His hands were clutching a silver picture frame that looked as though it had been on the nightstand. Sam was staring at the photograph with such intensity that he seemed to suck the very air out of the room.

"What's that?"

He stiffened, and it took a moment for him to pull his thoughts back from where they'd been. "Just an old picture."

Judging by his stance, the memento he held in his hands wasn't just an old anything. I watched his thumb rub back and forth slowly over the frame's beveled edge. The caress seemed involuntary; I doubted he was even aware he was making it.

"Of Sheila?"

Sam nodded, and held it out for me to see. "Happier times."

It was hard not to feel a pang when I saw the photograph. In it, Sheila was laughing, her head thrown back with delight. Her sleek, dark hair, longer than she'd worn it recently, was gathered back in a ponytail. Sunlight glinted off its depths. She looked young, and happy, and very beautiful.

Glare from the light filtering in through the filmy curtains obscured a portion of the glass. I tipped the photo so I could see it better. The image cleared and my breath caught.

What Sam hadn't mentioned was that he was in the picture too. This was Sam as I'd never known him—younger, more vulnerable; his T-shirt tight, his face unlined. His arm was slung casually around Sheila's shoulders; her hand rested on his chest, fingers like slim arrows pointing toward his heart. He, too, was laughing.

"Was this when you were married?" I asked.

"Before. The day we got engaged, actually. We were hiking in the mountains. I'd just asked Sheila to marry me. She said yes just as another hiker came up the trail. We handed him the camera and asked him to take a shot. This was it."

Sam reached out to reclaim the photo, handling it gently as though it was very precious. "This frame belonged to my grandmother. She gave it to Sheila and me when we got married. This is the only picture we ever put in it."

"You looked so young."

"And felt it." He sighed. "Back then, we thought anything was possible."

The wistfulness in his tone stung me like a slap. "It still is."

"On good days." Taking the photograph with him, Sam strode from the room.

I followed more slowly. We'd left the front door open and as we reached the hall, I heard the sound of a car bouncing up the rutted driveway. Together Sam and I walked out onto the porch.

It wasn't a car that approached, but rather a truck. A midsize Ford pickup that looked as though it had seen better days. The driver stopped in front of the house and got out.

He was a good six inches shorter and two decades older than Sam, with heavy jowls and a sunburn on his cheeks and nose. His Levi's jeans were faded; his boots, scuffed. He looked just as surprised to see us as we were to see him. Reaching back onto the seat of the truck, he slapped a baseball cap over his receding hairline before stepping forward warily.

"Help you?" he asked.

"I don't know," said Sam, eyeing the man's stance. "Who are you?"

"Chuck Andrews. This is my house." He looked past us to the open front door. "Mind telling me how you got in?"

"With a key. Given to me by the lady who rented the place."

"You knew Sheila?" Chuck squinted up at us. "I haven't seen you around here before."

It took me a minute to realize why his name sounded familiar. "You're the son of the woman who rented the house to Sheila. The man who's been doing repairs for her."

"That's right." He smiled slightly. "She mentioned me?"

"Um-hm. Just last week, she told me what a big help you'd been."

All right, maybe I was overstating things, but Chuck seemed to be relaxing. Besides, anyone who'd fixed it so that Sam didn't have to keep running to North Salem, was okay in my book.

I introduced myself and Sam. Chuck hopped up onto the porch and shook our hands.

"Sorry, but you can't be too careful. Especially after . . ." His gaze swung back and forth between us. "You know about what happened, right?"

"Sam came here yesterday and talked to the police,"

I said. "Sheila was his ex-wife. He and another friend took her dogs."

"Wondered about that," said Chuck. "As a matter of fact, that's why I'm here. I didn't find out there was anything wrong 'til last night. Took me 'til this morning to remember those dogs. I hated to think they might be sitting over here, neglected. It wasn't much, but I figured it was the least I could do."

"Thank you," said Sam. "I appreciate your concern, and I know Sheila would have, too. Actually, that's why we're here as well. One of the Pugs needs some medicine. We came to pick it up."

"You say you have a key?"

Sam took it out and showed it to him.

"You ought to know then that I plan on changing the locks. Probably tomorrow, which is about as soon as I can get a locksmith out here without paying overtime. Like I said, the way things are these days, you can't be too careful.

"It would just about kill my mother to see what things have come to. Thank goodness there's no reason for her to get involved in any of it. She made an arrangement with Sheila before she went into the nursing home, but I'll be handling things from here on in."

Chuck eyed Sam speculatively. "You say you're a relative?"

"Ex-relative," Sam corrected.

"Just wondering about the lease. I guess it's terminated now. I'll have to go about finding a new tenant."

"I don't know anything about Sheila's will. Or her estate. But I'm sure you'll be compensated for your trouble."

"That's good to hear. These days, with my mother doing as poorly as she is, I'm counting every penny."

"Do you want us to lock up?" asked Sam. He glanced at me, and I nodded. "We're just about done here."

"Nah, I'll take care of it. Now that I've come this far, I might as well have a look around. Don't forget what I said about the locks, though. After today, your key won't work, so if you think you're going to need anything else, take it now." Chuck looked pointedly at the silver-framed photo Sam still held in his hand.

"We're done," Sam repeated. "I'm sure someone will be by eventually to pack up the rest of Sheila's things. I assume her rent is paid through the first of the month?"

"That's right. Don't worry, I won't disturb a thing."

Sam stiffened at the inference we'd been snooping around, but before he could reply, Chuck walked past us into the house and closed the door behind him.

"He's pretty prickly for someone who doesn't have any more right to be here than we do," Sam said as we got in the Blazer.

"There's just been a murder committed in his mother's house," I pointed out; I could see how anyone might find that upsetting. "Under normal circumstances, he's probably a decent guy."

Sam started the car. His expression said he wasn't convinced. "*Did* Sheila mention him to you?"

"Briefly. Last week when we had dinner together. She said that Chuck had been making some repairs. That was why she hadn't been needing to call you nearly so often."

"That and because I stopped responding to all her 'urgent' messages," Sam said wryly.

"She was lonely," I found myself saying, though the

last thing I'd ever thought I'd do was defend Sheila's actions.

"And then she found Brian."

Judging by his tone, Sam still hadn't come to terms with that. Oprah would have a field day with this mess.

Scowling, he threw the car into gear.

Next stop, combat zone.

❦✱ *Ten* ✱❦

Brian Endicott's estate in Purchase looked just about right for a man who'd made millions in the computer industry. High stone walls, wrought-iron gate, curving, tree-lined driveway. Before I'd even seen the house, I was already salivating.

Sam watched my reaction with amusement.

"Let's buy a place like this after we get married," I said.

"Yeah, sure. If we win the lottery."

"We could pool our incomes." I grinned.

"And just about afford to build that stone wall."

Right, he was. Have I mentioned that the dedicated professionals who educate your children are severely underpaid?

The house was nice, too. Large enough to impress but not overwhelm, it was built of clapboard and weathered stone. The doors and shutters were painted ivory. Ivy climbed the walls, mature trees shaded the yard.

The driveway divided at the house; one section leading back to the kennel and garage, the other, forming a turn-around by the door. Sam parked out front. The door opened as we were getting out of the car, and Pugs came spilling out into the driveway.

"Want some?" Brian waved at the group as they ran circles around us, barking. "I've got Pugs coming out of my ears. Saint Bernards don't get as much done in an entire week as these dogs do in an hour. I'd forgotten how active little dogs could be."

"I thought we put them in the kennel last night." Sam reached down to scratch behind ears and in front of tails, both prime spots for getting the little bodies wiggling.

"We did, but they weren't happy. It's one thing for the Saints, they're used to it. But Sheila kept these guys as house dogs. And on top of that, they miss her. I figured bringing them inside might cheer them up."

"You're a nicer man than you want to admit," I said.

The comment caught Brian by surprise. "No, I'm not. Ask Sam, he'll tell you."

Sam ignored the invitation. "We've got the medicine you needed."

"Right. Thanks. Where are my manners? We don't have to stand out in the driveway. Let's go inside."

"I don't think we have time—" Sam began.

"Sure we do," I overrode him.

There was no way I was leaving so fast. First, I wanted to see the house. Second, I wanted to ask Brian about Sheila's murder and hear what, if anything, he might have learned from the police. Third, and most important, I wanted to observe these two together and try to figure out what made their relationship tick.

In the two years I'd known Sam, I'd never figured him

for the reticent type. Yet recently I'd discovered there were whole chunks of his life that he'd simply declined to discuss. Like his marriage to Sheila. Like his friendship, and his rivalry, with Brian. Things he deemed to be part of his past.

In the past maybe, but clearly not behind him.

A decade earlier, I'd married a man I thought I knew and understood. Only after he'd left me, disappearing one bright summer day when Davey was ten months old, did I begin to realize how wrong I'd been.

Sam and Bob, my ex-husband, were two entirely different people. But only an idiot wouldn't learn from her mistakes. Whatever had gone on between Sam and Brian—whatever was still going on—I wanted to know more about it.

"I guess we have a few minutes," Sam said curtly.

The three of us herded the Pugs up the steps and into the house. Boris, watching from the doorway, regarded our efforts with a bemused expression on his normally placid face. The Pugs' antics seemed to have worn him out almost as much as they had his owner.

We ended up in a kitchen that looked as though it had been designed for a magazine spread. Everything was black and white, and buffed to a high shine. No fingerprints anywhere; I looked. It was easy to tell Brian didn't have kids.

Even the mugs he poured our coffee into matched the decor. Glossy, black, ceramic tumblers that felt heavy and awkward in the hand; they seemed to have been chosen more for their looks than practicality. I wondered how often Brian actually used this room.

In my house, the kitchen is the hub, the place where

everyone tends to gather. Brian's kitchen was much too clean, much too sterile, to encourage anyone to make themselves at home. As if he felt the same way, he picked up his mug and led us to a sunporch in the back of the house.

Boris had flopped down happily on the cool kitchen floor. He didn't stir when we left, but the Pugs trailed along after us, scattering around the new room like a collection of plump throw pillows.

"What a mess," Brian muttered. He sank down into a cushioned chair. Since the sunroom, with its glass-topped tables and wicker furniture, was spotless, I assumed he was referring to the situation with Sheila. "It's hard enough getting the magazine off the ground without having something like this on top of it."

"Is that what Sheila's death is to you?" I asked pointedly. "An inconvenience?"

"Among other things." Absently, Brian smoothed the edge of his mustache with thumb and forefinger. "Looking at it from a strictly business perspective, this is really going to mess things up."

"You and Sheila were copublishers, right?"

"Yeah, partners. That was the way the agreement was structured. If the magazine took off, we both stood to profit equally. If it tanked, both our investments went down the tubes."

"Usually when lawyers draw up a partnership agreement, they make sure you get some protection against a loss like this," said Sam.

"You mean life insurance?"

Sam nodded.

"We have it. And you're right, the lawyers did insist.

Sheila and I probably wouldn't have bothered otherwise. Half a million apiece. Payable to the magazine."

Which Brian was now the sole owner of.

He shrugged as if reading my thoughts. "Big deal. Financially, it's a shot in the arm. Guess what? It's not like we needed one. *Woof!* wasn't started on a shoestring. I had money to invest and so did Sheila. As far as backing goes, we're sound as a rock.

"What the magazine needs is Sheila herself. Her enthusiasm for the project, the vitality she brought to the office. Not to mention her connections in the dog show world and her marketing savvy. I'll have a hard time finding someone to take her place."

One of the Pugs snuffled next to my knee. I ran my hand over the top of its smooth head. "If you don't mind my saying so, *Woof!* is intended to be a scandal sheet."

Brian's eyes narrowed. "Go on."

"Is there any possibility that Sheila's murder was connected to the magazine? Maybe to a story she might have been working on?"

"I don't know. I can't say the thought hadn't occurred to me. Hell, over the last twelve hours, I've considered all sorts of possibilities. It hardly seems likely, though.

"Most of the stories we're publicizing aren't exactly secret. They're just not very widely known. The news is already out there somewhere. In some cases we're even dealing with public records. All we're doing is exposing it to a wider forum."

"Maybe some people don't want their dirty linen laundered in public," Sam said. The phrase sounded like an argument he might have used before, perhaps with Sheila.

"People who care about that shouldn't behave badly in the first place," Brian shot back. "This is the age of information, and *Woof!* is a magazine whose time has come. If Sheila and I hadn't come along and done this, someone else would have. You can bank on that."

"Maybe," I said. "But you and Sheila did make the first move, and now she's dead. Did you mention that to the police?"

"No, and I'm not going to. There's no way *Woof!* needs to get caught up in a police investigation."

"You may not have a choice. The police would be crazy to ignore that aspect of Sheila's life."

"I guess I should have expected something like this." Brian sounded agitated. Obviously, he wasn't accustomed to having people argue with him. "Sheila told me you thought of yourself as some sort of amateur sleuth. The Miss Marple of the canine world. She even suggested we might want to do an article in a future issue of *Woof!* that turned the tables on you. Investigate your background and see how you liked it."

I stared at him in shock. So much for the we're-all-just-good-buddies-now demeanor Sheila had assumed the last time I saw her. It looked like I'd been more naive than I'd realized.

Brian took advantage of my momentary silence to deliver the last word. "Sheila's death is enough of a tragedy without you stirring everything up and making it worse than it has to be. The detective we spoke to thinks she was killed by someone who intended to rob the place, and until the police find any evidence to support a view to the contrary, that's what I intend to believe."

* * *

"Sorry about that," Sam said when we were back in the car. Gravel spun from beneath the tires as he turned in the driveway and headed out.

"You're sorry? Why?"

"Because I've known Brian a lot longer than you, and I know what a bastard he can be when things aren't going his way. I should have insisted that we just drop off the pills and leave."

"I'm the one who dragged you inside. If anything, I should be sorry. But I'm not. I found what he had to say quite interesting."

"Miss Marple of the canine world?" Sam lifted a brow.

"Not that part. Definitely not that part. Other things. Like the life insurance policies he and Sheila had taken out on each other."

"I know it sounds fishy, but considering they'd just formed a legal partnership over the magazine, it's probably on the up-and-up. I'd imagine the police, not to mention the insurance company, will have a good look at it."

"All right then." I settled back in my seat. "How about the fact that Brian is so sure that Sheila's work at *Woof!* had nothing to do with her death?"

"I doubt if he actually believes that quite as vehemently as he'd like you to think." Sam's gaze left the road and slid my way. "Brian's great at sleight of hand. Saying one thing and doing another entirely. Right now, he's looking to protect his new venture. If he has to tell a few lies along the way, I'd imagine it won't bother his conscience very much."

"You really don't think much of him, do you?"

"No. In fact, it's a policy of mine to think of Brian Endicott as little as possible."

Once again, he'd evaded my question. I wondered how long it would take before I finally got the truth. And what made him think that I'd give up before I did.

"Do you think Brian is capable of committing murder?"

Sam considered the question. "Under the right circumstances, I think he'd be very capable of committing the act. Are these those circumstances? I doubt it. He had no reason to want to see Sheila dead."

"Some would say he had five hundred thousand reasons."

"That only matters if he needed the money. Or, to be more precise, if he needed the money more than he needed Sheila. As far as Brian was concerned, she was performing an invaluable service."

"Sure she was smart and well connected," I said, frowning. "But I'd hardly say she was invaluable. Add that insurance money into the mix, and I'm sure he'll be able to replace her."

"At the magazine, maybe," said Sam. "But not in his personal life."

"Come on," I scoffed, beginning to grow testy. "She can't be *that* good. You replaced her."

"That's exactly the point. I moved to Connecticut what, two years ago? And I've been pretty visible at the shows around here since then. Brian's been living in Purchase this whole time. Our houses are probably no more than thirty miles apart. Yet we never crossed paths until recently. Until Sheila brought us back together.

"Once Brian had Sheila, he wanted to make sure I knew about it. He was really enjoying this whole three-way scenario. He was using her to get back at me."

I remembered the conversation I'd overheard the night we'd all had dinner together. Was this what they'd been arguing about?

"Did Sheila know that?" I asked.

"I tried to tell her. She didn't believe me. She accused me of trying to break them up because I was jealous of Brian."

"Over her?"

"No, although that might have been what she was secretly hoping. Sheila seemed to think that I resented the fact that Brian had been so much more successful financially than I had."

"Island of Mutant Terror?"

Sam shot me a surprised look. "What do you know about that?"

"Terry told me. He said Brian invented the game a decade ago and made a fortune."

"As usual, Terry's version of things is more or less correct. Brian patented the game, he didn't invent it."

Something in his voice alerted me. "Oh? Who did?"

"Some poor computer nerd who was in our class at B school. He'd been working on the prototype for months, refining the plot, perfecting the details."

"How'd Brian get hold of it?"

"You might say he got lucky. He knew about the game, we all did. We figured it was a lark, nothing too serious. We were happy to serve as the guy's guinea pigs. We were young, probably naive. We all thought it was just a game, something to fool around with. But Brian knew better."

"Are you trying to tell me that he stole Island of Mutant Terror from its creator?" I asked incredulously.

Sam waited a minute before speaking. When he did,

his voice was grim. "I told you not to be fooled by Brian's smooth style. That charm you see is all on the surface. Underneath is a man who knows exactly where he wants to go and doesn't care who he has to trample on his way there."

❧❀ *Eleven* ❀❧

Davey was still at Joey Brickman's house when we got home, but the dogs were happy to see us.

Sam let Tar out of Faith's crate and put both Poodles out in the yard. I got out a couple of cans of tuna and started making lunch. Tar and Faith were back inside within minutes. Poodles are confirmed people dogs. Given the choice of running and playing or being with their owners, they'll opt for the human connection any day.

I gave them each a peanut butter biscuit, and both dogs sacked out on the kitchen floor contentedly. Sam was the one who couldn't seem to stop moving. He toasted the bread and got out tomatoes. Dropped one knife and opened three drawers looking for another. This despite the fact that he knows his way around my house just as well as I do.

Finally, I couldn't stand it anymore. "Is something wrong?"

"No, everything's fine."

I motioned toward the cutting board. "Do you always

cut tomatoes you're planning to put in sandwiches into wedges?"

Sam swore under his breath.

"Better," I said. He looked up. "Talk to me. Yell at me if you have to. Just don't stand there and tell me everything's fine."

"Okay." Sam set down the knife and wiped off his hands. "I need to ask you something."

"That sounds serious."

"I guess it is. I need your help."

"Of course. Anything."

Sam didn't look pleased with my quick answer.

"It's about Sheila," he said. I got the impression he was testing the water, waiting to see if I'd change my mind.

"Okay."

This was looking like it might take a while. I kept working on the tuna salad. We might be fighting, but at least we'd be well fed.

"I was wondering if you might ask a few questions . . ."

I went still.

Sam hates it when I snoop around, and he's made that abundantly clear. The year before, some trouble my brother had managed to get himself into had nearly broken off our engagement before it was even started.

He couldn't be serious, I thought, stealing a glance out of the corner of my eye. Sam looked as though he'd meant every word.

But there was something else. He also looked concerned. Like he was afraid I might turn him down, and he had no idea what his next move would be after that.

"The police—" I began.

Sam didn't let me finish. "The police are going to find

what they expect to find. Detective Holloway told us yesterday that it looked as though Sheila had interrupted a robbery. He didn't care about where the dogs should or shouldn't have been because the facts he already had supported his theory."

"Maybe he's right."

"If he is, fine. The police will do what they're trained to do: take fingerprints, use forensics, find out if any suspicious people have been seen in the neighborhood. If Sheila was killed by an anonymous intruder, then the police are the ones to get the job done.

"But what if she wasn't? What if she was murdered by someone she knew? Someone *we* know? You have connections at the magazine and in the dog world that the police will never be able to duplicate. Doors will be open for you that they don't even know exist."

I didn't want him to plead, but it looked like he would if he had to. I felt lost, groping for the right decision when all the choices were wrong. How could I agree? Wasn't this the very thing that had driven a wedge between us before?

"You're asking a lot," I said.

Maybe too much, I thought.

"I know," Sam agreed. "And I feel like the worst sort of hypocrite. I wish there was another way, but I don't see one."

He lifted his hands in frustration, or maybe supplication. Sam wasn't any happier about the situation than I was. "It was one thing for me to put Sheila out of my life when she was alive. Her presence bothered you, and I felt I owed you that much. But now that she's gone, I feel as though I owe her something, too.

"I think the police are wrong about their assumptions,

but I want to know for sure. Until I do, it's going to gnaw at me. I won't be able to let go and move on."

Slowly I stepped away from the counter, walked over to a chair, and sank down into it without conscious thought. I heard what Sam was saying, but the words seemed to be coming from very far away. It was as if a fog had enveloped my senses, muffling sound, blocking out light.

Though he hadn't stated things that baldly, I knew perfectly well that the next thing Sam was supposed to be moving on to was his marriage to me. So where did that leave us?

From the moment Sheila had appeared on the East Coast, Sam's attentions had been divided. Much as he'd denied it, I'd felt the truth. Now she was gone, and I wanted it to stop. I wanted things to go back the way they had been, but no matter how hard I tried I couldn't seem to make that happen.

I drew in a deep breath and let it out. If this was what it would take, then I had no choice.

"I'll ask a few questions," I said slowly. "I'll see what people have to say."

Sam looked relieved. I felt slightly nauseated.

"Thank you," he said.

I didn't want his gratitude; I wanted his love.

It looked as though I was going to have to earn it.

By the time I picked up Davey later that afternoon, Sam and Tar had already left. Though I'd sprayed on conditioner and brushed through the puppy's hair, he still needed a bath to remove the last of the hair spray Sam had applied at the show. Besides, Sam needed to get back and check on his other dogs in Redding.

It's not like Davey and I couldn't have gone with him. Under normal circumstances, we probably would have. But nothing seemed normal anymore, and Sam looked as though he could use some time to himself.

I stood on the front step and watched him drive away. Tar had hopped over the seat of the Blazer and was looking out the back. He wagged his tail at me as I waved good-bye. Eyes facing front, Sam never even noticed.

Feeling utterly deflated, I retrieved my son, thanked Alice profusely, and drove over to Aunt Peg's house in Greenwich. Less than a day had passed since we'd seen each other at the dog show, but I felt as though I'd aged a decade. I hoped talking to Aunt Peg might cheer me up, but I wasn't counting on it.

Peg's house is smaller than Brian Endicott's, but every bit as beautiful. Set amid five acres of woods and meadow, the home itself was once the center of a working farm, and its graceful design reflects both its age and its original function. The clapboard siding is painted a creamy shade of yellow, and a wide porch wraps around three sides of the house. There's a kennel building out back, which now sits mostly empty. Aunt Peg's husband, Max, had died two years earlier and lately she'd begun scaling back on the number of Poodles she kept.

As always, our approach was announced by Aunt Peg's house dogs, who kept watch over the driveway and warned her of impending arrivals. All retired champions, these Standard Poodles sported the attractive and functional kennel trim, with a blanket of short, curly black hair covering their entire bodies. When Aunt Peg opened the front door, all half dozen came bounding out to surround the car.

Usually, I let Faith leap out and join in the fray. Now,

though I let Davey go on ahead, I held the Poodle back. Since she didn't seem to be making any concessions to her advanced state of pregnancy, I'd decided it was up to me to take precautions for her.

"For pity's sake," said Peg, coming down the steps. "She's not made of glass. Let the poor girl have some fun."

"Your dogs play rough," I pointed out, somewhat unnecessarily since the wild bunch was now gleefully engaged in pummeling my child. To his credit, Davey seemed to be enjoying the mayhem as much as the Poodles.

"Faith knows how to take care of herself. Mother Nature isn't stupid, you know."

This from a woman who had planned Faith's breeding with the same attention to detail that Michelangelo had brought to putting a mural on the ceiling of the Sistine Chapel. After Faith's genetic testing was complete, the next step had been to find a suitable mate: a Standard Poodle whose quality was every bit as high as Faith's and whose health and temperament were above reproach.

To my surprise, that part of the process hadn't taken very long. Like most breeders, Aunt Peg speculated about possible combinations every time she saw a good-looking male Poodle walk into the show ring. Over the last year and a half, she had mentally tried out and discarded dozens of potential candidates.

The dog Aunt Peg had finally decided upon was a young champion who came from a pedigree as illustrious as Faith's own. He lived in Pennsylvania with his breeder, a friend of Peg's who had taken meticulous care of Faith during her visit in the spring. Now, she was awaiting the outcome of the breeding as avidly as Peg and I were.

If the puppies turned out as well as we all hoped, she'd promised to take one herself and show it to its championship.

"I just don't want her to hurt herself," I said. "Or the puppies. This is her first litter. Maybe she doesn't understand what's going on."

"You only have one child," Peg pointed out. "Did you take foolish chances with him while you were pregnant?"

I sighed and unwound my arms from around Faith's neck. I've never won an argument with Aunt Peg yet. I don't know what makes me think I ever will.

Proving Peg's point, Faith sauntered over to the crowd of dogs and touched noses demurely with those closest to her. Davey, meanwhile, had managed to push the Poodles away and get to his feet. His T-shirt was rumpled and grass-stained; one sneaker was untied. His grin was wide and delighted.

"Ready to go inside?" I asked.

My son shook his head. "I want to stay out here with the dogs. You guys are just going to talk about boring stuff anyway."

No point in arguing with an offer like that.

Behind Aunt Peg's house was a large open field of at least two acres, all of it fenced. We left Davey and Peg's Poodles out there with a supply of tennis balls for tossing and fetching. Prudently, we took Faith inside the house with us.

"Well?" Aunt Peg demanded as soon as we'd closed the door behind us. "I'll have you know I've been waiting all night and most of a day to hear from you. Come in, sit down, and start talking. I want to hear everything."

I spent the next twenty minutes recapping the events that had taken place since we'd parted at the show. I told her about the police suspicions, Blossom's missing medicine, meeting Chuck the handyman, and the fact that Brian had recently taken out a large insurance policy on Sheila.

I didn't mention that Sam had shown up the night before drunk; awakened this morning morose; then disappeared again by midafternoon, apparently preferring to find solace in solitude.

I didn't have to. Aunt Peg has always been good at reading between the lines. "That's half the story," she said when I was done. "What about Sam? How's he taking it?"

"Badly."

"He would. I hope you're making yourself useful."

"I'm trying. Sam isn't sure he wants to let me."

"Oh pish, you're good at solving mysteries. Sam may not like it, but even he has to admit that."

"That's not what I meant," I said, thinking of all the things that had been left unsaid between us when Sam departed earlier. The comfort that I'd tried to offer that he'd refused to accept. "Oddly enough, right now, that's the one way—the only way—Sam does want my help. He's not sure the police investigation is heading in the right direction—"

"Nor am I, based on what you've told me."

"And he's asked me to look into it."

"There, you see." Peg sounded pleased. "That's a start, Melanie. He trusts you."

"No he doesn't," I argued. She and Sam were the best of friends. My relationship with him was much more complex. I wasn't at all sure I could make her understand. "I thought he did, but I was wrong. If he did, I would have known who Sheila was long before she showed up last spring.

"I've thought about that a lot, why she bothered me so much even though Sam kept saying that she wasn't important to him anymore. It's because when she arrived, I found out there were things that Sam had deliberately kept from me. Big things. Important things. And I can't help but wonder what else I don't know."

I knotted my hands in my lap. Thumbs first, then the fingers, twisting and tangling until Faith came over and pushed her cool nose into my hands and I looked up. "And now Sam has closed himself off from me. He's gone someplace where I can't touch him. Someplace he doesn't want me to go."

"Give him time," said Peg. "Sheila's death was a huge shock. Sam has to come to terms with it. And part of the process is finding out what really happened. That's where you come in."

"That's not where I want to come in."

She eyed me sternly. "Did he give you a choice in the matter?"

"No."

"There you are then. Resolve this problem first, then you can work on the next."

ᴅ❀ *Twelve* ❀ᴅ

Aunt Peg went to a drawer, got out a pen and a pad of paper, and began to make a list. There's nothing she enjoys more than playing investigator by proxy.

"You'll need to talk to the neighbor who found Sheila," she said. "Maybe she put the Pugs outside when she got there."

"She didn't. The reason Mrs. Benning knew something was wrong was because the dogs were barking all night long, which had never happened before. If the Pugs had been inside the house, she wouldn't have heard them."

"Maybe, maybe not. The police found open windows, didn't they? Trust me, the sound of a barking dog travels beautifully through screens. Have you any idea how far away Mrs. Benning's house is?"

"No."

"First question," Aunt Peg said with satisfaction, making a note. "Who let the dogs out? Second question: were Mrs. Benning and Sheila acquainted? Did they know each other well enough for her to be aware of who might have come and gone at Sheila's place?"

"I doubt it. Remember, Sheila was only renting that house. Her move to the East Coast was supposed to be temporary. It's not like she planned . . ."

Something, the merest flicker of knowledge in Aunt Peg's eyes, stopped me. "What?"

Peg developed a sudden fascination with the pad in her hand. I watched as she doodled the outline of a Poodle with an outrageous topknot. Fine, I thought. If she had all day to draw cartoons, I had all day to wait.

"Who told you that Sheila's sojourn in the East wasn't going to be permanent?" she asked finally.

"Sam did." I thought back. "And you did, too, after you first spoke to her. Sheila took a temporary assignment in New York, right? And after she got here, she met up again with both Sam and Brian."

"She knew Sam was here before she came," said Peg.

That was no surprise.

"Sheila never made any secret of the fact that she wanted Sam back. That was probably the real reason she came East. I guess she thought three months would be enough time to get him to dump me and go back to her. Sheila never did lack for confidence."

Aunt Peg sat for a moment, frowning. Her cartoon Poodle acquired bracelets on its legs and a large pompon on its tail. When she spoke again, her tone was seriously annoyed.

"Last March you were very angry with me when you found out I knew Sam had an ex-wife that I'd never told you about."

"Go on," I said carefully.

"It probably isn't my place to tell you this either."

Uh-oh. I didn't like the sound of this.

"Tell me what?"

"Sheila wasn't planning on leaving."

Whatever I'd expected her to say, that wasn't it. "What do you mean?"

"That house in North Salem? She had a lease with an option to buy."

"That can't be right. Sheila had no reason to buy a house here. She was only planning to stay for three months."

"She got here in March. It's nearly July now. You do the math."

"Yes, I know." I shook my head. Life is easier when you're in denial. "But I thought Sheila stayed on because she took the job at the magazine with Brian. You mean she intended to move here all along?"

"I would say so. Why else would she take an option on a house?"

"Maybe as a fallback if things went well with her job," I mused aloud. "Or maybe she wasn't as confident as I thought . . ."

Abruptly, I sat up. "Wait a minute."

Across the table, Aunt Peg seemed to brace herself, ever so slightly, for where my next thought might lead.

"How did you know about this?"

As soon as she sighed, I knew I wasn't going to like her answer. "Sam mentioned it once, when I asked him when Sheila might be heading home."

"*Sam* mentioned it. . . ?" I repeated the words just for emphasis. "He never mentioned anything like that to me."

"So I gather," Peg said dryly as she watched my expression darken.

"*Sam* told you about it?"

"And you wondered why I never brought up the ex-wife," she muttered audibly.

"Why would he tell you something like that and not me?"

"If you can't figure that out, go take a look in the mirror."

"Why, do I look angry? I am. If Sam's ex-wife was going to become a permanent part of our lives, I had a right to know."

"Maybe Sam didn't want to upset you," Peg said gently.

"Or maybe he thought it would make his life easier if he told me another lie. Lord knows, I bought the first one long enough."

"Sam never lied to you about Sheila."

Trust Aunt Peg to take Sam's side. My glare had a nasty edge.

"Not directly, maybe. But only because I never asked him flat out if he had an ex-wife. I never thought I *had* to ask. Sam told me about his life. I told him about mine. When I think of the things I owned up to . . ."

I threw up my hands. "A runaway ex-husband with a gushing oil well and a teenage bride . . . an aunt who left the convent to marry a former priest . . . a brother who thinks taking a job as a bartender constitutes a career move . . . not to mention you!"

"Me?" Peg asked innocently. "Sam likes me."

"No wonder. The two of you have a lot in common. You both think the truth is something to be told only when it suits you."

It was a low blow, and I knew it. It wasn't so much that Aunt Peg told lies, as that she had a habit of manipulating the facts to suit her version of the truth. That the

strings she pulled behind the scenes often worked to my
advantage seemed, at the moment, entirely irrelevant.

She pushed back her chair and stood up. Standing
nearly six feet tall, she towered over me. "If you were
Davey's age, I'd tell you that you needed a time-out.
Since you're supposedly old enough to know better, I
will remove myself from your presence. You may find
me outside with Davey when you come to your senses."

I watched, still angry, as she closed the back door
between us. Faith, who had listened to our rising voices
with pricked ears and anxious eyes, whined softly under
her breath.

"Come here," I said, patting my knees. I gathered the
front half of the large Poodle up into my lap. Her
extended middle pressed against my legs. "Nobody was
yelling at you. You're fine. I'm the one who's an idiot."

Faith's pomponned tail wagged in support of whatever
I wanted to say. Her damp nose poked at the bottom of
my chin. Studies show that people who keep pets have
lower blood pressure. It doesn't surprise me. This wasn't
the first time I'd discovered that having a dog in my lap
was a positive mood enhancer.

Why was I yelling at Aunt Peg? I thought. None of
this was her fault. She wasn't even the one I was angry
at.

I got up and walked outside. When I opened the door,
Faith ran on ahead, bounding down the steps to join the
Poodles in the yard.

"Watch!" Davey crowed, lofting a bright yellow tennis
ball toward the back of the yard.

My son doesn't have much of a pitching arm yet; the
ball didn't go far. The Poodles didn't care. As one, they
scrambled after it.

I watched long enough to make sure that Faith wasn't being jostled by the rush, then turned to Aunt Peg.

"I'm sorry."

"You should be," Peg replied. She let that sink in for a moment, then smiled to soften the words. "The Chinese revere their elder relatives. Think about that."

"We Puritans put them in nursing homes," I retorted. "You think about that."

Her smile turned into a grin. "Just try it."

"I wouldn't dare. Nevertheless, I shouldn't have taken things out on you. Sheila's the one I'm angry at."

"And Sam."

"And Sam," I echoed softly.

"He was probably trying to protect your feelings—"

"Or his own." I reached down, plucked a dandelion out of the grass, and twirled it between my fingers. "It scares me, you know. Sam and I are engaged to be married. And suddenly I've found out that I don't know him nearly as well as I thought I did."

"Talk to him," said Peg. "Make him talk to you. It's long past time the two of you got everything out in the open."

"That's just it." My fingers felt wet. I glanced down and realized I'd crushed the small yellow flower in my hand. "I thought we *were* talking. I thought I knew everything. Obviously, I was wrong. So now I have to wonder—what else was going on that Sam didn't see fit to tell me about?"

"Ask him. Call him when you get home. Demand some answers. That's what I would do."

Of course it was. That was Aunt Peg's way. She never took grief from anyone. If I were half as strong as she was, I wouldn't be in this predicament.

And I wouldn't be worrying about what else Sam might have to confess to.

After that, Peg all but pushed Davey, Faith, and me out the door. You've heard my advice, her expression said. Now go home and make good use of it.

To my credit, I tried.

I didn't succeed.

When we got home, I found that Sam had left a message on the answering machine. I played it through twice; the first time hopefully, the second, in frustration. Reach out and touch someone, my foot.

That's the whole problem with modern technology. It gives us too many options. If Sam hadn't been able to leave a message, surely he'd have kept trying until he reached me. Until we'd been able to talk. Now, I'd lost my chance.

"I'm sorry I missed you," he said on the tape. "I've spoken to Sheila's family. As I'm sure you can understand, they're really upset about what happened. Her parents have invited me to come out and stay with them for a few days."

There was a long pause before Sam's voice, slower now, started again. "They want me to tell them about how Sheila was doing these last few months. None of the family has seen her since she came East. They want to know that she was happy. They . . ."

He stopped again, cleared his throat. "They want more comfort than I'm going to be able to give. They want me to help them make sense of something utterly senseless. All I can do is try. They're going to be holding the funeral at the end of the week, so I'll probably stay in Illinois until then.

"I'm sorry we won't get a chance to say good-bye in person, but I've booked a flight to O'Hare this evening. I'm on my way out the door now. I've boarded the older dogs, and I'm taking Tar with me.

"I'm not exactly sure where I'll be staying so I can't give you a number, but I'll call in a day or two, okay? Give my love to Davey and tell Faith to hang on to those puppies until I get back, so we can whelp them together. I love you, Melanie. Bye."

I love you, Melanie. Bye.

Cruel juxtaposition, that.

Had he gone to Illinois to see Sheila's family, I wondered, or to try and heal himself? And why did I have the feeling that the more I tried to help, the harder he was pushing me away?

I'd wanted to offer solace. Sam wanted me to ask questions. It didn't take a genius to see that we were on two different wavelengths. And now he was gone.

So I'd give Sam what he asked for. I had almost a week until I'd see him again. Maybe by then, I'd have some answers.

Melanie Travis, intrepid girl sleuth.

I can do that.

❧ *Thirteen* ❧

First things first, however. Monday was my morning to drive the car pool to soccer camp. Wouldn't you just know it?

Davey had packed his gym bag the night before. At almost seven I was trying to let him take a little more responsibility for his own things. I could only hope it actually held cleats, shin guards, extra T-shirt, and a dry bathing suit and towel. Otherwise, he'd be bringing home another note.

The camp had drop-off at nine, pickup at four; with seven hours of freedom in between. Was it any wonder that every mother seemed to be smiling on her way out the driveway?

From there, I took the Merritt Parkway and headed south to White Plains. According to the masthead in my inaugural issue of *Woof!*, that was where the editorial offices were located. Sam wanted me to check things out, and the magazine seemed like a good place to start. I could only hope that Brian, whose Miss Marple crack still rankled, didn't object too strongly.

Woof!'s address turned out to be a boxy brick building on the edge of downtown. There were metered spaces on the street out front and a small parking lot in back. Since the lot was mostly full at nine-fifteen, I assumed it was intended for employees. That didn't stop me from snagging the last spot.

Inside, I found myself in a narrow, fluorescent-lit hallway. A roster near the elevator listed the building's occupants. *Woof!*'s office space was on the second floor. When I pushed the button, the door opened immediately. I stepped inside and rode up to another hallway, this one with two doors leading off from it.

The magazine took up the back of the building, a CPA's office occupied the front. *Woof!*'s door was standing open. There was no reception area and I entered directly into a large, well-lit room.

Two metal desks with matching credenzas had been stationed on either side wall, the furniture arranged to delineate separate work spaces. A copier and a fax machine took up more room, and a framed enlargement of *Woof!*'s first cover filled the wall above them. As offices went, it was pretty generic.

My gaze skimmed over those details, then came to rest on a fresh-scrubbed child with rosy cheeks and curly blond hair who sat behind a third desk, just inside the door. Carrie, presumably. She looked barely old enough to be in high school, much less part of the workforce.

I'd started to introduce myself when a shout from the other end of the room stopped me.

"Melanie, hey!" Tim Golonka came hurrying toward the door. "What are you doing here?"

Good question. I decided to wing it.

"The first issue of *Woof!* looked so good, I wanted to drop by and offer my congratulations."

"Oh. You probably want Brian then. I hope you haven't come too far because he isn't here. He left on a promotional trip this morning. Won't be back until the end of the week." He shrugged apologetically. "Not the best timing, under the circumstances."

"I wanted to talk to you about that, too."

"Really?" Tim perked up. He waved toward one of the desks. "Come on over to my office."

I lifted a brow.

"All right, my space. For now. I'm planning on working my way up."

"He wants my job," said Aubrey, emerging through a doorway in the back of the room. She hadn't seem relaxed at the dog show; today she looked positively stiff. Frown lines furrowed her forehead. "Hi, Melanie. Sorry about my big mouth the other day. Obviously, I was upset, and I wasn't thinking straight."

"Forget about it. We were all pretty upset."

"Thanks. And you . . ." Aubrey pointed at Tim. "Try to take a deep breath, would you? Haven't you ever heard of paying your dues?"

"Sure. A phrase coined to appease slow learners and losers. Not my problem. Besides, the way I see it we *all* move up."

"All?" I asked, following him to his desk.

"Sure. Aubrey can have Sheila's job."

"Tim—!"

He ignored her warning tone. "It's not like you weren't number two until she got here. You know you want it."

For a moment, the room was utterly silent, as if we were all holding our breaths for the blowup that would follow. Then, surprisingly, Aubrey laughed. "I hope you aren't planning to say that to the police."

"Only if they ask, boss." Tim smirked at Aubrey and waved me to a chair. "Just one big happy family, that's us."

"Except me," Carrie piped up from the other end of the room. "I'm not related to any of you."

"What did we tell you?" Tim asked in an undertone. "She thinks we're crazy."

"All dog show people are crazy," said Aubrey. "It goes with the territory. That's why *Woof!* is going to be such a smash. If everyone was normal, who would we write about?"

"Are you going to write about Sheila's murder?" I asked curiously.

"That's up to Brian," said Tim. "So far, he hasn't said yes or no. Come to think of it, he hasn't said much of anything."

"He will when he gets back," Aubrey said confidently. "Think how devastating it must be, having this all dumped on him just when the magazine's at its most critical stage. By the end of his trip, I'm sure we'll be back to business as usual."

Business as usual by the end of the week, when the copublisher had just been murdered? She had to be kidding. Maybe Aubrey was trying to put a good face on things in front of an outsider, I thought. Either that, or she was severely delusional.

"Aubrey," Carrie called, her hand cupped over the bottom half of the phone receiver. "Roger Lenahan on line one."

"Got it." Aubrey spun away and strode back toward

the room she'd come from earlier. Reaching the doorway, she paused. "Don't let Tim tell you too many lies."

"I'll try not to."

"Don't pay any attention to Aubrey," Tim said when she'd closed the door behind her. His fingers twirled a pencil on his blotter. "She has issues."

"About what?"

"Brian. Sheila and Brian. Aubrey and Brian. If you catch my drift."

Only an idiot wouldn't.

"So Sheila arrived and took Aubrey's job?"

"Sort of. Aubrey's always been managing editor. She's the one who has the experience, the know-how. She was with *Dog Scene* for nearly a decade."

His voice was reverent. As if *Dog Scene* was *The New York Times* or *Vanity Fair*, rather than a weekly wrap-up of dog show happenings; published on newsprint and chock full of ads placed by exhibitors who hoped to influence the upcoming judges. Ah, the innocence of youth.

"Wow," I said, matching his awed tone. "Brian was lucky to get her."

"You bet. When Sheila came on board, Aubrey's job and title didn't change, but she still got demoted. Because Brian made Sheila copublisher. They were like equal partners."

"So Sheila was Aubrey's boss."

"Supposedly, yeah. But you could tell Aubrey didn't buy that. She knew a lot more about the publishing business than Sheila did, so it's not like she felt she needed to defer to her or anything."

"That must have made for some friction."

"Friction. Good word!" The pencil stopped mid-spin. "You mean like a motive for murder?"

"I don't know," I said casually. "Why don't you tell me? You're the one who saw them together."

"They didn't fight a lot, if that's what you're asking."

"Did they fight at all?"

"Sure. Everybody here mixes it up at some point. Like Aubrey would have an idea to pitch and Sheila would say, 'Oh, God! Not another transvestite handler story. Like that's anything new!' "

His imitation made me smile. He had Sheila down pat.

"Then what would happen?"

"Usually Brian would step in and make a decision. Bottom line, it's his magazine, and he never lets anyone forget it, you know?"

"I thought you just said that he and Sheila were equal partners."

"They are. They were." Tim frowned. "But he was still in charge. I guess you could say he had seniority. I mean, we've all been here since winter. Sheila just started a couple of months ago. It's not like he was going to let her walk in and take over."

"Why do you suppose Brian took her on as a partner?" I asked. Privately, I had my own theory about that, but I wanted to see what someone who didn't know about their past history might come up with.

"I wondered about that myself," said Tim. "I know Sheila made some sort of investment in the magazine. I heard her say something about it once to Brian. But it's not like *Woof!* needed the money. For a start-up, this place is pretty solid.

"It's not like we needed another writer either. Brian and Aubrey and I were doing pretty well digging up stories. This is the dog show world; people gossip. Heck, they were all but throwing stories in our laps.

"Maybe we were all a little busier than we wanted to be, but nobody really minded. We were all really enthusiastic about getting *Woof!* off the ground, you know?"

I nodded. He was enthusiastic still. If I were starting a magazine, I'd have hired Tim in a minute. Aubrey, for all her supposed publishing expertise, would have taken longer to win me over.

"So then I wondered if maybe this was a personal thing," said Tim. "Like maybe Sheila was the one who needed the help. It's been pretty obvious to all of us around here that she and Brian were involved."

"Is that a problem?"

"Not for me."

Interesting answer. "Meaning?"

Tim lowered his voice, even though there was no one close enough to hear us. "I don't have the hots for Brian."

"Does Aubrey?"

Tim shrugged. "Maybe there was something between them in the past, nothing I'd know about for sure. Just a feeling I had when I first got here, that they seemed to know each other awfully well for two people who'd just started working together. Anyway, whatever it was, it's over now."

If it wasn't Aubrey's resentment he was referring to, there was only one other choice. "Carrie?"

"It's not her fault," he said. "It's just that she's so young."

Like he wasn't.

"And she was involved with Brian?"

"No, nothing like that." Tim looked horrified by my misunderstanding. "It's more like she kind of has a crush on him. When he's here, she follows him around the office like a lovesick puppy."

I smiled at the simile. "What does Brian think of that?"

"Funny thing, it's like he doesn't even notice. He thinks Carrie's just trying to be helpful."

"And is she helpful?"

"Well yeah, sure. I mean, how hard is it to be a receptionist? Answer a few phone calls. Type a few letters. But Carrie's always asking to do more. Asking Brian, that is. The rest of us she couldn't care less about. She wants to be near him all the time."

"Was that a problem for Sheila?"

"It was more like Sheila was a problem for Carrie. When Brian brought her in and introduced her around, you could tell Carrie was pissed. Of course, she smiled and made nice about it. She's not dumb. But after that, she'd get back at Sheila in little ways.

"Like she'd always fix a cup of coffee for Brian, but she never made any for Sheila. And when Sheila asked her, she'd make it wrong, fill the cup with sugar when she knew Sheila took it black. Or she'd manage to lose Sheila's phone messages.

"Then Carrie would be all apologetic, like she couldn't figure out how she could have gotten so mixed up. Sheila was usually pretty nice about it, even though Carrie's behavior must have been a real pain in the butt."

"Tim?" Aubrey's voice called from the back office. "Are you busy?"

"Yes," he shouted back.

"Are you working?"

He thought for a moment, grinned at me, then answered, "Yes!"

"Did you finish the edit on the Tar Heel Circuit story?"

Sheesh, I thought. The office wasn't that big. Rather than all this shouting back and forth, why didn't Aubrey just walk the dozen steps out to where we were?

"Hang on." Tim rifled through the papers on the top of his desk, grabbed up several sheets that were paper-clipped together, and strode into the back room.

Several minutes passed. I could hear Tim and Aubrey talking, but I couldn't make out the words. A glance in Carrie's direction revealed that she was sitting at her desk, thumbing through a fashion magazine. Since nobody seemed to mind my presence, I decided to wait it out.

Five more minutes passed. I got up and walked over to the door. Carrie was reading an article entitled "How to Land the Man of Your Dreams." How appropriate. She marked her page in the magazine with a finger and looked up.

"Which office was Sheila Vaughn's?" I asked.

She seemed surprised by the question. "That one." Carrie pointed to the room where Tim and Aubrey were conferring.

"She shared an office with Aubrey?"

"No." Carrie pointed again, this time at the remaining work space. The desk top was clear, the computer turned off. "That's Aubrey's desk over there. At least it was."

She hadn't wasted any time, I thought. Sheila was barely gone and Aubrey was already staking out her turf.

"What's in there?" I asked. Two doors remained; both were closed.

"Brian's office." Carrie gestured toward the first, then the second. "Bathroom. Can I help you find something?"

"No. I'm just being nosy."

"Oh." Carrie smiled. She seemed to like the idea. "Okay."

"I was a friend of Sheila's," I said, just to see what sort of response I'd get.

"Really? I didn't think she had many friends."

"Why's that?" I moved closer and perched on the edge of her desk. Nothing threatening, nothing confrontational about my posture. Just us girls, gabbing. It seemed to work.

"Mostly just that she was new to the area. At least that's what Brian said. When she came to work for the magazine, she was still getting settled in."

"I guess you must have been shocked to hear that she was murdered."

"Shocked doesn't begin to describe it." Carrie's pink lips made a round O. "I was blown away. I mean, you hear about things like that on the news, but you never expect it to happen to anyone you know."

"I realize you didn't know Sheila for very long, but while she was at the magazine, you had access to a large part of her life." I thought of the missing phone messages, wondered if any had been critical. "Can you think of anyone who might have wanted to kill her?"

"Who are you?" Carrie asked suspiciously. "Do you work for the police?"

"No, I'm just a friend who's trying to make some sense of what happened. Did the police talk to you?"

"Not yet." She sounded disappointed. "But they questioned Brian over the weekend. I'll bet it was just like on TV. Maybe they'll come here today. Do you think so?"

"Could be. From what you saw, was Sheila working on any stories that could have placed her in danger?

Maybe an exposé about something that someone would rather have kept quiet?"

"Sure, all the time," Carrie said proudly. "That's what we do here at *Woof!*. We've got freedom of the press on our side. Like the first amendment and everything."

"Is there anyone in particular she might have made mad?"

"Well Kenny Boyle, for one." Carrie giggled. "He was really steamed when he called last week. I left the message on her desk where she'd be sure to see it. Mr. Boyle told me to write down what he said, word for word, so I did.

"It said, 'Run that story and you'll be sorry. You ruin my life, bitch, and I'll ruin yours.' "

⇜❈ *Fourteen* ❈⇝

I sat up. "Since the police haven't been here to talk to you, maybe you should call them. I'm sure they'd want to hear about that."

"Really? You think? I heard on the news that Sheila was killed in a robbery. Kenny Boyle wouldn't have anything to do with that."

"No, but it never hurts to explore all the options. Did you keep the message?"

Carrie shook her head, and the blond curls danced. "Like I said, I put it on Sheila's desk."

"What did she do with it?"

"Read it, crumpled it up, and threw it away."

"Did she seem upset by it?"

"Nah. She just sort of made a face. Kind of like she used to do when Marlon Dickie called."

"Who's he?"

"Some photographer. He works freelance, but he takes lots of pictures for the magazine. Like if Brian wants to run a story, but we don't have any photos to accompany it. Sometimes he hires Marlon to go to a dog show and grab a shot.

"Brian says the people who buy *Woof!* like to look at pictures more than they like to read. Marlon says always make the picture as unflattering as possible. That way the readers will think the people in the stories are corrupt *and* ugly."

With a philosophy like that, it was no wonder Sheila used to grimace when Marlon called.

"And Sheila didn't like him much?"

"I think she thought he was an okay photographer. It's just that he called her a lot."

"A lot? About work, or about other things?"

"How would I know that? It's not like I listened in. Before Sheila came, Marlon used to check in once a week or so and see if Brian needed him for anything. After Sheila got here, he was calling every day. And he always asked to speak with her."

Interesting. I added Marlon Dickie to the list of people I wanted to see. It already contained Kenny Boyle's name. And Aubrey's. Someday I'd love to catch her with her guard down.

"Okay, Kenny Boyle was mad at Sheila because of the story she wrote. Was there anyone else who felt the same way?"

Carrie pursed her lips. She tilted her head to one side and propped her index finger under her chin as she thought. The effect was not so much one of concentration, but a studied attempt to look cute.

I wondered if she'd learned the pose in the magazine she was reading. And if it worked on me whether she'd try it on Brian next.

"Well there was Alida Trent . . ." Carrie paused, waiting to see if the name meant anything to me.

It didn't.

"You know," Carrie prompted. "The steel heiress?"

No help there. I live in Fairfield County. *Woof!*'s office was in Westchester. The entire region was lousy with heiresses. Alida Trent's name didn't ring any bells.

"I take it she shows dogs?" I asked.

"Sure." Carrie's head bobbed up and down. "Tons of them, according to Brian."

Good. That meant Aunt Peg would know who she was.

"And she had a problem with Sheila, too?"

"Sheila was researching her for a story about a Shih Tzu she'd leased. Alida Trent wasn't happy about it. And with all her money, you could tell she wasn't the kind of lady who was used to dealing with things she didn't like."

"Did you ever hear her threaten Sheila?"

"There was one time. Sheila had her on speaker phone and the whole office heard it. Mrs. Trent said she was going to sue Sheila's skinny hick ass all the way back to the Midwest where it belonged."

I felt my lips twitch. "Is that a direct quote?"

"Close enough." Carrie grinned. "Sheila didn't like being called a hick, I can tell you that. She slammed her office door so hard the whole wall shook. I think she was sorry she'd let all of us hear what Mrs. Trent had to say."

"I wonder why she did?" I mused.

"Sometimes she could be like that. She always wanted everyone to think that her stories were a big deal. I guess that was her way of drawing attention to how hard she thought she was working."

I noted Carrie's choice of words. Not how hard Sheila

was working, but how hard she'd *thought* she'd been working. Carrie, with her big blue eyes and her crush on the boss.

"Carrie, would you come here a minute?" Aubrey stuck her head out of the back office, where she'd been ensconced with Tim for the last twenty minutes. "Oh, Melanie, are you still here? I thought you'd gone."

"I was waiting for Tim—"

"Maybe you could set up an appointment for another time?" Aubrey suggested. "You can see how busy things are."

Actually I couldn't, but that seemed to be beside the point.

"Especially with Brian and Sheila both out of the office, we're all having to do double duty. I'm sure you can understand."

"Certainly." What I could understand was that Aubrey wanted me gone. I guessed this wouldn't be a good time to ask to have a look at Sheila's desk. "Please tell Tim good-bye for me."

"Will do."

"Nice meeting you, Carrie."

"Likewise." She was already heading across the room.

"If the police don't come here, you might want to contact them about some of the things we've talked about."

"Yeah." She turned and shrugged, her plump shoulders moving beneath her form-fitting T-shirt. "Maybe."

In the doorway behind her, Aubrey frowned. "Don't worry. I'm in charge of things while Brian's gone. I'll take care of it."

Yeah, I thought, just as Carrie had done a moment earlier. Maybe.

* * *

From White Plains, I headed north, taking 684 to the Katonah exit. Then I drove east on Route 35 to 121 north. It was just before noon when I reached North Salem.

Turning onto Sheila's road, I slowed as I approached her driveway. On my two previous visits, I hadn't paid any attention to the other houses in the area. Most seemed to be of a more recent vintage than Sheila's cottage: large colonials on spacious lots, probably built twenty years ago to offer harried city dwellers a suburban option when it came time to raise a family.

Luckily, most of the driveways sported custom-made mailboxes; big, buff-colored fiberglass bins with pictures of Labrador puppies or ducks flying off into the sunset, and the home owner's name personalized along the bottom. I located the house belonging to THE DONALD BEN-NING FAMILY with no problem.

The Benning house sat much closer to the road than Sheila's did. As I turned in the driveway, I wondered if her property ran along behind this one. If so, it would explain why Mrs. Benning had been able to hear the Pugs. Still, as with all the houses in the area, a buffer of woods separated the Benning house from its neighbors. Nancy Benning might have been able to hear some of what went on at Sheila's house, but I doubted she'd been able to see much.

A scooter and a tricycle littered the driveway. I drove carefully around both and had just stopped in front of the door when it opened.

"See?" a small girl demanded. She turned and stuck her tongue out at someone standing behind her. "I told you someone was here!"

Another little girl appeared, identical to the first, except for her clothes. One wore a T-shirt and shorts; the other, a frilly dress. Both had dark, wiry hair, and fair, freckled skin. I guessed their age at five or six, just younger than Davey.

"Who are you?" the second girl asked as I walked up the step. "We're waiting for our friend, Sarah, to come and play. You're not Sarah's mom."

"No, I'm Melanie Travis." I hunkered down to their level. "I was hoping to talk to your mother. Is she home?"

"She's out back." The child in shorts spun on her heel and raced away. "I'll go get her."

"No, I will!" The other girl dashed after her.

Since I hadn't been invited to follow, I waited on the step. The open front door provided a view of a wide front hallway, a curved stairway leading up to the second floor, and an expansive living room. If I'd been a burglar, I'd have been inside in a second.

One minute passed. Then another. Considering that the Bennings' neighbor had just been murdered in what the police had characterized as an attempted robbery, it was amazing that their security was so lax.

Then Nancy Benning appeared, hurrying down the long hallway, wiping damp hands on her shorts. She smiled tentatively, brushed her fingers back through thick hair much like her daughters', and pulled the open door partway closed, blocking the space that remained with her body.

Rather like closing the barn door after the horse was already gone, I thought.

"Thank you for waiting," she said, her words tumbling out in a rush. "The girls aren't supposed to open the door, but they thought you were someone they knew. Can I help you?"

"I hope so." I extended a hand and introduced myself. "I was a friend of your neighbor, Sheila Vaughn. I wonder if you might have a minute to talk?"

"I guess so." She glanced behind her. "Molly, Jessie, you girls go upstairs and play, okay? I'll keep an eye out for Sarah and let you know when she comes."

Giggling, the twins fled. Nancy waited until they were gone, then opened the door and invited me in.

"They're adorable," I said, following her into the living room. With its hardwood floor and polished antiques, the room was pristine; I could only imagine that the twins did their playing elsewhere.

"They're a handful. Don't ever let anyone tell you that two are barely more trouble than one. Nancy perched on the edge of a plump cushion and smoothly switched gears. "Now then, what can I do for you?"

"The woman who was killed over the weekend was my fiancé's ex-wife. We were just here visiting her. I guess we're trying to understand what happened . . ."

"I'll never understand," Nancy said, her voice low and angry. "The police told me they believe Sheila interrupted a burglary and that the burglars killed her. I don't think I've slept a single night through since. Why did they choose that house and not this one? Because it's back in the trees? Because she was a woman living alone?"

She paused briefly, gnawing on her lip. "I was here that night. My husband, Don, was traveling, so it was just me and the girls. Sheila's dogs kept barking. You know, the little Pugs? I would never have imagined they could make so much noise."

"So it wasn't normal for them to be allowed to bark like that?"

"Not at all. I almost never heard them. Sheila seemed very conscious of the fact that they might bother the neighbors, and she took care to keep them quiet. If she and I hadn't met one day out on the road and gotten to talking about it, I would never even have known she had so many."

"When did the Pugs start barking?"

Nancy thought back. "I don't really know. Of course, now it seems like it might matter. But then, it was just background noise. I put the twins to bed around nine. The windows in their room were open, and I could hear the dogs barking then. I remember hoping that the noise wouldn't keep them awake."

She and I shared a mothers' smile. Bedtimes are never easy.

"So you didn't call Sheila and ask her to shut them up?"

"Oh no. I would never have done something like that. Especially knowing how hard she tried to keep the dogs from being a nuisance. Actually, I thought maybe she'd gone out. I couldn't imagine she was home listening to all that noise. I just figured she'd quiet them down eventually."

"But the barking kept up all night?"

"Yes. So the next morning I did call, but there was no answer. That's when I began to think maybe I should go have a look, just to make sure everything was okay. I cut through the woods in back."

"Your property and Sheila's are adjoining?"

"That's right. Most of the newer houses around here are on two or three acres. But Mrs. Andrews—she's the lady who leased the house to Sheila?—her house was built years ago. It's got seven or eight, which is really nice for us because the girls like to play in the woods, and we don't feel like we have a neighbor right on top of us."

Above us, I heard a loud boom. The ceiling seemed to vibrate, and the movement was accompanied by a loud, delighted shriek. Nancy stood. "Excuse me for a minute, would you?"

She stepped out of the room and walked to the foot of the stairs. "Girls! No jumping on the bed!"

Though she sounded annoyed, I couldn't help grinning. Sometimes it was nice to be reminded that it wasn't only the mothers of little boys who had their hands full.

"Okay," Nancy said, coming back in. "Where were we?"

"You went over to Sheila's Saturday morning?"

"Right."

"And when you got there, the door was locked?"

"No, it wasn't. It wasn't even closed all the way. When I saw that, I got a really creepy feeling."

"Did you go in?"

"No. I rang the bell, and when no one answered, I walked around the side of the house. You know, calling Sheila's name? The Pugs were out back in that fenced area. They must have been pretty tired by then because when they saw me, they ran over to the gate and began whining like they wanted me to let them out."

"So they weren't in the house when you got there?"

"No, I just told you that, didn't I? The Pugs were outside in the yard."

So much for the random robbery theory.

Sheila had been home when her attacker arrived. She'd probably let him or her inside. Sheila wasn't stupid; she wouldn't have opened her door to just anybody.

The police could search all they wanted for a stranger. I knew we were looking for a friend.

ᶜᵃ❋ *Fifteen* ❋ᵖ

"What's the matter?" asked Nancy. I looked up to find she was watching me closely. "What do you know that I don't?"

I debated what to say only briefly. Nancy had a right to know. "Based on what you just told me, it's highly unlikely that Sheila was killed by a burglar, no matter what the police think." I outlined what Sam had said about the way Sheila cared for her dogs.

"I don't know whether to feel better or worse," she said when I was finished. "Until Sheila was killed, I would have said that this was one of the safest neighborhoods we could have found. This whole thing has really shaken us."

I could imagine. "How well did you know Sheila?"

"Not very. Like I said, we met for the first time out on the road. She was picking up her mail, and I was driving by. I stopped and introduced myself. This isn't Donna Reed-ville, believe me. Nobody comes and greets the new neighbors with a homemade cake.

"I invited her to stop by for coffee sometime, but as

you can probably imagine, our schedules were totally opposite. I would love to have some company during the week, but of course that's when Sheila was working. She finally came by one Saturday, but we didn't get much chance to talk."

"How come?"

"Don. My husband? He was here when she got here. Let's just say they really hit it off."

Her tone wasn't quite bitter, but close. Call it seriously annoyed. What do you know? Nancy and I had something in common.

"Don't tell me. Sheila roped him into doing a few things for her around the house."

Nancy looked surprised. "How did you know?"

"Been there. I thought it was only Sam."

"I thought it was only Don."

We both smiled.

"It's not that I minded Don playing good Samaritan, just that if he was going to do it, he should have started a little sooner. When Mabel Andrews was living all by herself in that house, she could have used someone looking out for her. She's in her eighties and the last time I saw her, she was looking quite frail.

"Before she went into managed care, I used to stop by and check on her every few days or so. Mabel always said she was fine, but I think she just didn't want to be a bother. By the end, even the basic upkeep had pretty much gotten away from her."

I nodded. That jibed with what Sheila had told me. "The other day, over at the house, I met Mrs. Andrews's son."

"Chuck? Mabel used to keep his picture on the mantel, and she spoke about him occasionally. Frankly, if you ask me, he could have been paying a little more attention. Anyway, I don't want to give you the wrong impression about Sheila. It's not that I didn't like her, more that I never really got to know her."

I heard a giggle, followed by a thump. A small voice whispered, "You go!"

"No, you go!"

Nancy frowned. "Molly? Jessie? Aren't you girls supposed to be upstairs?"

"We were upstairs." One of the twins, I wasn't sure which, slid into the doorway. It looked as though she'd been propelled there by a disembodied pair of hands. The girl batted the hands away, added another slap for good measure, then turned back to Nancy and me with a grin. "We came down to wait for Sarah. She was supposed to be here by now."

"I'm sure she's coming any minute, Jessie. Were you listening when you weren't supposed to be?"

"No!" This accompanied by an emphatic shake of the head. Then she ruined the effect by adding, "Are the police going to catch the man who hurt Mrs. Vaughn?"

Nancy and I exchanged a look. I had no idea what she might have told the twins about the murder. Probably not much. "Did you know Mrs. Vaughn?" I asked.

"Sure," said Jessie, as Molly appeared to stand beside her. "We used to see her all the time."

"You did?" Nancy's eyes narrowed. "When?"

"When we were playing in the woods. Her house is right back there. Sometimes she let us pet her dogs. Once she gave us each a cookie."

"We liked her a lot," said Molly. "But we didn't like the man."

"What man?" Nancy and I asked together.

"The mean man." Jessie made a face. "He came to visit, and made her unhappy. Sometimes he yelled."

Brian? I wondered. Not necessarily, but his was the first name that came to mind.

"What did the man look like?" I asked.

"He was tall," said Jessie.

"Way taller than us," Molly added.

That wasn't saying much.

I looked at Nancy. "Do you have any idea who they're talking about?"

"None. I didn't even know that they were visiting Sheila through the woods. I guess I should have been paying more attention." Her gaze focused steadily on the two girls. "Is there anything else going on that I should know about?"

Both heads shook back and forth in unison. If I hadn't seen the same innocent expression on Davey's face when I knew full well that he was up to something, I might have been tempted to believe them.

"Kids." Nancy sighed. "You can't keep watch them every second of the day. And until recently, I had no idea I needed to."

A car horn tooted outside. The two girls shrieked, and ran to the front door. "Sarah's here!" cried Molly, as Jessie unlatched the door and threw it open. Immediately, they both ran out.

"I know you spoke to the police," I said to Nancy as we followed them. "But did they ever talk to your girls?"

"Of course not. Detective Holloway didn't ask, but even if he had, I wouldn't have allowed it."

"But considering what they just said—"

"No," Nancy cut me off firmly. "There's absolutely no way I would ever allow the twins to get involved. My husband, Don, is a lawyer, and between the two of us, we would block any attempt to make them part of the investigation."

We'd reached the front porch. In the driveway, Sarah's mother had pulled her car up behind mine. Sarah was already out of the backseat and running in the yard with Molly and Jessie. Her mother sketched a cheery wave out the window.

"I guess you'd better move your car," said Nancy. The dismissal was clear in her tone.

I fished my car keys out of my pocket. "Thanks for your time."

"No problem."

Nancy turned away and strode over to the car behind mine. Ducking down, she leaned her head in the window and began to talk to Sarah's mom. Feeling vaguely guilty about having wrecked her day, I slid behind the wheel of the Volvo.

I understood how Nancy felt, but unlike her, I couldn't just stick my head in the sand. Somewhere, a murderer was still free. She might be able to ignore that fact, but it sure gave me the willies.

Back on the road, I considered my options and headed south. If nobody was going to take their information to the police, then I figured I was going to have to do it for them. However, there were two immediate problems with that.

First, I knew from past experience that the police were not likely to jump for joy when handed proof that someone had been meddling in one of their cases. And second, I had no idea where the state police barracks in Somers was located. Actually, I knew nothing about Somers at all, except that it was north of North Salem. I learned that from the map. Davey's soccer camp was south, and the afternoon was passing.

I probably don't have to draw you a picture.

So I headed home. I figured I could call Detective Holloway just as easily as talk to him in person. Besides, considering that I was going to tell him I was doing legwork that his men should have covered, I wouldn't mind having some distance between us.

Faith was waiting for me in the front hall, and her dark, almond shaped eyes were filled with reproach. Usually I take her with me almost everywhere. Now that she was pregnant, however, I was trying to cut down on the amount of stress she was exposed to; and that meant leaving her home. The house was cool and quiet, and she should have been napping. Instead, I could see by her anxious expression, she'd been waiting for my return.

"What's the matter?" I asked. "Did you miss me?"

Faith woofed her reply. Then she turned and raced toward the back door. That signal was clear. Faith needed to go out. Now. By the time I flipped the latch, she was whining softly under her breath.

As soon as the door was open a crack, the Poodle dashed down the back steps and squatted immediately. A wave of guilt washed over me. Single mothers get used to juggling everybody's needs, but Faith was usually so easy I'd gotten into the habit of taking her for granted. Obviously I was going to have to start trying harder.

And if Faith herself hadn't just managed to convey that thought, the message that was waiting for me on my answering machine would have.

"It's me," said Aunt Peg, secure in the knowledge that I would recognize her voice. "Why aren't you there?

Who's watching Faith? Do you have her with you? Have you started to take her temperature yet? I hope you're keeping records."

I grimaced at the barrage of questions. No doubt Aunt Peg would find my answers highly unsatisfactory.

"I'm calling to tell you that I'm stopping by later with a whelping box for Faith," she continued. "It's high time you started to make preparations."

"Yes, Aunt Peg," I muttered dutifully, as Faith scampered back up the steps. I got a biscuit out of the box in the pantry and handed it to her.

"I'll be there about five-thirty. Don't worry about dinner. I'll bring something with me. I hope Davey likes Chinese. By the way, have you lined up a supplier for goat's milk yet?"

Goat's milk? I spun around and stared at the machine. Like it was going to offer me answers. No dice. Instead it clicked off, signaling that Aunt Peg was done giving orders. For the moment, anyway.

Since I still had some time before Davey got back, I dialed information and got the number for the state police in Somers. So far, so good. Then I called and asked for Detective Holloway.

I sat on hold for three minutes, plenty of time to calculate how much money I was spending in long-distance rates to listen to dead air. By the time Holloway picked up, my patience was wearing thin. Maybe I should have written him a letter.

"This is Detective Holloway," he said brusquely. "What can I do for you?"

"My name is Melanie Travis. I'm calling about Sheila Vaughn. You met my fiancé, Sam Driver, at her house on Saturday."

"Yes?" The single word didn't sound encouraging. More like he wished I'd hurry up and get to the point.

"Sam told me it was your impression that Sheila had interrupted a burglary, that she was killed by someone who broke into her house."

This time when I paused, Holloway didn't bother to reply. He simply waited. All at once, none of the interesting things I'd planned to tell him seemed very interesting.

"Sam told you about Sheila's Pugs, right? That they wouldn't have been outside unless she was home?"

"Yes, I believe he did mention that."

"So that meant that Sheila let her killer into the house."

"Not necessarily. What if the robber arrived first and let the dogs outside himself so that they wouldn't be in his way?"

"I guess that's possible," I conceded. "But it doesn't seem very likely. If you were looking for a house to rob, would you choose one that was filled with guard dogs?"

"Guard dogs?"

I couldn't see Holloway, but I swear I could hear his smile.

"You are referring to the Pugs, aren't you?"

"Yes, of course," I said huffily. I wasn't getting anywhere and we both knew it. The heck with it, I thought, and went in another direction. "Are you aware that Sheila recently became partner in a magazine whose primary function is to expose the sordid secrets of the dog show world?"

There was a brief moment of silence. I heard the sound of papers being shuffled, then Holloway was back. "*Woof!*, right? Brian Endicott is the other managing partner, and I met him on Saturday as well."

"Did he tell you that several of the people Sheila had written stories about had made threats against her?"

"We spoke about the magazine briefly. Mr. Endicott was of the opinion that there was no way that their business could be connected to Ms. Vaughn's death."

"Well, the receptionist at his office has a different opinion. Also Sheila's neighbor, Nancy Benning? She has twin daughters who saw someone they called a mean man visit Sheila on more than one occasion."

"How old are these girls?"

"I'm not sure. Five or six."

"And did they have any idea who this man was?"

"No."

"I see. Is that it?"

I sank down into a kitchen chair, feeling deflated. "Yes."

"In that case, thank you for your interest. I'll have someone look into these issues you've raised."

I hung up the phone, frowning.

Let's just say I wouldn't be holding my breath.

⮞❖ *Sixteen* ❖⮜

Promptly at five-thirty, Aunt Peg blew in like the gale force she is. A jumbo-size canvas tote was slung over one of her shoulders, and she carried two big plastic bags in her hands. The aroma of Chinese food filled the hallways as she neatly sidestepped the inevitable onslaught by dog and child, marched to the kitchen, and set our dinner down on the counter.

"Much better," she said, turning to Davey. "Where's my hug?"

"You had your chance." Davey pouted.

"I had my hands full. What good is a hug if you can't hug back? Come on, don't be shy."

She gathered my child into her arms and squeezed him hard. Davey's eyes bulged. A squeak emitted from between his lips. Aunt Peg laughed at his theatrics. For a moment, I didn't know whether to join in the merriment or call the paramedics.

"Harder!" Davey cried gleefully.

I guess that settled that problem.

"There's my girl." Aunt Peg released Davey and turned to Faith. "Don't you look splendid! It won't be long now."

"One more week," I said.

"If she's right on time. Sixty-three days is the average gestation period, but bear in mind that's only an average. It's not uncommon for dogs to be a few days early, or even a day or two late. That's what taking her temperature can help you predict. You have started, haven't you?"

"Not exactly." With everything else that was going on, I'd forgotten.

Aunt Peg sighed, loud enough to make the point that her relatives were no source of comfort in her old age. "You have to establish a base temperature now. Otherwise, you won't notice when it drops."

That sounded vaguely familiar. It had probably been part of the copious lectures she'd delivered on the art of whelping puppies eight weeks earlier when Faith had been bred. I knew I should have been taking notes.

"We'll talk about it over dinner," I said. "Do you mind eating right away? Davey's starving. He's been playing soccer all day."

"Fine by me," Aunt Peg said, then turned to Davey. "I want to hear all about camp. Don't they feed you anything? Maybe your mother should pack you a lunch."

"I did."

Davey's eyes shifted away.

"A sandwich, an apple, and three cookies. They were supposed to give you a carton of milk."

As if we weren't talking about him, my son busied himself rolling a tennis ball across the kitchen floor for Faith.

"Davey, what happened to your lunch?"

He shrugged.

I sat down on the floor beside him. "You didn't eat it, did you? That's why you're so hungry."

"I guess I lost it."

"You had it this morning when I dropped you off. Didn't you put it in your locker?"

Aunt Peg was frowning. She pushed me aside and took my place. "Did you lose your lunch or did someone take it from you?"

Davey rolled the ball again. "Maybe someone took it."

"Someone like who?"

"Randy Bowers." He thrust out his lower lip. "He said I had to give him my lunch or he would punch my lights out."

"Punch your lights out?" I was outraged. Aunt Peg poked me in the shoulder.

"Is Randy bigger than you?" she asked.

"No," Davey admitted with a small sniffle. "Just meaner."

"We'll just see about that!" Aunt Peg reached for a chair and levered herself up.

"Aunt Peg, what are you going to do?"

"I'm not sure yet. But no bully is going to run rough-shod over my nephew. Give me a chance to think about it. In the meantime, let's get out some plates and eat."

True to form, Aunt Peg had brought enough food to provision the Mongol hordes: spring rolls, egg drop soup, chicken lo mein, curried beef, and roast pork egg foo yung. Davey showed off his proficiency with chopsticks, shoveling food into his mouth as though it had been days since his last meal. While we ate, Aunt Peg got back to her original topic.

"The normal temperature for a dog is higher than that of a human. It ranges from one hundred point five to a hundred one point five and is usually higher in the evening, which is why you should be checking twice a day. When a bitch is due to whelp, her temperature will drop by a degree or two twenty-four hours ahead of time. After that happens, you shouldn't leave her alone at all."

"I'll start tonight," I said, helping myself to more lo mein.

"Yes, you will. We'll take Faith's temperature after dinner. Then we can set up her whelping box. I've brought you mine; it's in the van. You and Davey can help me bring it in and decide where to put it. I'm thinking your bedroom will probably be the best place. And I've got bedding as well."

Aunt Peg was relishing this. She's at her best when she's taking charge of other people's lives. But for once I wasn't complaining. I was the one who'd chosen to place Faith in a delicate condition; now it was my duty to do my best for her. Aunt Peg's expert guidance was more than welcome.

Davey gobbled down two fortune cookies and helped unload Peg's van. Then he and Faith removed themselves to another part of the house where they wouldn't be subjected to adult conversation and could, presumably, have more fun. That was Aunt Peg's cue to ask me what I'd found out so far about Sheila Vaughn's murder.

"I started this morning in White Plains," I told her as we decided which corner of my bedroom to place the low-sided, wooden whelping box in. "I went to visit the *Woof!* offices. Brian wasn't there. According to Tim, he's traveling on business."

"Interesting. I thought the police always told their chief suspects not to leave town. Or am I watching too many cop shows on TV?"

"Probably. But the police don't seem to view him as a suspect. I talked to Detective Holloway this afternoon. They're still holding pretty tight to the notion that Sheila surprised a burglar in her home."

Aunt Peg looked exasperated. "Didn't you explain about the dogs being outside and what an important clue that was?"

"I tried. He didn't seem impressed. I also told Holloway that he should take a trip down to White Plains and talk to Carrie, Brian's receptionist."

"About what?"

"She fields most of the calls that come in to the office. Apparently, Sheila researched and wrote several stories that their subjects weren't too happy about."

"Let me guess. Kenny Boyle is probably one."

"You're good."

"Of course I am, though it wouldn't take a genius to figure that out. Did you read the article about him in the first issue?"

"I meant to." Unfortunately, reading *Woof!* had gone the way of taking Faith's temperature. As soon as I had a free moment, I planned to get to it.

"Really, Melanie. If you expect to figure out who murdered Sheila, then you have to try and stay on top of things."

"I *am* trying."

Aunt Peg snorted. Rudely. "I don't imagine you've ever met Kenny Boyle, have you?"

"No."

"He handles mostly working breeds. You know, Dobermans, Rottweilers, Bernese Mountain Dogs? He has a wonderful hand on a dog, and over the years, his clients have enjoyed a great deal of success in the show ring."

"It doesn't sound like Sheila would have had much to say about that."

"That's just background, so you'll have a context for what came next. It seems to be a truism in the dog show world that the more people win, the more they want to win. Someone has the top working dog on the East Coast, and the following year they want to be number one in the country."

"That makes sense, I guess."

I watched as Aunt Peg spread out a waterproof tarp over the corner of the rug near my bed. The wooden whelping box had four sides, but no bottom or top. Once the tarp was in place, Peg maneuvered the box on top of it, then pulled out a thick bundle of newspapers. Together we began to lay down the next layer.

"The more you show, obviously, the higher the bills get. And with the way some of those specials dogs travel these days, it can be very hard to keep track of which expenses are legitimate and which have been padded. I gather from the article that one of Kenny's clients simply issued him a credit card."

"One of Kenny's very rich clients," I muttered. I had a hard time mustering sympathy for people who had so much money they didn't even notice when some of it disappeared.

"I think we can assume that," Aunt Peg said dryly. "Apparently nobody was scrutinizing the bills very closely. By the time the client's financial advisor actually sat down and had a look, Kenny had bought himself a new van and financed part of his son's private-school education at the client's expense."

"It sounds like Kenny is a pretty industrious guy."

We'd finished with the newspaper, and Aunt Peg went

back to her canvas sack. Watching her unpack was like watching clowns spill out of a Volkswagen at the circus. Now she pulled out a stack of cotton-backed, waterproof pads. Placing six in an overlapping pattern filled the floor of the whelping box, and I thought we were done. Instead, Peg unfolded another eight.

"This is the actual surface you'll use when the puppies are being born. Whelping is a messy business, and you want the newborns to stay as warm and dry as possible. As each pad gets wet and soiled, you simply slip it out from under the bitch and go on to the next."

"Got it." Once again, I found myself wondering if I should be taking notes.

"Kenny *is* industrious," Peg went back to our earlier topic. "But as I said, he's also an excellent handler. So while he may have been charging his client plenty, he was also getting results. I believe this supposed breaking story Sheila wrote about is actually a year old. In the meantime, Kenny and the client have come to terms and continued their relationship."

"Even though the client knew that Kenny was stealing from him?" I asked incredulously.

"Kenny was winning with the man's dog, didn't I just tell you that?"

"And winning is everything?"

"Close enough," Peg said crisply. "Kenny apologized and promised to clean up his act. And the client's Doberman was the number one working dog, all systems, last year. In the end, everybody went home happy."

"I don't get it," I said. "If that's how things ended, what was Kenny so upset about? Why did he threaten Sheila?"

"Sheila took a story that a few people had gossiped

about privately and made the whole thing very public. I imagine Kenny could make a case that she had cost him a bundle in future business. He and his client had a long-term relationship which, obviously, both felt was worth salvaging. But suppose you were new to the dog show game and shopping around for a handler, would you even think twice about hiring Kenny Boyle? I know I wouldn't."

"Me either," I agreed, rocking back on my heels and surveying our handiwork. "Now what?"

"We're just about finished." Sheepskin pads were the last thing to emerge from the tote back, and Aunt Peg laid them on top. "Leave these here until she goes into labor. You want Faith to get used to being in the whelping box. I'd like to see her sleeping here at night, so make it as comfortable and appealing as possible. After the puppies are born, you'll put the pads back. They make a wonderful surface for baby puppies to keep warm, and they offer good traction besides. Where's your heating pad?"

I thought for a moment, then got up to check in the linen closet. "By the way," I said, returning a minute later, heating pad in hand. "Do you know a man named Marlon Dickie?"

A frown creased Peg's brow briefly. "The name doesn't sound familiar. Who is he?"

"A photographer Brian used sometimes for the magazine. Carrie said he was awfully interested in Sheila. Used to call her a lot, though she didn't seem to return his interest. How about Alida Trent?"

This time Aunt Peg nodded. "Shih Tzus," she said. "Been in dogs forever. She's a client of Crawford Langley's."

"According to Carrie, Sheila was researching a story about her, and Alida had threatened to sue."

"Over what? I don't recall hearing about any scandals that had to do with Alida. What was the story about?"

"I'm not sure. A lease, I think. Or maybe a co-ownership? I was hoping you could give me an introduction."

"Crawford would be a better bet, if he'll do it. Alida and I have crossed paths occasionally, but no more than that. I think she lives somewhere in Duchess County. Maybe Millbrook? There's lots of old money there."

"And there isn't in Greenwich?" I teased.

"Actually"—Peg harrumphed—"it feels like we've begun to specialize in new money."

I cocked a hand on the side of my ear. "What's that? Are those violins I hear?"

"You might be more sympathetic." Peg gathered her things and stood. "And since we're on the subject, how's Sam doing?"

I felt a pang. All day long, I'd tried to keep thoughts of him at bay. I hadn't been entirely successful. I hadn't expected to be.

"Gone."

"Gone where?"

"Illinois to visit Sheila's family. He didn't phone you?"

"No." Aunt Peg looked bemused. "I take it he did call you?"

"He left me a message," I admitted.

"I hope he's all right."

Tell me about it, I thought.

❧❀ *Seventeen* ❀❧

As I got Davey ready for camp the next morning, it occurred to me that Aunt Peg hadn't followed through on her promise to solve the problem of Davey and the lunchtime bully. I offered to write a note for him to give to the counselors—an idea my son firmly rejected in the belief that it would make him look like a wuss. Speaking as a mother, I wasn't sure that was an all-bad thing.

But when Davey rolled his eyes and assured me that a girl would never understand, I capitulated; instead packing a spare sandwich and extra cookies in his bag, in the hope that he could use the additional food to negotiate a truce.

As soon as he was gone, I took Faith's temperature, adding the morning's normal reading to the chart Peg and I had begun the night before. Earlier, Faith had begun to exhibit the first signs of nesting. I heard her burrowing beneath the dining-room table and trying to slip into the narrow space behind the couch. Her nails scraped as she dug furiously into the carpet, attempting to ready a spot or her puppies' arrival.

She'd been introduced to the sumptuous accommoda-
tions Aunt Peg and I had prepared in my bedroom, but
so far her only response had been to sniff the box disdain-
fully and walk away. In her own doggy way, she was
rolling her eyes just as my son had. A human, she seemed
to be saying, just wouldn't understand.

I spent the next hour browsing through the inaugural
issue of *Woof!*. Aunt Peg had been right about Sheila's
story on Kenny Boyle. There was scant mention of the
fact that he and his client had resolved their differences,
and the facts were presented as sensationally as possible.
Not only would the tone of the article keep future clients
from seeking him out, I could see how some of the ones
he had might be tempted to jump ship.

Several photographs accompanied the article. One, of
course, was of the top winning Doberman. Kenny was a
tall man, built along the same elegant lines as the dog
he was handling. In the picture, taken to celebrate a group
win at the prestigious Tuxedo Park show, they seemed
to complement each other well.

The second photo was considerably less flattering. It
was a candid, snapped under the handlers' tent. Kenny
was leaning over a grooming table, talking to someone.
Judging by the sneer on his face, he wasn't very happy.
The tone of the photograph matched the article it accompanied, and when I checked for the credit, I wasn't surprised to find Marlon Dickie's name.

I got up, walked over to the phone on the counter, and
dialed the magazine's office. When Carrie answered, I
identified myself and reminded her that we'd spoken the
day before. Even so, it seemed to take her a minute to
place me.

"Oh yeah," she said finally. "You're the lady that ticked off Aubrey."

I was? Interesting.

"What was she mad about?" I asked.

"Like I would know. When Brian's not around, nobody tells me anything. They treat me like a piece of furniture. All I know is after you left Aubrey spent the next hour in a ferocious snit. Even Tim had to stay out of her way, and he's usually her favorite."

Before her tone degenerated into a complete whine, I interrupted. "Listen, I was calling to find out where Marlon Dickie lives. And could you give me his phone number, too?"

"Sure," Carrie said.

I heard the sound of pages being flipped.

"It's in the Rolodex. D . . . d . . . d . . . Oops." She giggled. "It's not here. Hang on a minute. Sometimes I try to get a little creative with my filing system. It livens up the day, you know? I'll try the M's. Hold on."

Carrie was young, I told myself as another minute passed. Very young.

"Damn! Not here either. Maybe P."

"For photographer?" I asked.

"No." Carrie chuckled again. "Pain in the butt. Hey, what do you know? Here it is. Marlon Dickie, 319 West River Road, Stamford."

Stamford? That made life easy. Carrie reeled off the phone number, and I wrote it down. I thanked her, hung up, and dialed again.

Marlon Dickie answered his phone on the first ring, and seemed delighted by the prospect of having me stop by his studio. I should probably confess that I might have left him with the impression I was looking for a

photographer to record my upcoming wedding. He gave
me directions, and River Road turned out to be only a
few miles away.

Once again I opted to leave Faith home, the knowledge
that she would be safe and cool winning out over the
pleasure of her company. I took her upstairs, stepped
her into the whelping box, and told her to lie down.
Obligingly, Faith did.

Now came the tough part. Her stay command is a little
iffy. Besides, stay is an absolute. If I used it, it would
mean she was to remain in the box until I got home. I
was hoping Faith would regard the whelping box as a
haven, not a prison. Instead, I patted the comfortable
sheepskin surface encouragingly and left her.

Faith reached the bottom of the stairs before I did.
When I shut the front door behind me, her nose was
pressed against the window next to it. So much for good
intentions. If things didn't improve soon, she was going
to be popping out these puppies under the kitchen sink.

Marlon's studio was located on a side street off Long
Ridge Road where small houses sat on small lots, and
once-quiet neighborhoods were now disrupted by the
deluge of commuter traffic heading toward the over-
developed areas to the south. I found the house by the
number on the curb, then saw a small sign he'd posted
in his front window. "Marlon Dickie, Professional Photographer for All Occasions. Walk-Ins Welcome."

The house itself was a raised ranch, dark red in color
with black shutters and white trim. The style and color
screamed fifties. Was it just me or would most people be
turned off by a photographer who didn't have enough
of an artistic eye to see that his house had been in its
prime nearly a half century earlier?

Steep concrete steps led up to the front door; black paint flaked off the spindly wrought-iron railing that accompanied them. I had to ring the doorbell three times before Marlon appeared. Maybe he spent his days sitting by the phone.

"You must be Melanie," he said cheerfully, extending a hand. "Glad to meet you."

Perhaps because of Carrie's less-than-flattering assessment, the image I'd formed of Marlon Dickie wasn't very complimentary. I certainly hadn't expected curly black hair, mischievous green eyes, and an infectious smile. I reached out to shake his hand and Marlon's fingers curled possessively around mine.

"Come on in," he said. The front door opened onto a small landing, which faced two staircases. One led up to a combination living room/dining room. Marlon pointed down the other way. "Studio's down there. Come on, I'll show you some of my work."

He skipped down the steps, turning lights on as he went. The bottom half of the house was refreshingly cool and consisted mostly of one large room. A small grouping of furniture filled half the space. The rest was taken up by the tools of Marlon's trade: a backdrop, lighting, reflectors, and several cameras.

"Have a seat. You said a wedding, right? Let me get the right book. I also do birthdays, bar mitzvahs, anniversaries . . . You name it, I'm game for it."

As he dug into a cabinet on the side wall, I sat down on a couch that was pushed against one wall. The cushions were old and soft; they sucked me in like quicksand.

"Dog shows?"

Marlon glanced back over his shoulder. "Those, too. How'd you know?"

"That's how I got your name. From *Woof!* magazine."

"Sheila recommended me?" He sounded pleased.

"Not exactly." I struggled to sit up straight, pushing myself to the edge of the cushion. "You have heard . . . ?"

"Oh yes, of course." An aggrieved expression settled on Marlon's face. He didn't look so much grief-stricken as determined to play the part well. "What a shock! It makes you wonder what this world is coming to. I saw a story about it on the news."

"How awful for you, finding out that way. I heard you were a friend of Sheila's."

Marlon found the scrapbook he was looking for and placed it on the table in front of me. Then he sat down on the couch as well. Maybe it was because he had longer legs, or maybe he was just used to the couch. It didn't seem to swallow him as it had me.

"Don't tell me," he said, flipping to the first page. "You've been talking to Aubrey. That woman spends so much time minding other people's business it's a wonder she ever gets anything done."

"No," I said, "Aubrey didn't mention you."

To keep up the pretense, I let my eyes skim over the first few pages of the photo album. Eight-by-ten color glossies showed a succession of brides; and much to my surprise, the pictures were gorgeous. Marlon was really talented.

"Tim then?"

"No, I—"

"Carrie, that little minx behind the desk? I always thought she had it in for me."

I looked up. "Then you weren't Sheila's friend?"

"Not like I wanted to be. And not for lack of trying

either. God knows she needed someone to be on her side."

"Did she? Why?"

"If you knew Sheila, then I imagine you knew her life was in a bit of turmoil. First there was the bit about the awful ex-husband."

"The . . . what?" Quickly I lowered my gaze before he read something in it I didn't want him to see. The pages of the scrapbook flew by.

"My words, not hers. Poor Sheila never had a bad word to say about anybody."

"You must be joking."

He was, I realized, when I saw the grin on his face. I flushed slightly. Marlon didn't seem to notice.

"Let's just say she was deluded where he was concerned. Always thinking she was going to get him back."

"She talked to you about that?"

"Why not? I make a pretty good listener. And I've been married myself. Trust me, once you get out, stay out. You can't go back, and you shouldn't want to."

Marlon stopped suddenly. He gulped heavily, his Adam's apple bobbing in his neck. "Sorry. I guess that's not the right tack to take with a bride-to-be."

"Don't worry about it. I can be pretty cynical myself about some things. Your photographs are beautiful."

"Thank you."

"They're not at all like the others I'd seen, the pictures you took for *Woof!*."

"Give the client what he asks for," Marlon said breezily. "That's my motto. You want someone to look stupid and snarky, I can do that. You want to look beautiful . . ." His hands came up to form a frame around my face. "I can do that, too. In your case, it would be easy."

Flatterer, I thought. Hadn't I just told him I was a cynic?

"So Sheila hired you to make people look ugly and stupid?"

"Not Sheila. Those were Brian's instructions. You know him?"

I nodded.

"Mr. Perfectionist. Mr. Nothing You Ever Do For Me Is Right The First Time." Marlon grinned. "Not that it matters now. I expect I'll be having the last laugh shortly."

"Why is that?"

"High-and-mighty *Woof!*, the tome that was going to revolutionize the dog fancy's reading habits? It's on the verge of going bankrupt."

❧❖ Eighteen ❖❧

I sucked in a breath. "Where did you hear that?"

"From the lord of the manor himself. Not that he said so in as many words. No, Brian's explanations were all couched in accountant-speak. You know, bottom line, cost-effective, maximizing the investment. Let's just say that the bottom line for me was that Brian wouldn't be needing my services anymore."

"But they just published their first issue," I protested. "Everyone was wildly enthusiastic about it."

"Sorry to be the bearer of bad news, but that's the way it is." Marlon shrugged, looking anything but apologetic. "I imagine they'll struggle along for a while, while Brian tries to put the best face on things. Heaven forbid one of his projects doesn't turn out to be a huge success.

"My guess is, in about six months, he'll see the light. Realize in a very public way that the dog show game isn't really as nasty and underhanded as he thought it was. Sorry, folks, we're going to have to close down now. We've plumb run out of bad news."

I found myself smiling. "Maybe in six months time, he'll have been able to pull things back together."

"With Sheila there, maybe. That lady was working her tail off to make the magazine a success, and I wouldn't have bet against her. But now? I don't think it has a chance."

I spent the next fifteen minutes looking through the rest of Marlon's scrapbook and checking out his price list. When I left, I had one of his cards tucked in my purse. But delighted as I'd been with his work, I couldn't decide what to make of what he'd said.

I wondered if Sheila had known about *Woof!*'s financial straits when she'd signed on. With all her supposed business acumen, I was sure she would have checked things out pretty thoroughly. Perhaps she'd thought her own investment would be enough to turn things around.

Or maybe Marlon was just plain wrong. The fact that Brian had said he didn't want to work with the photographer anymore didn't necessarily mean that the magazine was going under. Maybe Brian had found someone whose work he liked better.

Or maybe Marlon had been let go after the two men had had an argument over something else entirely.

Or someone.

Marlon hadn't made any secret of his antipathy for his ex-employer. I wondered if he knew about the insurance policies the two copublishers had taken out on each other. Or that his version of things gave Brian the strongest motive I'd found so far.

That afternoon my brother, Frank, dropped by. He lives in Cos Cob, a small town on the coast between Greenwich and Stamford. From the amount of time we spend together, however, he might as well live in Timbuktu.

At twenty-eight, Frank is four years younger than I, and if you think Peter Pan is charming, you'd love my brother. He doesn't want to grow up either. Usually an unexpected visit means he wants something, and this one was no exception.

"Mel!" he cried expansively, throwing open the front door and letting himself in.

Faith and I were in the kitchen, baking brownies as a surprise for Davey when he got home from camp. Startled by the unexpected intrusion, the Poodle leapt up and galloped into the front hall. I went running after her.

With her recent weight gain, Faith's not nearly as balanced as she thinks she is. I had visions of her skidding into a wall and falling, but when I caught up a moment later, everything was fine. She was sniffing Frank's leg, and he was frowning at her. Just like usual.

"Hey, Mel. Hi, dog. Do I smell brownies?"

"Her name's Faith," I said, a fact I was sure I'd mentioned at least a hundred times before. "And the brownies won't be ready for twenty minutes."

"Faith, of course. I knew that." My brother tried out an ingratiating grin. "Twenty minutes it is. I've got time. Where's Davey?"

"Soccer camp. He'll be back around four-thirty."

Frank walked past me down the hall. In the kitchen, he opened the refrigerator and helped himself to a soda. "Camp, right. He told me about that. Is it going well?"

"Davey loves it. You should see him dribble."

"I bet the kid's a natural. He probably gets it from me."

As I recalled, my brother had played basketball desultorily in high school and joined an occasional game of pickup softball since. What is it about men that they all remember themselves as former sports stars?

"How's the Bean Counter doing?"

Just before Christmas, my brother had opened a coffee bar in north Stamford. He was manager and part-owner and I'd heard nothing but good reports. Before that, Frank's employment history had been pretty spotty. Half-afraid I would jinx his new endeavor, I'd tried not to check up on him. I hoped the coffee bar wasn't the reason he'd stopped by.

"Terrific. Couldn't be better. Starting next week, we're going to have live entertainment on Friday and Saturday nights."

"Sounds great," I agreed, then added casually, "Do you need a permit for that?"

What can I say? Old habits die hard. I'd been looking out for my brother since we were children and, as subtle queries sometimes go right over his head, I'd learned not to beat around the bush.

"Don't worry. Everything's in order. This is real life, Mel. A real business. I'm not a little kid anymore."

"I know that." I pulled out a chair and sat down. "So why'd you stop by?"

"Does there have to be a reason?"

Answering a question with a question wasn't a good sign.

"No . . ."

"You see?" said Frank. "That's the whole problem with our family. We're not close. We hardly ever get together."

Funny, he'd never thought of that as a problem before.

"I was thinking we ought to do something about that."
This was getting interesting. "Like what?"

"I was thinking of a big family dinner, sometime soon. Maybe a week from Saturday. Are you free?"

I thought for a moment. "If you don't count the fact that I should have a litter of very young puppies in my bedroom by then, yes. But what do you mean by a big family dinner? I'm sure this won't come as a shock to you, but we don't have a big family. Who are you planning to invite?"

Frank's finger traced a circle around the rim of his can. "You and me, of course. And Davey. And Bertie."

His voice dropped as he said the last name. I wasn't sure I'd heard him right. "And who? Did you say Bertie?"

My brother nodded.

"As in Alberta Kennedy?"

Now he looked exasperated. "Do you know any other Berties?"

"No, but since when did she become part of our family?"

Bertie Kennedy was a professional dog handler whom I'd met eighteen months earlier when Aunt Peg had tried to convince me that I needed to join the local all-breed kennel club. She was bright and vivacious and gorgeous to look at. Not unexpectedly, my brother had been entranced. The one date I knew they'd been on seemed to have gone well enough, but I'd never heard that anything further had come of it.

I guessed I should take this as a gentle reminder from the fates that I should have been staying on top of things. "Frank, what are you trying to tell me?"

His face grew pink. "Don't start jumping to conclusions. It's not like we're getting married or anything."

"Well what exactly *are* you doing?"

"We're seeing each other."

"Seriously?"

"I guess."

"Don't you *know*?"

He shot me a look. "Men never know these things. It's the woman who figures out where you stand. If you're lucky, she might clue you in."

I bit back a smile. "And has Bertie done that?"

"Kind of."

"Meaning?"

"Her parents are coming to visit next week, and she thinks we should meet." Frank paused. "Over dinner."

It only took a moment for the implications of that to make themselves felt. "This is the big family dinner you were talking about?"

"Come on, Mel. Be a good sport. You don't have to do anything fancy. Maybe we could just throw some steaks on the barbecue."

"Wait a minute." I stared at him. "Are you saying you want to bring Bertie's parents over *here?*"

"Sure." The ingratiating smile was back. "Why not?"

"Because they're coming to meet you, not me."

"They're coming to meet my family, Mel. And you and Davey are it. Unless you'd like to add Aunt Peg and Aunt Rose to the guest list."

Not if I could help it. Every time those two women got together, something seismic happened.

I glared at my brother. His eyes shifted away. "You've already told Bertie I'd have her parents to dinner, haven't you?"

"Sort of," Frank admitted. "I said I'd have to check and make sure."

More likely Bertie had been the one to insist that he check on the arrangements before making any promises.

My brother and Bertie a couple, I thought. Who'd have guessed? I didn't know Bertie well, but what I knew, I liked. She was smart and hardworking; and I had no doubt she'd make a mark in her chosen profession. I supposed it was no use wondering what she saw in Frank.

I glanced up. When I'd stopped talking, so had Frank. Sensing he might be winning, he'd prudently decided not to push things. He was leafing through the issue of *Woof!* that I'd left on the table earlier.

"This guy's an idiot," he said.

I leaned over and had a look. "Who?"

His finger poked at the win photo accompanying Kenny Boyle's article.

"You mean Kenny?"

Frank nodded. "He's Bertie's ex. Thinks he's some real hotshot because he has some dogs who've done a bunch of winning. He's always trying to lord it over her, saying she had her chance to be somebody when she was with him."

I rocked back in my seat. "Bertie was seeing Kenny Boyle? I didn't know that."

"It was a while ago. Last fall, I think. Bertie doesn't talk about it much, but I think he gave her a pretty rough time of it."

"Do you think she'd talk to me about Kenny?"

"Sure. Why not?" Frank flipped the magazine shut.

"Give her a call. Then you two can make some plans for the dinner, too."

"Right." I glanced at my watch. The brownies were just about done. "You owe me, Frank."

My brother only shrugged. "So what else is new?"

Frank stayed until Davey got home. He said he wanted to see his nephew, but I think the real reason was that it took the brownies that long to cool. Fortified by a big square of fudgy cake apiece, the two of them went out in the backyard to kick a soccer ball around.

Davey had wolfed his snack down, but he hadn't gone back for seconds. I hoped that was a good sign. Maybe he'd gotten to eat his lunch at camp earlier.

While the two of them were keeping each other busy, I picked up the phone and called Bertie. Tuesday is the best day of the week to call a handler. The weekend rush is over. They've spent Monday recovering and calling clients, but it isn't yet time to start gearing up for the next weekend's shows yet.

Bertie answered the phone in her kennel. I could tell that by the background noise, which all but drowned out what I was trying to say.

"Hang on," Bertie yelled. "I'm going to switch phones. I'll be right back."

A minute later, she picked up again. This time the line was blessedly quiet. "Melanie, is that you? I couldn't hear a thing."

"Yes, it's me. I've been talking to Frank."

"Good." Bertie paused, probably considering what she knew about our relationship. "That *is* good, isn't it?"

"Sure. I hear your parents are coming to visit."

"Sheesh. Don't tell me he led with that. Look, getting everyone together at your house was Frank's idea. I'm perfectly happy to go to a restaurant or do something here. There's no reason we need to impose on you."

"You wouldn't be imposing," I said, crossing my fingers in my lap. "It's fine."

"Are you sure?" Bertie needed to be convinced. "The only reason I went along with this is that I think Frank is nervous about meeting my folks. I've told him it's not a big deal, but he really wants to make a good impression.

"He's worried that my parents won't like him, and he seemed to think that having you and Davey around would help. I think he figures that if they hate him— which they won't—they'll still be charmed by the rest of his family and see that he has potential. Like if he was related to a really cute kid and a woman who had her whole life pulled together, how bad could he be?"

"Frank said that?" I asked, amazed.

My brother was much more likely to make fun of my sedate, school teacher lifestyle than to compliment it. Unless he wanted something from me, of course. Then I began to look like a pretty good provider.

"I'm paraphrasing, but that was the gist. Still, it doesn't mean we can't make other arrangements."

"Don't be silly. We'll do a barbecue here. I have to admit, though, this whole thing kind of caught me by surprise."

"Me and Frank?" Bertie chuckled. "Yeah, me too."

"I didn't even know you guys were seeing each other."

"Since right after Christmas. I'd just gotten out of a really bad relationship. Something I never should have hung on to as long as I did. And then, out of the blue, Frank called.

"I remembered that dinner I had with him and you and Sam last summer and how much fun it was. And how sweet Frank was, just a nice, normal, undemanding guy. I thought maybe seeing him a few times would be just what I needed to get my head back on straight."

Bertie sighed. "The last thing I was looking for was anything serious. But when we got together again, Frank and I really hit it off. I don't think either one of us expected that. Six months later, here we are."

"Good for you," I said. It was nice to hear that the possibility of an uncomplicated relationship actually did exist. "Since you kind of brought it up, I have a question. Was the guy you were seeing before my brother Kenny Boyle?"

Bertie hesitated for so long that I wasn't sure she was going to answer. When she finally did, her voice was small. I'd always thought of Bertie as unflappable, but mentioning Kenny's name had certainly pushed the wrong button.

"Yes," she said finally. "How did you know?"

"It was something Frank said. If you don't mind, I'd love to get your impression of him. Did you know Sheila Vaughn?"

"The woman who was killed? I knew who she was from being at the shows. I don't think we'd ever met. Why?"

"She wrote an article about Kenny that appeared in the first issue of *Woof!*. Apparently he wasn't too happy about some of the things she said."

"That doesn't surprise me." Bertie's tone was bitter. "Kenny isn't a happy kind of guy."

"According to the secretary at the magazine, Kenny made some threats against Sheila shortly before she was murdered."

"What do you want to know?" asked Bertie. "Do I think Kenny is capable of something like that? Hell yes, Kenny could kill someone. I was lucky he didn't kill me."

❧❖ *Nineteen* ❖❧

I nearly dropped the phone. "Bertie, what are you talking about?"

I heard her sigh; felt her reluctance to answer. I waited, giving her time to gather her thoughts.

"Look," she said finally, "I don't want to do this over the phone. You want to know what Kenny's like, there's one surefire way to find out. What are you doing tomorrow?"

"After Davey leaves for camp, I'm free all day."

"Good. I'll swing by around nine and pick you up. By the way, you don't mind being used as a human shield, do you?"

I was so relieved to hear some of the usual spirit back in her voice it took me a moment to realize what she'd said. By then, it was too late. Bertie was already making plans.

"I left some things at Kenny's that I've been meaning to pick up forever. I could never seem to face going back there, especially after the way I left. I guess I didn't want to go alone, either. But this will work out well, if it's okay with you. We'll go together, and you can see the great man in action for yourself."

"Sure," I said. Great man? "I'll be ready."

As I hung up the phone, I realized I'd half expected Bertie to come back and say she'd been kidding about that human shield crack. She hadn't, though. I hoped I wasn't meant to take it literally.

Later that night, after I'd put Davey to bed, I found myself back on the telephone. Sam called from outside Chicago to let me know that he was okay and staying with Sheila's parents. The funeral was scheduled for Thursday, he expected to be home sometime over the weekend.

I acquiesced to all his plans and tried like crazy to read between the lines. Sam said he was fine, but I knew how hard this trip had to be for him. I was sure he was holding his emotions tightly in check; his voice was unusually flat, and he didn't remember to ask about Davey until the very end of the conversation.

If he'd been there, we'd have discussed Davey's lunch dilemma. I would have liked to have Sam's input; I was sure he'd have had something useful to say. But it didn't seem like the time to add to his worries.

Instead, I told him that I'd been speaking to some of Sheila's coworkers and would see a few more before he got back. Sam seemed pleased to believe that I was making progress. Whether that was actually true or not, I was happy to let him believe it.

"I love you, Melanie," Sam said at the end. "You know that, don't you?"

Briefly I wondered why he would feel the need to ask.

"I know," I said. "I love you, too."

After I hung up the phone, I sat and stared into space. Usually I feel a rush of warmth when Sam says those words. There's a tug of emotion when I say them myself. But tonight, it seemed as though we'd professed our love for each other by rote.

I hoped it was only my imagination because all I'd felt between us was a long stretch of empty space.

Bertie has auburn hair, green eyes, legs a mile long, and the kind of figure that men pant over. There, I got that out of my system. Now I feel much better.

When we first met, I'd thought she was prickly and standoffish. Then again, Bertie was a young woman alone, trying to build a career in a tough, highly competitive profession. And I was investigating a murder and considered her a suspect. You can see why we might not have hit it off right away.

Fortunately over the last year, we've managed to move past that rocky beginning. I wouldn't say we're real friends yet, but we're heading slowly in that direction. Considering Bertie's many assets, she hasn't had things easy. Women tend to be intimidated by her looks; men, by her competence.

Aunt Peg, who doesn't notice what people look like (though she can sort out their dogs at twenty paces) and who values the ability to get things done above all else, calls Bertie a pretty sharp cookie. I'd say that assessment is right on the mark.

Bertie picked me up in a maroon Chevy van whose odometer had just passed one hundred thousand miles. This wasn't a minivan like those favored by droves of suburban mothers; this was a working truck, used for hauling crates and equipment to shows. The rubber-matted back was empty; the seat next to the driver's, padded and comfortable.

Bertie was used to traveling in the van, and it showed. There were two mugs of coffee in the cup holders and a dog-eared book of maps in the side pocket of the door. As I climbed in, she grinned a welcome and shifted into reverse.

"I guess I didn't sound too grim yesterday," Bertie said as we backed out of the driveway. "I was half-afraid I might have scared you off."

"Who me? You should know better than that."

Her grin widened. She'd been on hand when I'd confronted one murderer, and she'd probably heard about others. "Yeah, I guess I should."

The other times I'd seen Bertie had been at dog shows or functions, so she'd always been dressed up. Today she looked very different in jeans, a T-shirt, and sneakers, with her hair pulled back into a casual ponytail. She wore no makeup, no jewelry, nothing intended to draw the eye. I wondered if that was the way she normally dressed on her days off or whether the drab look she'd aspired to was a calculated response to the fact that we were going to visit her ex.

"You didn't tell me where Kenny lives," I said. "Where are we going?"

"North Haven. It'll take about an hour each way. I hope that's okay."

"Sure." I settled back in my seat. "I've got all day."

"I brought coffee. Help yourself. I didn't know how you took it so I added a little milk and sweetener."

"Close enough, thanks. You want to tell me about you and Kenny now, or would you rather beat around the bush for a while first?"

Bertie cast a startled glance my way, then quickly recovered. "Now's fine. But first, I have a question for you. Why do you care? What's your interest in this?"

"I told you yesterday. Kenny was heard making threats against Sheila Vaughn just before she was murdered."

"Isn't that a problem for the police?"

"It should be, except that they seem to think she was killed in a random act of violence by robbers who had broken into her home."

"How come you don't agree?"

I explained about Sheila's Pugs being outside. Bertie's a dog person. She understood immediately and was nodding before I'd even finished.

"All right, I'll go with you on that. But still, so what? Who was Sheila to you?"

"My fiancé's ex-wife."

"No shit." Bertie choked on a strangled laugh. "Sam was married to *Sheila*?"

"You didn't know?"

"No, why should I?"

I shrugged uncomfortably. "I didn't find out myself until recently, and I have to admit the news came as a shock. But since both of them were involved with dogs, I wondered if everyone had known all along but me."

"Not me. Maybe I'm out of the loop."

Bertie? Never.

"Sam and Sheila." She shook her head, still surprised. "You don't get things easy, do you?"

"Apparently not." I waited a beat, then added, "I gather you didn't have things too easy with Kenny either."

"That's putting it mildly. Have you ever met Kenny?"

"No. My Aunt Peg told me some stuff about him, but I don't think I've ever even seen him."

"Considering all the showing you've been doing, you probably have, you just didn't know it. If there's a show with halfway decent judges, Kenny's there with a big string of dogs. Picture someone tall, with neatly trimmed hair, always in place. Wire-rim glasses. Strong cheekbones." Bertie looked sideways at me. "Great lips."

"Sounds interesting. Too bad he's a jerk."

"Yeah." Bertie yanked the wheel and changed lanes. "He's a jerk, all right. Most people don't realize that right off. Certainly there are plenty of owners and judges who think that Kenny's an all-around great guy."

I thought about the article I'd read in *Woof!*. Even though Kenny had been exposed as a thief, he was still doing business with the man he'd stolen from. It seemed amazing that some people were able to skate through life without ever being held accountable, and I said so.

"That's Kenny all over," Bertie said. "Nothing's ever his fault. No matter what goes wrong, he's never the one to blame. I'm sure he found some perfectly reasonable explanation for how that money got spent—something that didn't implicate him as the son of a bitch he is."

I reached for my coffee and took a sip. It was sweeter than I normally take it, but hot and strong. "If Kenny's such a louse, what were you doing with him in the first place?"

"I know it seems crazy now, but in the beginning I didn't realize what he was like. I was fooled, just like everyone else. I mean there he was, this older, very successful man—his dog won the Nature's Recipe Award for Pete's sake—and he was interested in me. I was flattered. Hell, let's face it. I was smitten."

"Smitten?" I smiled at the old-fashioned word.

Bertie fluttered her lashes. "You know what I mean."

"Yeah. I do."

"At first, everything was fine. Kenny was the big, important handler, and I was the lowly sycophant."

"No, you weren't. You had your own string of dogs, too. Bertie, you've been out on your own, earning a living as a handler, for five years."

"Maybe, but we sure weren't equals. Kenny knew it, and I knew it, too. So when he said something uncomplimentary about my technique or my performance, it was easy to believe, like he said, that he was doing it for my own good. I figured being with Kenny would be good for me. I thought there was a lot he could teach me."

She stopped and grimaced. Her eyes stared straight ahead out the windshield.

"And did he?" I asked, even though I was sure I knew the answer.

"No. Kenny wasn't interested in helping anyone else, though it took me a while to figure that out. Why should he bring someone along and try to make them better? In the end, they'd only be more competition for him.

"Kenny didn't say those awful things to me because he wanted me to improve. He did it because he wanted me to feel worthless. The lower I got, the more important it made him feel."

I thought back to what she'd said the night before. It wasn't hard to see where this was heading. "Did he hit you?"

"Once." Bertie spat the word out. "He gave me a black eye. At the time I was appalled. Now I realize it was a good thing because it brought me to my senses. I got up the next morning, looked in the mirror and thought,

Alberta Kennedy, if you think any guy in the world is worth this, you must be out of your friggin' mind."

"Good for you."

"Yeah, it was." She nodded. "Finally. I packed up most of my stuff that morning and left. The kicker was that Kenny was surprised, shocked even, by my reaction. He came back all full of apologies and bullshit and couldn't understand why that didn't make everything all right between us."

"Idiot," I muttered.

"You can say that again. That happened right before Christmas, so I ended up spending the holiday alone."

"I wish I'd known."

"It wouldn't have mattered," Bertie said matter-of-factly. "It's not as if I was going to let anyone see me looking like that. And besides, it gave me time to think. It wasn't just the black eye, it was everything that had led up to it, too. Kenny Boyle took me to the lowest point of my life, and the really rotten thing is, I think he enjoyed doing it."

"Have you seen him since?"

"Seen him, sure. We go to the same shows all the time. In the beginning, I couldn't even stand to look at him. But I'm getting better now." Bertie smiled. "I can even talk to him without clenching my fists.

"Kenny's been bugging me for months to come and get this stuff I left behind. I doubt if it's in his way; I think he just wants to erase all sign of my presence from his life. Which probably makes sense when you consider that I feel the same way about him.

"It should only take us a few minutes to load. It's just some kennel stuff—a couple of wooden crates and a box of supplies. The only thing I really missed is the big hair dryer. It'll be nice to finally get that back."

"Does Kenny know we're coming?" I asked.

"He knows. I called him last night. Heaven forbid we should show up unannounced. Kenny doesn't like surprises."

I rolled my eyes. "Is there anything he does like?"

"Sure. He likes attention. He likes flattery. He likes to win. Brace yourself, we're just about there. Oh, and Melanie?"

Her tone was serious. I looked at her and lifted a brow.

"Whatever you do, don't tell him you think he might have killed somebody. Trust me, with this guy news like that wouldn't go over well."

∞✿ *Twenty* ✿∞

Most of the kennels I've visited have been small, private operations, tucked away in residential areas and usually hidden discreetly behind high fences. Not Kenny Boyle's. A large sign, posted next to the four-lane highway, announced that we'd reached our destination.

GOLDEN TOUCH KENNEL, it said. KENNY BOYLE, OWNER. BOARDING, GROOMING, AND SHOWING AT THE HIGHEST STANDARD.

"Golden Touch?" I read incredulously.

"Yeah, can you believe it?" Bertie put on her blinker and turned in. "And to think, I didn't see that as an omen."

A short, paved driveway led us to the kennel, which turned out to be a complex of one-story concrete buildings, painted a cheery shade of yellow and grouped around a middle courtyard that was filled with dog runs. A quick survey estimated that the kennel could hold nearly a hundred dogs.

"This place is huge," I said as I got out of the van.

"Like Kenny's ego."

Bertie held up a hand. "Sorry, I didn't mean that. I didn't come here to pick any fights. I just want to get my stuff and go home. Come on, I'll take you around back. That's probably where Kenny will be."

Bertie bypassed the front door with its dog-bone-shaped welcome mat, walked around the first building, and led the way through the courtyard. Most of the runs we passed were occupied. Dogs of various breeds threw themselves at the wire mesh that enclosed them, barking frantically.

Each, I knew, was hoping we'd come for him. Each was going to be disappointed. Feeling pleased I'd left Faith at home, I hurried to catch up to Bertie, who'd reached another entrance.

"This is where they do all the grooming," she said. "Kenny only works on the dogs he shows and sometimes not even all of them. The staff takes care of the rest."

"How big is the staff?"

"It varies, depending on the season, but usually around ten or so. It takes a lot of people to run an operation this size."

Not to mention a lot of clients. It was easy to see that Kenny would have plenty to lose if a prominently placed article were to question his integrity. Considering what I already knew—and didn't like—about him, it was nice to find another reason to settle on Kenny Boyle as the number one suspect.

The large front room of the building we entered was a dog groomer's dream. Several large bathtubs lined one wall, another held built-in crates. There were rubber-matted tables in the middle and bright lighting over-head.

Only one table was currently in use. A young, red-headed man was working on a Scottish Terrier. He glanced around as the door opened, swung back, then quickly looked again. It was a classic double take.

"Bertie, hey! Um . . . good to see you."

"Hi, Cal." Bertie breezed past him. "Is Kenny in back?"

"Yeah." Cal dropped the Terrier's nose, scrambled across the room, and angled himself between us and the door. "I'm sure he's busy, though. Is he expecting you?"

"He knows we're coming," Bertie said firmly. "Get out of the way, Cal."

He stepped to one side, but he didn't look happy. "I guess this is why he's been in such a foul mood all morning."

"I hope so." Smiling sweetly, Bertie pushed past him and strode into the next room. I followed.

The second room looked just like the first, only smaller. The outer grooming area was probably for the boarding clients. This inner sanctum was where Kenny and his top assistants would work on the show dogs.

The room was empty save for a man who was perched on the edge of a grooming table, thumbing through an issue of *Dog Scene* magazine. I recognized Kenny from Bertie's description and the pictures I'd seen in *Woof!*. He looked up and immediately smiled.

"Hi, Kenny. I'm here to get my things," Bertie spoke up before he had a chance. "This is a friend of mine, Melanie Travis. She came to help me load." She sent me a look, warning me to remember what she'd said in the van.

"Hi," I said. "Nice to meet you."

Kenny stood up and walked forward. He barely glanced at me. Instead he went straight to Bertie, arms outstretched. Despite what Cal's behavior had implied, Kenny looked delighted to see her.

"Hey, doll," he said, folding her into a tight embrace. "I'm glad you came."

"I'm just here to get my stuff." Bertie stood stiffly, but didn't pull away until Kenny had stepped back. Then I saw her shudder slightly.

"Sure. How about we go inside and have a cup of coffee? I've been working all morning, I could use a break."

"Sorry. We don't have much time. Melanie has to get back."

"Too bad." Kenny finally glanced my way. "I'd have been happy to help you load. You know that."

A casual observer watching the interchange would have thought that Kenny was the reasonable one, and that Bertie was being churlish. Even though I knew better, I had to admit that Kenny was a charmer. I could see how he'd been able to parlay a decent amount of talent and a confident swagger into a position of power in the dog show game.

On some level, all professional handlers have to be actors. They sell themselves, and they sell their dogs: good dogs, bad dogs, indifferent dogs. Very few handlers can afford to pick and choose among them. Regardless of the quality they have to offer, it's their job to make the judge believe that whatever they've brought into the ring is the best.

A Poodle with cow hocks? Scissor them out. A faulty

topline on a Terrier? Comb the hair to cover the problem. Weak rear end on a Rottweiler? Angle the dog away and showcase the glorious head.

I had no doubt Kenny knew all those tricks and more. He hoodwinked people for a living. That was his job. Evidently he used the same skills in his private life to cover a multitude of sins.

"I wanted to come," I said, stepping forward. "I wanted to meet you."

Now I had his full attention. Just as Bertie had said, Kenny liked flattery. "Is that right? You must show dogs, then."

"Standard Poodles. I've been going to shows for the last two years."

I saw his gaze flicker and knew what he was thinking. *Neophyte.*

"I read an article about you recently in a new magazine. It was very interesting."

"Not that piece in *Woof!*, I hope?"

"That's the one."

Kenny's lip curled. Out of the corner of my eye, I saw Bertie take a reflexive step back. "It just goes to show you can't believe everything you read. That whole thing was a pack of lies. A hatchet job. They were out to get me."

"You're kidding," I said, aiming for an air of innocent curiosity. "Why would they do something like that?"

"Because that's what that magazine does. Takes decent people and tries to make them look bad for the sake of sales. It's all sensational crap, every bit of it. If what they said was true, would I have a place like this?"

It seemed to me that would depend on how many

clients' credit cards he'd managed to appropriate. I decided not to mention that.

"I guess you weren't too upset, then, about what happened to the woman who wrote the article."

Kenny shrugged, but his satisfaction was pretty evident. "Hey, what can I say? Sometimes bad things happen to bad people. Lucky for that scandal rag, I guess. Now they've got a lead story for their next issue."

As we'd been speaking, Bertie had opened a door in the side wall, and peeked into what appeared to be a storage area. Now she turned back to Kenny.

"I left my things piled in a corner in here, but I don't see them. Do you know where they went?"

"Yeah. Out back. The storeroom got too full, and I had Cal move everything out to the garage." He held out his hands, palms up, expressing his innocence. "If you'd bothered to return my calls and let me know you were coming back for that stuff, I might have waited. As it was, I thought maybe you'd just decided to junk it."

"Junk it?" Bertie's brow lifted. "Custom-built wooden crates and a Speedy hair dryer? I don't think so."

Grumbling under her breath, she headed for the back door, with Kenny striding along behind. I wondered if I should go out the other way and bring the van around so we could load up more easily, but Bertie had the keys and before I thought to ask, she was already outside and crossing the driveway to yet another long, low building.

The garage had three bays. One door was open; the slot within, empty. The second door was also open, and a gold Lexus was parked inside. The third door was closed.

Bertie stopped there, waiting for us to catch up. Passing

her, Kenny walked into the middle bay and pushed a button. The garage door rose.

As soon as it was halfway up, Bertie ducked down and scooted beneath it. It was semidark inside the garage, and as my eyes took a moment to adjust, I heard Bertie gasp.

"You bastard!" She whirled and came striding back out.

"What?" Kenny sounded puzzled. He and I both looked to find the source of her anger.

"Look at my stuff!"

I knew what the equipment Bertie had left behind should have looked like, but it was barely recognizable now. Instead, a mangled assortment of wood and metal littered the garage floor. Shards of polished wood lay scattered over the area; a mesh door balanced on empty hinges. The long nozzle of a free standing blow dryer tilted upward at an odd angle. Its engine lay beneath it, crushed.

"Uh-oh," said Kenny.

I turned and stared. That was the best response he could come up with?

Bertie fell to her knees beside the hair dryer, trying to dig the machine out of the rubble. It wouldn't do any good. I could tell from where I was standing that it was never going to work again.

"Gee, I'm sorry." Kenny produced a contrite look. "I guess one of the kids must have run over this stuff with the truck. You know how teenagers are—they never look behind when they're backing up."

Bertie glared up at him. "You don't let the teenagers that work here drive your truck, Kenny."

Besides, I thought, the crates had been big, substantial.

They wouldn't have crumpled with the first nudge, and anyone backing into them would have felt the hit. Judging by the extent of the destruction, those crates hadn't been hit by a car, they'd been demolished by an ax or a sledge-hammer.

"I knew you had problems, Kenny, but I can't believe you would do something this crazy." Bertie sounded like she was in shock. She gave up trying to salvage the blower and dragged herself to her feet. "That hair dryer cost five hundred dollars!"

"So sue me. I told you, it wasn't my fault. Nobody asked you to leave all your junk lying around here any-way. That's negligence on your part. Any court would see that."

"Come on," I said to Bertie. "There's nothing here worth salvaging. I think we'd better go."

"In a minute. Let me just look . . ." Angrily she leaned down and began to claw through the debris.

Kenny glanced at me and shook his head, willing me to take his side, to see him as the sane and injured party, burdened with an unbalanced ex-girlfriend and trying to make the best of things. Annoyed, I looked away. His attitude goaded me past the warning Bertie had given earlier.

"Did you ever meet Sheila Vaughn?" I asked. "You know, the woman who wrote the article about you?"

"Yes." His eyes narrowed. "We spoke, briefly. Why?"

"Did you ever visit her at her house?"

"I may have. I don't remember."

Right. "She lived fifty miles from here. I would think you'd remember a trip like that."

"Fifty miles is nothing," said Kenny. "I travel around

a lot going to shows. I don't keep track of every trip. What difference does it make, anyway?"

"I was just remembering that after Sheila was murdered, the state police dusted her house for fingerprints. Maybe you ought to contact them, Kenny. You know, so there won't be any misunderstandings? I mean, I'm sure everything's fine ... unless your fingerprints happen to be on file somewhere ..."

Bertie stood up, grabbed my arm, and wheeled me around. I thought at first she was angry, but then I realized she was struggling to keep a straight face.

"Are you nuts?" she whispered as we hurried away. "Or just looking to start World War Three?"

"Come on, he deserved it," I said, as we strode around the front building and left Kenny behind. "What an imbecile, standing there looking smug while all your stuff was in pieces. I just wanted to tweak him a little. You know, kick his pompous, self-important butt."

"You did that all right," Bertie said, climbing in the front seat of the van. After a minute, she grinned, and added, "Thanks."

"Don't mention it."

We didn't talk much on the way home. Bertie and I both seemed to have plenty to think about. Despite what I'd told Kenny, he probably had nothing to fear from the police. Not unless he had a record for back-country break-ins in Westchester County, anyway.

Bertie delivered me to my door in plenty of time to play with Faith and run some errands before I had to drive the car pool. Because it had been on my mind, I asked her what she would do about the camp bully who'd been taking Davey's lunch.

"That's easy," Bertie said. "I'd march down to that

camp, find out who the little troublemaker was, and beat the ever-loving crap out of him.''

As solutions went, I wouldn't put it at the top of my list, but I could see where she was coming from.

It had just been that kind of day.

⤌❧ ✿ 🐾 *Twenty-one* ✿ 🐾 ❧⤍

"Terry, I need help."

It was the next morning and Davey had just left with Alice, who was driving the car pool to camp. That meant it was time to hunt down another suspect, and Alida Trent was the next person I wanted to see. According to Aunt Peg, Crawford was the one to speak to, but with a request like this I knew I'd have better luck going through his assistant, Terry.

"Darling, what else is new?" He paused to slurp loudly at what I imagined was a cup of coffee. Though it was nearly nine o'clock, Terry is not a morning person. "What is it this time? Another haircut? Makeup tips? Oh wait, I've got it. You want some help with your wardrobe."

"No, I—wardrobe?" My voice squeaked. Faith glanced up at me from the floor and cocked an ear. "What's the matter with my wardrobe?"

"Nothing if you're aiming for Preppy-of-the-Month. You know, the Post-Deb Meets June Cleaver look."

"Bitch," I muttered.

"Flatterer," Terry shot right back. "Whatever you're looking for, doll, I've probably got it."

"I never doubted it. Luckily, all I need is an introduction."

"Sounds promising. You're not thinking of stepping out on that hunky fiancé of yours, are you? Good for the goose, good for the gander, that sort of thing? I hear he's out of town for a few days."

It was no use wondering how Terry knew Sam was away. When it came to who was doing what with whom and where, Terry seemed to know almost everything. And speaking of which . . .

"Terry, do you know Kenny Boyle?"

"Of course. Working dogs—Dobermans, Rottweilers." His voice dropped an octave. "Manly dogs. I wouldn't have thought he'd be your type. Is that who you want to meet?"

"No, actually I met Kenny yesterday. Bertie Kennedy took me up to his place."

"Bertie? Word is, she and Kenny are through. In a big way, if you know what I mean. Mention him in her presence and smoke comes out of her ears. She's been seeing some scrawny new guy with no dogs and a job in the real world."

I laughed into the phone. "The new guy is my brother, Frank."

"Oops. Scratch the scrawny part. I'm sure he's stunning, just like you. So what was Bertie doing up at Kenny's?"

"She was supposed to be picking up some stuff she'd left behind when she moved out. Except when we got there, it had all been destroyed."

"Our boy Kenny has a temper, doesn't he?"

Interesting that Terry had leapt immediately to that conclusion. He hadn't even asked if it might have been an accident.

"Apparently so. Have you seen it in action on other occasions?"

Terry paused. I wondered if he was going to pass on something really juicy, but for once, he decided to be circumspect. "Let's just say I'd rather be around Kenny when he's winning than when he's losing."

The reason for his rectitude became apparent a moment later when I heard someone say something in the background. Terry replied to the other person, then came back to me. "Crawford just walked in. Hang on a sec, okay?" He turned away from the phone, and said, "It's Melanie. She wants to know about Kenny Boyle."

There was more rumbling I couldn't quite make out, then Crawford's voice came on the line. "Melanie?"

"Hi, Crawford," I said meekly. The handler tends to take a dim view of my investigations into his dog show cronies. And though he'd never said as much, I also suspected he thought I was a bad influence on Terry.

"Don't tell me, you're trying to figure out who killed Sheila Vaughn, right?"

"How'd you guess?"

"It would take a moron not to see this one coming. Do me a favor, leave Terry out of it. Enemies like Kenny, I don't need."

"Just one question, then. Was Sheila's article accurate?"

"What makes you think I read it?"

I couldn't see him, but I knew Crawford well enough to know that his eyes were twinkling. "You read it. If you didn't, Terry told you all about it. Come on, Crawford, give me something."

"Sheila was good. Her research and her conclusions were both spot on. Which means exactly that. Kenny did get himself into some trouble last year, but he managed to get out of it, too. Do I think he was angry at Sheila for exposing the whole mess to the world? Yes, I have to think he probably was. That's as much as I know, okay?"

"Sure. Thanks. Enough about Kenny. But can you manage one more thing? I want to meet Alida Trent."

For a minute, Crawford was silent. Unlike Terry, he never blurted anything out without thinking first. I knew he was turning the request over in his mind and wondering what to make of it.

"I assume it's all related," he said finally. "Where does she fit in?"

"Sheila was planning an article about her in an upcoming issue of *Woof!*. I gather Mrs. Trent had threatened to sue."

"And in your mind, that makes her a murder suspect?"

"Not necessarily. I'm just trying to cover all the bases."

"Look," said Crawford, "Alida Trent is what some might call a feisty old broad. She never does anything she doesn't want to do. I don't know a thing about an article or any lawsuit, but I'll give Alida a call. She's a bit eccentric. Something like this might just pique her interest. If she wants to meet with you, I'll let you know."

"Thanks, Crawford. I appreciate it. I don't want to rush you or anything, but I'm free today."

"Now you're pushing your luck."

I smiled. "I always push my luck, Crawford. You know that."

"Bye, Melanie." The phone clicked in my ear.

I spent the next twenty minutes with Faith. First, I took

her temperature and recorded the result on my chart. It still hadn't dropped, which was good because if Alida Trent would see me, I'd have to be gone most of the day. I couldn't leave Faith alone if whelping was imminent.

After that, I took her upstairs and reintroduced her to her whelping box. Obligingly, Faith climbed in, turned a circle, and lay down. Then she looked up at me expectantly. You put me here, she seemed to be saying. Now what?

Now what, indeed. While I was pondering how to make the box seem like a more appealing nest, the phone rang. I wasn't surprised to find it was Crawford. Not that I'd ever dream of telling him so, but when it comes to getting things done, he's a little anal.

"Alida's heard of you," Crawford said after we'd exchanged greetings. He didn't sound happy about this turn of events. "She said she always loved Nancy Drew books, and she can't wait to meet you."

"Great." I grabbed a pad to scribble down directions.

"Alida wants you to have lunch with her in Greenwich."

"Greenwich? Aunt Peg told me she lived in Millbrook."

"She does, but she's got friends in Greenwich she can visit and there's an exhibit at the Bruce Museum she's been wanting to see. This way she figured she could kill two birds with one stone." Crawford named a restaurant on Greenwich Avenue. "Is noon good for you?"

"Perfect." Now I wouldn't have to leave Faith alone for nearly so long. "I'll make a reservation."

The phone clicked in my ear again before I could even thank him. I owed Crawford one. Actually, now that I thought of it, I owed him several. I was sure he'd find a way to collect eventually.

* * *

The restaurant Alida Trent had chosen was near the bottom of Greenwich Avenue, almost across from the train station. Of course, I couldn't find a place to park. Finally, on my third time around the block, I snagged a space on Mason Street. I shoved some quarters into the meter and hurried around the corner so I wouldn't be late.

After the hot, bright sidewalk outside, the interior of the restaurant was cool and dark. I'd been wondering how I would recognize Mrs. Trent, but it turned out not to be necessary. As soon as I entered the vestibule, I was accosted by an older woman, who'd obviously been waiting for me.

Alida Trent was probably in her seventies, but one look at the woman told you that she knew she was in her prime. She had silver hair, a face creased with a lifetime's worth of lines, and a glowing smile. Her fingernails were painted shocking pink, and a jaunty scarf around her neck picked up the same shade. She wore tennis shoes on her feet and crossed the restaurant lobby with a stride as long as mine.

"You must be Melanie Travis," she said, grabbing my hand and giving it a shake. "I had Crawford describe you for me. I must say he did a pretty fair job. I knew he would. That man has an artistic eye, that's why he's so good at what he does."

I nodded, smiled, sputtered. Before I could answer, she was talking again.

"Call me Alida. And I'll call you Melanie. You're punctual; I like that so you've scored some points already. They tell me our table's ready. Come on, right this way.

Have you eaten here before? The food's pretty good. What do you suppose they recommend today?"

I followed Alida and the maître d' through the maze of tables to a booth near the front window. It was amazing; the woman had forty years on me, and I could barely keep up. I'd planned this meeting so I could ask her about Sheila, but at this rate, I'd be lucky to get a word in, much less a whole question.

I studied my menu quickly while Alida conferred with the waiter about what was fresh. I suspected we'd be ordering right away, and I was right. The waiter had his pad out before I'd even finished reading. Alida seemed to have that effect on people. She opted for clam chowder and a cobb salad; I ordered the French dip. Within moments, our iced tea had already been delivered.

Alida took a quick sip, then said, "As you can probably tell, I don't believe in wasting time. Realistically, at my age, how much do you think I have left? Pack it all in, that's my theory. Crawford said you wanted to talk to me about Sheila Vaughn. All right, I'm here. What's up?"

I couldn't see any point in beating around the bush.

"As I imagine you know, she's dead."

"Not just dead." Alida leaned toward me across the table. "Murdered. I hear that's your specialty. So Sheila Vaughn is your new case. What's that got to do with me?"

Now that we were sitting face-to-face, the idea seemed pretty ridiculous. On the other hand, I've met unlikely murder suspects before. None, though, who seemed to take such delight in the situation.

"I was told that you threatened Sheila shortly before she was killed."

"Threatened her?" Alida's brows knit together. "Oh you must mean that stupid story about Belle."

"Belle?"

"My Shih Tzu. Well, she's mine now anyway. Originally, I'd leased her from her breeder as a specials bitch. She's a gorgeous Shih Tzu and deserved every moment of glory I was able to give her. Her breeder's another story. Even though we had what my lawyer called a cover-all-the-bases contract, we still ended disagreeing about the terms."

"What was the dispute about?"

Alida selected a warm roll from the basket on the table and broke it into pieces on her bread plate. "According to the lease we signed, I was to assume all the expenses of giving Belle a specials career and Belle was to live either with me or my handler while she was being shown. When we stopped showing her, she was to return to her breeder, Carlotta, to have puppies."

"That sounds pretty straightforward."

"You would think so, wouldn't you? The problem arose last fall when Crawford and I began to feel that Belle was getting a little stale from the constant grind of being on the road. Those top dogs work pretty hard, you know.

"Crawford and I decided that it was in Belle's best interest to stop showing her briefly, giving her some time off before Westminster. She'd been third in the Toy Group the year before, and Crawford and I agreed that this time around she had a good shot at doing even better. Westminster was to be her last show, and we both wanted Belle to go out with a bang."

"And Carlotta didn't agree?"

"Oh she thought taking the bitch to Westminster was

a fine idea. Why wouldn't she? I was the one who was paying for it all. But she also said that, according to the contract, once Belle stopped being shown she was supposed to go home and have puppies. Carlotta interpreted that to mean that Belle should squeeze in a quick litter between October and February."

I ticked off the months in my mind. It wasn't impossible, and I said so.

"Of course it's not impossible!" Alida's gaze narrowed. "But that doesn't mean it's a good idea. This is Westminster we're talking about, not some backwater specialty show.

"Do you know what bitches do after they whelp a litter of puppies? They blow coat. And I had no intention of taking Belle to New York looking like a plucked chicken. What would be the point? She'd have been beaten in the breed, and I'd have ended up looking like an idiot."

The waiter appeared with our food, arranging the plates and bowls on the table with care, then hovering solicitously until he'd made sure everything had been prepared to our satisfaction. I figured he'd already pegged Alida as a heavy tipper.

"So what happened?" I said impatiently, when he'd finally gone.

"Didn't you go to the show? Or at least watch it on TV?"

I'd gone into the Garden the first day, Monday, when the Non-Sporting breeds were judged, and I'd watched the group judging both nights on cable. Shih Tzus weren't my breed, however, and the winner hadn't made a big impression on me. Thinking back now, I had no idea what had happened in the Toy Group.

I glanced over at Alida. She was grinning.

"Belle won, didn't she? You showed her and she won."

"Exactly right. And well she should have. After four months off, Belle was raring to go. The judge said in his critique that he couldn't deny the Shih Tzu the win. She was asking for it every minute she was in the ring."

"So you and Crawford were proven right. But how did you get Carlotta to agree to what you wanted?"

"I imagine you can figure out the answer to that. M-O-N-E-Y. The great problem solver. But just because I had enough to buy Carlotta off doesn't mean I should have had to do it. Our contract spelled out the terms of our deal. She was the one who tried to renege."

I dipped my roast beef sandwich into the juice, held it over the plate and took a large bite. The beef was rare; the baguette, chewy. "And Sheila didn't see things that way?" I asked after I swallowed.

"No, though that was hardly surprising considering that she never even bothered to hear my side of the story. The only person she spoke to was Carlotta, and you can imagine the spin *she* put on things. Thank goodness I found out what was going on because Sheila never made any attempt to call and make sure she had her facts straight."

"So you called her."

"You bet your bootie I did. I phoned her office half a dozen times at least. I'd already been taken advantage of once over this deal. I wasn't about to let it happen a second time. Especially when I heard that the focus of the article was going to be how wealthy backers were using their money to bully poor little breeders into acceding to their unfair demands."

"That doesn't sound right." I considered what Brian

had said about responsible journalism. "I can't imagine why Sheila wouldn't have wanted to talk to you."

"That's what I thought, but I could never get through to her. Every time I called, I got switched over to another editor instead. A woman named Aubrey."

"Couldn't she help you?"

"Maybe, if she'd wanted to. But it was pretty obvious she didn't. I don't know what kind of an old fool she took me for, but that Aubrey made me madder than a wet cat.

"I'll tell you one thing. It's too bad that whoever squeezed the life out of Sheila didn't have the leash wrapped around Aubrey's neck instead."

❧❧ *Twenty-two* ❧❧

"I don't understand," I said. "What did Aubrey have to do with Sheila's article?"

Alida smiled. "Now that's a good question, isn't it? I wondered about that myself. Aubrey told me she was managing editor. I figured that ought to mean she could get something done if she wanted to. So the first time we spoke, I spent some time explaining what the problem was. She assured me she understood my concerns."

"And?"

"And nothing!" Alida snapped. "The two of them must have been in cahoots with each other. One to write the article, and the other to run interference until it was finished."

Remembering what I'd heard about Aubrey's resentment of Sheila, I doubted it. It seemed more likely that Aubrey had been waylaying Sheila's calls in order to undermine her efforts, not assist them.

"So you called again."

"And again, and again. That article was going to sully

my good name. There was no way I would let that happen without a fight."

"And you kept getting transferred over to Aubrey."

"Every time but the last. By then I was really mad. By then, I was ready to contact my lawyer."

And Aubrey had accomplished what she'd set out to do. She'd screwed things up royally for Sheila, then dropped the mess in Sheila's unsuspecting lap and left her to deal with it. In front of the whole office, and over the speaker phone, no less. I wondered if that little touch had been Aubrey's idea as well.

It was almost enough to make me feel sorry for Sam's ex-wife. She hadn't made many friends after moving to the East Coast, but she certainly had piled up enemies.

"I'm curious about something," I said. "The piece you objected to was in the researching and writing stages, yet you seem to have been remarkably well informed about its progress. Since you've already told me that Sheila never contacted you, I'm wondering how you found out about it in the first place."

Alida glanced down at her salad, using the tines of her fork to pick among the greens and spear a thick chunk of chicken. "Crawford told me you were sharp," she said finally.

I recognized stalling when I heard it. "Thank you. I'm delighted Crawford thinks so. He would never dream of saying as much to me."

"He told me you were looking for suspects in Sheila's murder. Actually, I was quite tickled to think that I might be on your list. Imagine, at my age. Just when I thought I'd seen and done everything. There's nothing like a little excitement to get the old juices flowing."

"You find murder exciting?" I asked dryly.

"Of course." Alida waved a hand in the air, dismissing my tone. "You do, too, Melanie, or we wouldn't be here. So now I've presented you with a bit of a puzzle, haven't I? Things aren't so simple as they first appeared."

"No, they're not."

Alida Trent was proving to be a challenge. Not only that, but she seemed to be enjoying herself enormously. I couldn't help but wonder if that was because she assumed she was going to get the better of me.

"Let me help you along," Alida offered. "Did I have means? Did I have opportunity? Of course. I'm rich, so both those things can be easily acquired. Did I have a motive, though? That's the stickler."

"You were angry at Sheila."

"I was angry at the magazine. Killing Sheila wouldn't necessarily have killed the article."

Because she was having so much fun, I decided to play along. "Do you have a temper, Alida?"

"Of course I do. And I'm well-known for putting it to excellent use. Ask Crawford, he'll tell you. Or better still, ask Terry."

"You lose your temper with Terry?"

"Occasionally. And only when he deserves it."

"What about Sheila? Did she deserve it? Did you lose your temper with her?"

"This is good." Alida grinned. "Is this what they call the third degree?"

"No. I think that requires a small, uncomfortable room and hot lights." It was getting harder and harder to keep a straight face. "But you still haven't answered my question."

"Did I murder Sheila? No, I didn't." Alida placed her

hands on the table in front of her, fingers neatly laced together like a schoolgirl's. "Does that help?"

I shook my head. "That wasn't the question I was talking about. How did you know someone was writing an article about you at *Woof!* magazine? Who was your spy?"

"Goodness," Alida said. "You make it sound so dramatic. This wasn't international intrigue we were engaged in. I didn't have a spy. What I had was more of a facilitator. Someone who was willing to slip me a tidbit of information every now and then in return for a small remuneration."

Facilitator, spy: there didn't seem to be much of a distinction to me.

"Tim," I guessed.

"Right you are."

Alida looked so pleased by my accomplishment, that I felt obliged to admit, "It wasn't that hard to figure out. It's a very small staff."

The waiter came, cleared our plates, and took an order for coffee from Alida. I waited until he had gone, then said, "How did the arrangement come about? Did you approach him, or did he approach you?"

"The latter, of course. I may show dogs, but I certainly don't keep tabs on every facet of the sport. If Tim hadn't contacted me, I never would have known about Sheila's article until it was too late. Not unexpectedly, he seemed to think that information might be worth something to me."

"And you agreed to his terms. That sounds suspiciously like extortion."

"Not to me. I prefer to think of it as a business arrangement between two mutually agreeable partners. Besides,

I think you might be surprised to discover what he wanted in return."

"What?"

"Tim wants to be an author, and like most writers he thinks he's written the great American novel. He's quite sure he has the talent and determination to be the next Hemingway."

"Does he?"

"I have no idea." Alida picked up her spoon and stirred her hot coffee absently. "And it hardly matters, does it? Tim needed an entrée into the publishing world. He wanted me to get his manuscript read. I imagine it's no secret that my former husband, now deceased, worked in publishing for many years. All I had to do was call upon one or two old friends and make an introduction."

"So you helped Tim and he helped you."

"Precisely. So you see, what looked like an intriguing question turns out to have had a perfectly ordinary explanation."

Perfectly ordinary, my foot, I thought. There was nothing about Alida Trent that was even vaguely ordinary. Not only that, but the information she'd given me was leading me to consider the staff of *Woof!* in a whole new light.

"About the story," I said. "Do you know what's happened to it now that Sheila's gone?"

"Poof!" Alida said gaily. "It seems to have vanished. It turns out Aubrey did have some clout after all. I've been told it's been tabled indefinitely."

"So you got what you wanted."

"Of course, Melanie. I always do."

That was a sobering thought.

Our waiter reappeared to discreetly slip our check on

the edge of the table. Alida and I reached for it at the same time.

"My treat," she said firmly.

"I asked you," I pointed out.

"That may be, but I've had entirely too good a time to allow you to pay." Alida slipped a platinum American Express card out of her wallet. "You will keep me informed as to how your investigation progresses, won't you? I'm sure you'll get the whole thing sorted out in no time."

Call me suspicious I thought as the waiter spirited the bill away, but it was hard not to suspect that my acquiescence was being bought. For the price of a lunch, no less. Who knew I looked that cheap?

I thanked Alida politely and told her I'd keep in touch. But until I became convinced of her innocence, I was keeping my theories to myself.

Whoever thought up the expression, never a dull moment, must have had my life in mind. That afternoon, I was ready for some serious downtime. Alas, it was not to be.

The problems started when I arrived at camp to pick up Davey and his friends. Bradley and Jason, two boys who were in Davey's class at school and who lived in our neighborhood, came running out as soon as my car reached the front of the line. My son and Joey Brickman were nowhere in sight.

"Hi, guys," I said as the two seven-year-olds climbed in the backseat. My eyes scanned the milling horde of young soccer players looking for Davey's sandy head and Joey's darker one. "Where are Davey and Joey? Have you seen them?"

The two boys exchanged a look. Not the sort of look a mother wants to see in answer to a perfectly reasonable question. I put the Volvo in gear, pulled out of line, and parked by the curb.

"They might be in the locker room," Bradley volunteered. Watching in the rearview mirror, I saw Jason elbow him sharply. Something was definitely up.

"That's downstairs, right?" I asked. Both boys nodded reluctantly. "You two stay here. I'll be right back."

Inside the school building, I came almost immediately upon one of the counselors, easily recognizable by his clipboard and black-and-white-striped referee shirt.

"I seem to be missing a couple of kids. Which way is the locker room?"

"Down those stairs." He pointed. "But everyone should be outside by now. It's pickup time."

As if I couldn't see that for myself.

"There may be a problem," I said.

"What sort of problem?" He waved to another counselor, who came to take his spot by the door, and followed me down the steps.

"I'm not sure. My son's been having some trouble with one of the other boys, Randy Bowers."

"And your son would be?"

"Davey Travis."

The counselor smiled. "Blond hair, good dribble. Great kid. He's in my group. I'm Jeff, by the way. And I probably shouldn't say this, but you're not the first mother to say something about Randy."

I stopped at the foot of the steps. "I'm not?"

"Randy's a bit strong-willed. He's not above pushing the other kids around when he doesn't get his own way."

I glanced down the dimly lit hallway. All was quiet.

It looked deserted. "What do you intend to do about that?"

"Well . . ." Jeff's eyes slid away. "When it gets really bad, we step in and tell him to cut it out. Otherwise, this is the type of thing we prefer to let the boys handle on their own."

"That's not working," I said flatly. "My son handles the situation by giving away his lunch."

"Umm." He still wouldn't meet my gaze. "I'll see what I can do. The locker room is over here."

Jeff pushed the door open and I followed him inside. The smell—equal parts wet floor, metal lockers, and old gym socks—instantly brought back memories.

"Davey?" I called. "Joey? Are you in here?"

"Mom?"

A locker slammed shut, then both boys came running around the corner. Davey ran straight into my arms. Joey hovered uncertainly behind him.

"What's up?" I asked, giving him a quick hug. "What are you guys doing down here?"

"We couldn't go outside," Davey mumbled.

"How come?" I glanced at Jeff. He was frowning.

"It was Randy," Joey said helpfully. "He told Davey he'd be waiting in the hallway. He was going to kick Davey's ass."

"Watch your language," Jeff warned.

Language be damned, I thought angrily. "What are you going to do about this?"

The counselor looked unhappy. "Maybe it was a misunderstanding." He turned to Davey. "Randy isn't outside. There's no one out there. He's probably gone home."

"It doesn't sound like a misunderstanding to me," I

said. "Davey's usually pretty clear on what he hears. And apparently Joey heard the threat, too."

"Come on, let's go upstairs." Jeff held the door open for us. "I'll talk to the rest of the staff tomorrow morning, and we'll see what we can do."

Feeling far from reassured, I escorted the boys out.

The day's excitement wasn't over yet, however. That evening Faith decided to exhibit all the signs of first stage labor outlined in the book Aunt Peg had given me. Though the Poodle's temperature hadn't dropped, she was restless and moody. She wouldn't eat her dinner. She nested and dug incessantly—inside my closet, beneath Davey's bed, everywhere but in the whelping box we'd prepared for her.

And just in case I still wasn't getting the message, Faith would stop every so often to turn her head and stare at her body in obvious puzzlement. I knew that for a fact because I followed her around all evening, waiting for something to happen.

When Sam called shortly before eleven, Faith was finally snoozing on my bed. I was a nervous wreck. Judging by the Poodle's current tranquillity, it was beginning to look as though it had all been a false alarm. Try telling that to my pulse rate.

I snatched up the phone so it wouldn't wake Davey. Faith lifted her head inquiringly; but when I patted her shoulder, she settled back down. Lying on the bed beside her, I rested a palm on her stomach and smiled as I felt tiny feet kicking within.

"It's me," said Sam. "How are you?"

"Fine." Not exactly true, but the easiest answer under the circumstances. "How are things out there?"

"Okay. Everything's getting done. Sheila's will was read today. She named me executor of her estate."

I knew I shouldn't have felt a stab of irritation, but I did. Even after her death, apparently, we were never going to be free of Sam's ex-wife. I wondered if she'd planned things that way. It was a petty thought, but I entertained it anyway.

"Exactly what does that mean?"

"Mostly that I have to tie up all the loose ends. Make sure her bequests are distributed as she intended. File her insurance. Sell her place here. Do something about the house in North Salem."

"It sounds like a big job."

"Pretty big," Sam said. He sounded tired. "But I can do almost all of it from Connecticut. That's why I called. I wanted to let you know I'll be coming home Saturday."

"Good. I've missed you."

"I've missed you, too." His voice dipped. "I wish I was holding you right now."

"Me too." I sighed. "Will we see you Saturday?"

"You'll be my first stop."

Hallelujah.

ᵔ✻ *Twenty-three* ✻ᵔ

It was time to visit *Woof!* again. Brian was supposed to be back in the office at the end of the week, which meant he should have returned by now. And if not, I'd talk to Aubrey. Or Tim. It's not like the place had a shortage of suspects.

Less than a week had passed since we'd all been together at the dog show; it seemed like much longer. The last time I'd seen Brian, I'd asked some questions. But not the right ones, apparently. Now I had a better set.

Was *Woof!* going under? And if so, had Sheila known how precarious things were when she became his partner? Was Aubrey undermining Sheila's efforts as publisher, and, more importantly, how was she getting away with such behavior? Who was Tim "facilitating" for aside from Alida Trent? How many times had he sold out?

Friday shaped up much as all the others had that week. Davey at camp. Faith at home. Me on the road. And to think, this was supposed to be my vacation.

As soon as I reached the magazine office, I knew that

Brian was in. The sight of Boris, lying on his side in the middle of the linoleum floor just beyond Carrie's desk, was a dead giveaway. Though it was morning, with the full heat of the day yet to come, the Saint Bernard was sacked out.

Air conditioning kept the room cool; I'm sure the floor was cooler still. Even so, Boris's mouth was slightly open, his breathing heavy. A ribbon of drool spiraled down to the floor.

"Hi, Boris!" I said as I pushed the door open. "How are you doing, big guy?"

The dog's bushy tail flopped up and down in greeting. The eye he rolled in my direction had a devilish-looking gleam. Added to the effect of the open mouth, I could swear he was grinning at me.

"Oh please." Carrie grimaced. "Don't encourage him. He just lay down, for Pete's sake. If you talk to him, he'll get up and come and drool on me again."

Obviously Brian's campaign to turn Carrie into a dog lover hadn't yet succeeded.

I walked over to the Saint Bernard, squatted beside him, and reached out a hand to scratch behind his ears. His whole body wiggled with pleasure. That's what I love about dogs. Find their spot, and they're yours for life.

"You're Melanie, right?" Carrie asked brightly. "Am I good with names, or what? Who do you want to see? Tim? Aubrey?"

Though I could hear voices coming from one of the other offices, she and I were the only ones in the room. I looked up over my shoulder. "How about Brian?"

"Brian." Carrie looked thoughtful. Or maybe she was trying for a dreamy expression, like one she might have seen in her magazine. "I don't know. This is his first day back, and he said he was going to be busy all morning."

"Why don't you check and see?"

"Umm . . . okay."

Carrie rose from her chair and walked toward Brian's office. The door was standing slightly ajar. Just for the heck of it, I stood up and followed.

The publisher's office was a fairly nondescript room that looked as though it had been outfitted with furniture ordered from a rental catalogue. Brian was seated behind a large desk, his chair swiveled sideways to face a computer on a console. Beside the monitor, a cigarette sat burning in an engraved crystal ashtray, probably an old dog show trophy. A thin stream of smoke spiraled toward the ceiling.

Brian glanced over as Carrie pushed open the door. He saw me, and smiled. "Melanie! Come on in. What a nice surprise."

Carefully he closed his file before standing. The screen wiped clean. "I didn't expect to see you today."

"I know you've been away," I said. "But I was hoping you could spare me a few minutes."

"Sure. Have a seat."

Carrie withdrew. I noticed she didn't shut the door behind her.

"How's Sam doing?" Brian asked. "Is he handling things okay?"

"Actually, I thought maybe you'd seen him. I heard you were traveling and wondered if you went to Sheila's funeral. It was held yesterday in Evanston."

"No." He reached for his cigarette and sucked in a lungful of smoke. "I didn't make it. I didn't want to intrude on her family's grief."

"I'm sure no one would have thought you were intruding. You were Sheila's business partner. And her friend."

"Nevertheless." Brian frowned apologetically. "I was busy working. Distributing copies of the first issue, visiting some of the major dog food companies that I'm hoping we can count on for contract ads. I've never been one to dwell on what might have been. Sheila's gone, and I couldn't see how rearranging my schedule to help other people cope with that would help anything."

Was it just me, or was his reaction cold enough to freeze mud?

"Maybe I misunderstood then. The night we had dinner at Sheila's house, I got the impression that the two of you were quite close."

"We were," Brian said. "Look, don't get me wrong. I'm sorry about what happened. But it's not like I'm going to spend the rest of my life in mourning. Things move on. People move on. I'd already lost Sheila once before. This time around, there was no way I was going to get that involved.

"Sheila and I were running a business together and having some fun on the side. That's all it was. That's all I was going to let it be."

I wondered if Sheila had known that. And if she had, whether the realization had come to her before or after she'd invested in Brian's magazine.

"I guess you needed to visit those major accounts," I said, settling back in my chair. "I've heard that *Woof!* is heading for bankruptcy."

"Who told you that?"

I certainly had his attention now. "Marlon Dickie."

Brian snorted. "Nobody listens to what Marlon says.

The man's an opportunistic bastard. I never should have given him the chance I did."

"Then it's not true?"

"Does this *look* like an operation that's going down the tubes?"

He hadn't, I noticed, answered my question. "I'd say it looks like an operation with problems. For example, your editorial assistant, Tim."

"What about him?"

"He was keeping tabs on what Sheila was up to for Alida Trent."

"Really?" To my surprise, Brian looked almost pleased. He tapped a long gray column of ash into the ashtray. "If we've captured her attention, that is something."

"Sheila was writing a story about her. Alida wasn't very pleased with the slant Sheila had chosen to present."

"That's hardly our fault. Sheila and I discussed that article just last week. I think it will make an excellent cover story for our third issue."

"Then you'd better tell Aubrey. She assured Alida the story had been scrapped."

Brian frowned. "Aubrey is reporting back to Alida, too?"

"Apparently she's been running interference between Sheila and Alida, making sure that Alida's calls never went through. Tim told me that Sheila had been having trouble with her phone messages. He thought Carrie was behind it."

"Carrie? She's just a kid."

"A kid with a crush on the boss."

Brian colored, looking slightly uncomfortable. "Carrie's too innocent for her own good."

"Too bad you can't say the same about the rest of your staff."

"Don't be ridiculous. I don't need to defend them."

"Are you sure?"

"Of course I'm sure. Why would you even ask such a thing?" Brian glared at me, then his gaze narrowed. "Oh good God. You're investigating us, aren't you? You didn't buy the police theory about a break-in, and now you're trying to solve Sheila's murder.

"I should have known. Sheila warned me about you, but at the time, your macabre hobby seemed like a joke, an amusing anecdote. I had no reason to suspect that I might ever become the victim of one of your little mysteries."

My little mysteries? All at once, I was as angry as he was. I felt my face growing hot. The rest of the questions I'd meant to ask seemed unimportant now. It was Brian himself who was going to have my undivided attention.

"Let's not lose sight of what happened," I snapped. "Sheila is the victim here. Not you."

Amazingly, he still managed to find a way to make himself the center of attention. "That depends, doesn't it, on how far you intend to go with your meddling? This is a very delicate time for the magazine. Make or break, you might say. This kind of bad publicity now could kill us."

"Funny thing about that. I thought *Woof!* was built on bad publicity. That's the whole point, isn't it?"

"Look." Brian stubbed out his cigarette, grinding the butt into the glass until it broke apart between his fingers. "We need to talk about this. There are things you don't understand. Things you should know."

"About you and Sheila?"

His gaze was hard and direct. "And Sam. Despite what he's probably told you, he's not the angel in this situation. And I'm not the villain."

"Fine." My stomach muscles clenched. In that moment, I knew I'd rather be anywhere else than sitting in that chair waiting to hear what he had to say about Sam. And the worst thing was, I knew I had to listen. "Let's talk."

"Not here."

Brian glanced at the door, and I heard voices in the outer room. Aubrey and Tim, arguing about the sequence of some pictures that were meant to accompany an article.

"We'll take it to Brian then," said Aubrey.

"Fine," Tim shot back.

I heard papers shuffle and knew they were on their way. "Where?" I asked. "And when?"

"My place," said Brian. "Tonight."

"I'll be there." I'd have to juggle a few things, and find a sitter for Davey. Bearing Faith's condition in mind, maybe Aunt Peg could be convinced to fill in.

"Eight o'clock?" Brian said, and I nodded.

As I stood up, Aubrey and Tim pushed through the doorway together, both trying to be the first into Brian's office. Grow up, I thought irritably. It was just as well they both ignored me.

As I walked out, I glanced back over my shoulder. Judging by the look on Brian's face, he wasn't in any mood to deal with whatever they brought him. Aubrey pushed the door firmly shut behind me.

Shaking my head, I started across the room. Boris was still sleeping in the middle of the floor. Carrie jumped up from behind her desk and grabbed my arm.

"Wait!" she said, sounding almost plaintive. "You like

dogs, right? I mean, you were petting Boris before. You're
not afraid of him or anything?"

"No," I said, surprised by the question. "He doesn't
scare me. I love big dogs. Why?"

"I was wondering if you could do me a favor."

"Maybe." With this crowd, I wasn't about to take anything for granted.

"It's time for him to go outside and . . . you know, visit
a few bushes? He's been in here a couple hours and that
always makes me nervous. I mean, if he has an accident,
he's going to flood the place."

Judging by Boris's languid demeanor, the only way he
was going to pee soon was in his sleep. He was a grown
dog, with a bladder that could probably wait more than
an hour or two. Carrie looked genuinely worried, however.

She was a cat person, I reminded myself. She didn't
know the drill.

"Won't Brian walk him?" I asked.

"Sure, when he thinks of it. But once he gets locked
in with Aubrey and Tim like that, he might not surface
for hours. And in the meantime . . ."

My guess was that Carrie was too intimidated by
Boris's size even to consider walking him herself. There
was probably no point in mentioning that most Saint
Bernards are placid, gentle dogs with impeccable temperaments. Carrie didn't look likely to be convinced.

"Where's his leash?" I asked.

"Right here." Her worried look vanished, replaced by
a smile and a rush of words. "Brian hangs it by the door.
Boris doesn't like the elevator, but you can take the stairs.
You don't have to go far or anything. Brian usually just
walks him around the edge of the parking lot."

I took the six-foot leather leash and hooked it to Boris's collar. "Come on, boy," I said. "Want to go out?"

That phrase sends Faith running to the door. Boris managed, with effort, to lift his head. I clucked encouragingly and gave him a nudge. Boris groaned.

After a moment, he shifted his weight and heaved himself to his feet. We lumbered to the office door. Carrie held it open for us.

"Be right back," I said.

Once outside, the Saint Bernard knew what was expected of him. He strolled over to the nearest tree and lifted his leg obligingly.

"Good boy," I said. Boris wagged his tail, and went to sniff another spot.

We'd completed a walk around the perimeter of the lot and were heading back inside when the door to the building flew open and Tim came running out. Seeing me and Boris together, he slid to a stop.

"I was hoping to catch you. I didn't realize you'd been given dog duty."

"Carrie asked. I think she was afraid to do it herself."

Tim reached down to stroke Boris's broad head. "I'm glad you were willing to help. Because that's what I wanted to talk to you about. There's something important I have to do. And I need your help, too."

❧❖ *Twenty-four* ❖❧

"What are you talking about?" I asked.

Unfortunately, Boris chose that moment of inattention on my part to notice that there were chipmunks running beneath the foliage that formed the border of the parking lot. He plunged toward the bushes, and I found myself flying after him, courtesy of the leather lead that connected us.

"Give me a minute," I said to Tim, as the dog stuck his head into the hedge and woofed loudly. I glanced up at the office windows, hoping the noise wouldn't draw anyone's attention. Obviously Tim had wanted privacy for what he had to say. "Boris is finished out here. Let me just take him back upstairs and then we can talk."

"Sure. I'll be waiting."

Nothing illustrates the term *deadweight* like a Saint Bernard who doesn't want his walk to end and has to be cajoled up a steep flight of steps. By the time I got back to the parking lot, I was hot and out of breath.

Tim was leaning against my Volvo, talking on a small

cell phone. As I approached, he ended the call and slipped the phone onto a clip hooked to his belt.

"Do you mind if we get in the car?" he asked. "I'd just as soon everyone not know . . ."

"That you're talking to me?"

"What we're up to," Tim finished, as I unlocked the doors and he slid into the Volvo's hot interior.

"We're not up to anything yet," I pointed out, though I certainly wasn't ruling out the possibility. I climbed in beside him. "Why don't you tell me what this is all about?"

"I need you to go with me to North Salem. To Sheila's house. There's something there I have to pick up."

"What do you need me for?"

"Directions, company." Tim managed a lopsided smile. "Moral support?"

"Sounds interesting. What are we picking up?"

"It's kind of complicated. Why don't I explain while you drive?"

I had to admit he'd piqued my curiosity. I turned the key in the ignition, opened the windows, and put the car in reverse. Still, there were a few details that needed attending to.

"How are we going to get into Sheila's house?" I asked. "Do you have a key?"

"No, but I called the caretaker and told him that the office needed some files Sheila had been keeping at home. I offered him twenty-five dollars, and he agreed to meet us there."

I looked both ways and pulled out of the parking lot. "Is that true?"

"Possibly. I have no idea whether Sheila took stuff

home from work or not. Anyway, it's not what we're looking for."

"Which is?"

"A set of photographs and negatives."

"That belong to Sheila?"

"They were in her possession."

"So I gather," I said dryly. "What are these photos of, exactly, and how did Sheila come to have them?"

"That's the part that gets complicated." Tim glanced out the window as I turned up onto the highway. "You know where you're going, right?"

"Right. You've never been to Sheila's house?"

"No. Why would I have gone up there?"

"No reason," I said casually. "But the fact that you don't even know where she lives makes me curious as to how you would know that there's a handyman who has a key. Much less how to contact him."

Tim looked a little sheepish. He cleared his throat and stared out the window for a minute. If he didn't answer soon, I was turning off at the next exit and driving straight back to the office.

"I guess I might have found that information in Brian's office," he said finally.

"I take it Brian wasn't there at the time?"

"Not exactly."

"So you searched Brian's office. What were you looking for, the photographs and negatives?"

"You're a pretty good detective."

"And you're pretty lousy at explaining what's going on." I eased the car over to the shoulder of the road. "Before we go any farther, why don't you tell me what you're up to."

Tim turned in his seat to face me. "Okay, here it is. I

think I told you before that Carrie kind of has a crush on Brian. She thinks he's like the big, important boss-man and she's always working really hard to get his attention.

"He doesn't even seem to notice her much, at least not in the way she wants him to. But the guy who did notice her was this photographer named Marlon. He does some work for the magazine."

"Marlon Dickie," I said. "I've met him."

Tim nodded. "Then you probably know . . . I guess a girl might find him attractive in a slick sort of way. And he can be pretty persuasive, too. Anyway, he got this idea . . ."

He paused and swallowed heavily. His Adam's apple bobbed in his throat. "He told Carrie that she'd make a great model. He wanted her to pose for what he called artistic shots. He said he could make her look really beautiful, and that she could give the pictures to Brian and he would realize how grown-up she was."

Uh-oh.

"By artistic, do you mean nude?"

Tim's chagrined expression confirmed my guess. "You have to understand—Carrie never would have come up with something like that on her own. It was all Marlon's doing. He talked her into it."

"But Carrie's just a kid," I sputtered. So much for thinking I'd found a photographer for my wedding.

"She's twenty. But she looks younger, and she's still pretty naive. I think that's why Marlon got such a kick out of the whole thing. I guess Carrie wouldn't take all her clothes off, but she did let him take some pictures topless."

"Then what happened?" I flipped on my signal, checked the lane, and pulled back out into traffic.

"Marlon showed the pictures to Brian."

"And what did he think of them?"

"According to Carrie, he was really shocked. She'd only done it because she thought it would please him, and it didn't please him at all."

Score one for Brian's side, I thought. At least the man had some ethics.

"He demanded that Marlon give him all the photographs he'd taken, and every negative, too."

"Did Marlon do that?"

"I think so. At least he said he did. Once Brian had the package, he told Marlon that the magazine wouldn't be needing his services any longer."

Good for him, I thought. "How does Sheila fit into all this?"

"Brian told her about the pictures, and she got really mad."

"At Marlon?"

"At Marlon, at Brian, pretty much at men in general. Believe me, it was something to hear. She took the photographs and negatives away from Brian. I'm not sure what she intended to do with them, but she died before she had a chance to do anything."

I thought about that, turning the information over in my mind and seeing if I could piece it into the puzzle. It didn't seem to want to fit.

"The first time I came to the magazine, Carrie told me that Marlon had been calling Sheila a lot over the last few weeks. Was that what those calls were about?"

"Probably. Marlon has a pretty high opinion of his touch with the ladies, if you know what I mean. I guess he figured he had a better chance of getting Sheila to forgive him. Then she could talk Brian into rehiring him. Of course that never happened. Sheila wouldn't give him the time of day."

Chalk one up for her, too, I thought reluctantly.

"Did the whole office know about this?" I asked.

"Not at first, but eventually, yeah. It's just not that big a place, and you tend to hear things. I really felt bad for Carrie. It's not like any of this is her fault."

Debatable, I thought, but I didn't interrupt.

"She was really broken up about the whole thing. Marlon had convinced her that this would be an adult thing to do. She thought Brian would be really impressed. Then she saw his reaction and began to feel like she'd done something really cheap and stupid. And it's not like Brian went out of his way to make her feel any better either. So I figured it was up to me to help her."

I detected more than a note of jealousy in Tim's tone. Carrie had a crush on Brian; it looked like Tim was interested in Carrie. And now he'd fashioned himself as her white knight, riding to her rescue.

"What makes you think the pictures are at Sheila's house?" I asked.

"They have to be somewhere and they weren't in her office. I looked there first, before her stuff was all boxed up and shipped home. Then I checked Brian's office for good measure. He never bothers to lock his door, even when he's out of town. I know Sheila had the pictures, so I figure they've got to be at her house."

It sounded like a reasonable assumption to me.

When we arrived, Chuck's pickup truck was parked beside Sheila's garage. He was waiting in the shade on the porch. He stared speculatively at the Volvo and at us as we pulled up. Even considering the twenty-five dollars Tim had used as an incentive, Chuck didn't look very happy to see us.

He introduced himself to Tim and nodded at me when I reminded him that we'd met before. Chuck didn't hand over the key, but rather used it to unlock the front door himself. Then he quickly pocketed both the key and the money Tim passed to him.

"How long you think you're going to be?" he asked. "I'll have to lock up again when you leave."

Tim and I looked at each other. "Maybe an hour?" I said. "It could be less. It depends how long it takes us to find what we're looking for."

"That's another thing. Seeing as this is my house, I'm thinking I ought to have a look at anything you remove from it."

Beside me, Tim paled slightly. Before he could protest, I spoke up. "You may be the owner of the house, but you're not the current occupant and you have no right to the contents. They belong to Sheila's heirs, not to you."

Chuck scowled. "Don't forget, it was a furnished rental."

"Don't worry, we won't be removing any furniture. You're welcome to stick around and watch, if you like." I pushed past him and went inside, taking Tim with me.

"Thanks," Tim said. "I should have realized he was bluffing. Or maybe angling for more money."

"Don't mention it."

Chuck sat back down on the porch. Obviously he was planning to keep tabs on what we were up to. Fine by me, as long as he stayed out of our way.

"Where should we start?" asked Tim.

I looked around the small house. Much of the ground

floor was visible from where we stood just inside the front door. "I've never been upstairs. I wonder if there's another bedroom up there, maybe one that Sheila turned into an office."

Together, Tim and I trooped up the narrow stairway. The second floor of the house contained only a small amount of finished space that looked as though it had been reclaimed from the attic. A tiny bedroom was paired with an even smaller bath. The ceilings of both rooms sloped with the roofline.

My guess had been right, though. Sheila had done her best to convert the dark, cramped space into a home office. A twin bed and nightstand had been pushed to one side. An old pine desk and dresser set were angled next to each other, near the only window.

A laptop computer sat closed on the desk, next to the only lamp in the room. The dresser top held a fax machine and telephone. A waist-high file cabinet completed the furnishings.

There were some papers in a neat pile on the desk, and a few more in the in tray of the fax, but the three desk drawers were empty, as was the wastebasket. Clearly Sheila had done most of her work in her office at the magazine.

"Why don't you get started looking around downstairs?" I said to Tim. "We don't want to keep Chuck waiting any longer than we have to."

"Got it." He spun on his heel and clattered down the steps.

It only took a few minutes to rifle through the file cabinet. I found plenty of papers, but no photographs, and no negatives. A minuscule closet was also empty. I got down on my knees and looked under the bed, then went through the drawers of the pine dresser that matched the desk. Still nothing.

I gave the bathroom a glance, then went downstairs. Tim was in the kitchen. He turned around hopefully as I approached. "Anything?"

"Not yet. Where else have you looked?"

"Just the living room so far. Nothing there either." He gestured toward the refrigerator. "Somebody ought to do something about that. There's a ton of food in there that's going bad."

"Why don't you see if you can find some garbage bags? You can clean it out and we'll toss it when we leave. Meanwhile, I'll check the other rooms."

The sideboard was the only enclosed piece of furniture in the dining room, and I didn't see anything inside that looked like a package of photographs. That left only one place to look. I dragged my feet toward Sheila's bedroom. Nothing had changed since Sam and I had been there the weekend before. The bed was still rumpled; filmy curtains still framed a charming view.

A light coating of dust now covered the night table where the picture of the newly engaged Sam and Sheila had sat. Ignoring the lump that seemed to be expanding in my throat, I yanked open the drawer underneath and hit pay dirt. Two books, a magazine, and a bulky manila envelope filled the space.

I pulled the envelope out, twisted its clasp open, and spilled the contents onto the bed. Black-and-white photographs, eight-by-ten glossies, poured out. In the top photo, Carrie was clothed and smiling.

Maybe it was a trick of the lighting, or maybe Marlon really was as talented as I'd believed that day in his studio. In the picture the unexceptional child who sat behind the *Woof!* desk looked beautiful, almost radiant. Too bad the photographer didn't have some moral fiber to go along with his skill.

Quickly I flipped through the rest of the package, confirming that these were the shots Tim had been looking for. The negatives were there, too. I gathered everything up and shoved it back inside the envelope.

"Tim?" I called, walking out of the bedroom.

"Out here."

The front door was still standing open. Tim and Chuck were in the yard. Each was carrying a large black-plastic trash bag, and they were heading for Chuck's pickup.

"I found those files you needed."

"Great." Tim flashed me a grin over his shoulder. "Be with you in a sec." He reached the truck and hoisted his bag up onto the bed. "Chuck offered to dump this for us."

"Thanks," I said.

"No problem." Chuck threw his bag up after Tim's. "No way I want all that stuff going bad in there and stinking up the place."

"That's right. You mentioned you were going to be looking for another tenant soon."

"Yeah." Chuck swiped his cap off his head and wiped his forehead with a handkerchief. "I'd like to get someone in here by next month. Worst case, the month after. I ought to be thinking about running an ad."

"You don't have to do that," said Tim. "I heard Brian talking about the house. He said he's going to take over the lease."

Chuck and I both stared at him.

"Whatever for?" I asked, surprised.

"Who's Brian?" said Chuck.

"Sheila's business partner," I told him. "Brian Endicott. He lives in Purchase. I can't imagine why he'd want to rent another place up here."

"Don't ask me." Tim shrugged. "I only know what I heard. He said Sheila wasn't sure when she took the place whether she was going to stay on the East Coast long-term or not. Brian thought it was a pretty good deal, so he cosigned the lease with her."

Chuck scratched his head. He looked as baffled as I felt. "That can't be right," he said.

I thought back, trying to remember what Sheila had said about the arrangement. "Did you draw up the lease?" I asked Chuck.

"Nah. My mother did all that, right before she went into the nursing home. I know she's been a little dotty lately, but she never mentioned anything about there being two names on the lease."

Tim pulled out a business card. "Here's the number at the office. Maybe you want to call Brian and check with him about it."

"Thanks." Chuck pocketed the card. "I'll do that."

Tim stared meaningfully at the envelope under my arm. "Is that it? Is that what we came for?"

"Yes. I looked through it and I'm pretty sure everything's here."

"Great." He made no attempt to hide his relief.

"That's it?" Chuck looked at the two of us. "All you wanted was that little bitty envelope? Heck if I'd have known that, I wouldn't have given you such a hard time."

"Don't worry about it," I said. "And thanks for helping with the kitchen. My fiancé's been named executor of Sheila's estate, so I'm sure he'll be contacting you soon about moving the rest of her things out."

"Tell him to call me anytime." Chuck walked up onto the porch, pulled the door shut, and locked it. "I'm happy to be of service."

"Sure," Tim said under his breath. "At twenty-five dollars a shot."

"Don't complain," I told him as we got in the car. "It's a small price to pay for getting these back. In Carrie's eyes, you'll be a hero."

"Yeah." He smiled happily. "With any luck, she'll want to shower me with gratitude."

Jeez, I thought, turning back toward White Plains. Was there anyone who didn't have an ulterior motive?

ᴒ✲ *Twenty-five* ✲ᴒ

First thing I did when I got home was phone Aunt Peg. She assumed I was calling to fill her in on what I'd been up to all week, which bought me some goodwill. Unfortunately, as soon as I mentioned that I was hoping she could baby-sit that evening, the jig was up.

"That's why you're calling?" Censure coated her tone. "Because you need a baby-sitter?"

"Actually, what I need is a dog-sitter. If it was just Davey, I could get Joanie from down the block. But as you know, right now Faith has to be looked after, too."

"Has her temperature dropped?"

"Not yet."

"Maybe you missed it," she considered. "What day is it?"

"Sixty." Of a normal gestation of sixty-three.

"Then of course you're not going to leave her with some witless teenager from down the block!"

Joanie wasn't witless. Far from it. If she had been, I never would have left Davey with her. Somehow, things like that never seemed to occur to Aunt Peg.

"What time do you want me?" she asked.

"Six o'clock for an early dinner? I'll make lasagna."

"And be prepared to give me a full report."

"Yes, ma'am."

"Don't be fresh, Melanie."

"I wouldn't dream of it."

Actually I would. But not when I was asking a favor, and hoping she might grant it.

By the time Davey got home after being picked up at camp by Alice, then playing for a while at the Brickmans' house, the lasagna was in the oven and the ingredients for salad and garlic bread were laid out on the counter. Faith, who'd been fed a nutritious dinner which she'd mostly declined to eat, was waiting by the door for his arrival. Together, they came bounding into the kitchen, Davey still dressed in the mud-streaked clothing that had weathered a day of soccer.

"Come over here." I beckoned to my son.

He grimaced. "Not another hug. You just saw me this morning."

I hadn't hugged him that morning. In fact now that he mentioned it, I couldn't remember the last time I'd had my arms around him. It must have been several days.

"No, not a hug," I said, as he advanced warily. "I need your clothes."

"What clothes?"

"The ones you have on." I lifted his arms and pulled the T-shirt off. "They're filthy."

Another mother might have sent him up to his room to change. Not me. I've tried that tack before. Best case, he puts on clean clothes and the dirty ones end up in a ball at the bottom of his closet. Worst case, as he walks up the stairs, he remembers something he meant to look at, gets engrossed, and never changes at all.

With a windy sigh, Davey stepped out of his shorts. It's a sad thing when your six-year-old thinks he's humoring you. Just to complete his degradation, I grabbed a paper towel, wet it under the faucet, and swiped at his face, hands, and knees.

"Camp okay?" I asked as he squirmed to evade the threat of cleanliness.

"Yeah. I scored two goals in scrimmage."

"Get to eat your own lunch?"

"Yup. I think Randy got switched to a different group. I didn't see him all day. Joey and I shared our lunches. He traded his cupcake for my apple." My son chortled. "How dumb is he?"

Just the kind of story that warms a mother's heart. Then again, at least he was eating.

"Aunt Peg's coming," I said when he was reasonably clean. "Go upstairs and get dressed. She'll be here in fifteen minutes or so."

As he and Faith raced away, I opened the basement door and tossed the dirty clothes down the steps in the direction of the washing machine. Tomorrow's problem.

The term fashionably late was not coined with my aunt in mind. She believes in being punctual. Or early, depending on her mood and level of curiosity.

Davey had barely gone upstairs when I saw her headlights flash through the living-room window. I opened the front door and waited on the step. Aunt Peg got out of her car empty-handed.

"You didn't bring dessert," I said as she came up the walk. It was hard not to sound accusatory. "You always bring dessert. I didn't buy any."

"I'm trying not to be so predictable," she said, a declaration that left me temporarily speechless. "We'll have to make do."

Aunt Peg swept past me and into the house. "Is Faith okay? Davey well?"

"Everyone's fine. They're upstairs."

"Good place for them. Then you can tell me all about Sheila's murderer."

"I would if I could." I followed her into the kitchen.

"You mean you don't know who did it yet?"

"I'm working on it. By the way, have you spoken to your nephew lately? He's apparently serious enough about Bertie Kennedy that he's going to meet her parents."

Aunt Peg's brow lifted. "Isn't Davey a little young to be dating?"

I supposed I should have seen that coming. Technically, Davey was Aunt Peg's great-nephew, but most of the time it was entirely too much trouble to stand on ceremony. Hence the confusion.

"Frank," I said. "Your other nephew."

"Frank," Aunt Peg mused. "I haven't heard a peep. I figured that meant he was staying out of trouble."

A sad but true commentary on the state of our family relations.

"He is. At least as far as I know. But he and Bertie have been seeing each other."

"Poor girl," Peg murmured.

"Don't worry about Bertie. She can take care of herself. Which brings me to my point. Did you know that last year she and Kenny Boyle were living together? And that when he's not busy cheating his clients he's into emotional and physical abuse?"

"Now why doesn't that surprise me? The part about the abuse, that is. Not Bertie, I had no idea she and Kenny were a couple." Aunt Peg sank into a chair at the kitchen table and thought for a minute.

I got out a cutting board and started chopping up vegetables for the salad.

"Kenny was married once upon a time," Peg said. "His wife left him. This was pretty far back, five years ago at least. There were all sorts of whispers at the time. Unsubstantiated rumors, you know, the sort of things one doesn't pay any attention to."

Like hell, I thought.

"Of course his wife wasn't a dog person, so everyone was pretty much inclined to take Kenny's side. We had to, don't you see? It was the only side we really heard. His ex-wife just disappeared."

"Disappeared, like from dog shows?" I asked. "Or off the face of the earth?" Where dog people are concerned, this is often considered to be one and the same.

"From the show circuit," Aunt Peg said stiffly. That was her way of reminding me that she doesn't like it when I take a poke at her avocation. "I have no idea what happened to her in real life. She's probably remarried and living a perfectly normal life in Hoboken."

"Maybe she's dead," I said cheerfully. "Strangled under suspicious circumstances. That would help clear things up."

"You have a very odd sense of humor," Aunt Peg muttered. "And I'd feel better if you didn't say such things while holding a sharp knife in your hands."

"Point taken." I smiled over my shoulder. "Would you like to cut up the cucumbers?"

"If I must."

She got up, came over, and went to work. This could take a while. Aunt Peg has spent so much time scissoring Poodles that she tends to aim automatically for clean lines and rounded edges. I stuck the garlic bread in the oven, got out some place mats, and began to set the table.

"All right," Peg said. "So we know Kenny was angry at Sheila, and we think he's capable of violence."

"No, we know he's capable of it. At least against inanimate objects." I told her about the pile of rubble Bertie and I had found in Kenny's garage. "And don't forget Alida Trent. She was also mad at Sheila. Not only that, but she had set herself up with a spy in the *Woof!* office."

"Must have been that boy, Tim."

I stared at her in amazement. "How did you know that?"

Peg shrugged, unconcerned by her acuity. "He just seems like the type."

"Well, you're right. And aside from his dealings with Alida, Tim also has his eye on Carrie, the receptionist. He and I spent this morning driving up to Sheila's house to retrieve some compromising pictures Carrie allowed Marlon Dickie to take after he convinced her that they would impress Brian."

Aunt Peg pondered that for a minute while slices of cucumber continued to fly from her blade. "And she wanted to impress Brian because?"

"She apparently has a crush on him."

"Good Lord. Isn't there anyone in that office who isn't all tangled up with everyone else?"

I folded three napkins into triangles and placed them on the mats. "Aubrey Jones. Maybe. Although she seems to have been running interference between Sheila and Alida. And Tim thinks she has some sort of history with

Brian. I have no idea what that's about. Maybe I'll ask him tonight."

"Tonight, right," said Peg. "Aside from the fact that you're going to serve me a delicious dinner, tell me again why I'm here."

"So I can go talk to Brian."

"Whom you just saw this morning."

"He didn't want to talk in the office. And I couldn't blame him. Even with the door shut, you still get the impression there are curious ears listening everywhere."

Aunt Peg snorted. "So Brian's been hoist by his own petard. Pardon me if I'm feeling rather short on sympathy."

"I agree. But I have to admit I wanted privacy for this discussion, too. Brian implied that he has things to tell me about Sam. Things that Sam would never have told me himself."

"Brian may be lying," Peg said crisply. She's always been a staunch defender of Sam's. "Have you considered that?"

"Of course. And I'm sure he's also interested in covering his own butt. From what I've been able to learn, he had as good a motive for killing Sheila as anyone. Maybe better."

"Money?"

"Lots of it."

Aunt Peg had a whole medley of vegetables chopped up by then. She scraped them off the board and onto the lettuce in the bowl. "I wouldn't count him out then. And I'd be careful tonight. Are you sure you want to go to his house alone?"

Now that she mentioned it, no.

Aunt Peg saw my hesitation. "I have an idea."

"You're not coming with me," I said firmly. That was the unwelcome direction her ideas usually veered in. "Who would watch Davey and Faith?"

"I can't come in person, but I can be there in spirit."

I stopped just short of rolling my eyes. I hoped this wasn't some sort of religious thing.

"You have a cell phone, don't you?" asked Peg.

"Sure, I usually keep it in my car."

"Well, charge it up and put it in your pocket. Just before you get to Brian's house, call me here and we'll leave the line open. That way, I'll be able to hear what's happening. If anything goes wrong, I'll dash out to my car phone and call for help."

It wasn't a bad idea. Of course, Aunt Peg couldn't leave it at that. She had to embellish.

"We need a code word," she mused. "Something you can say if you begin to sense that things aren't going well. You know, to alert me *before* I hear screaming."

Comforting thought. If I had my way, there wouldn't be any screaming.

"Poodle," Peg decided. "That's the word we need. Not likely to come up in conversation on its own, but something you could work in quite handily if you had to."

I'd been thinking along the lines of *mayday, s.o.s.*, or just plain *help!*

"Poodle it is," I agreed.

Aunt Peg and I had spent so much time chatting before dinner that I ended up having to leave as soon as we finished eating. Peg encouraged me to leave the dishes to her and accompanied me to the front door.

"Don't forget," she whispered heavily into clandestine mode. "Poodle."

"Got it."

Of course when I was off by myself, driving down the Merritt Parkway, the whole thing began to seem pretty silly. It was nice to take precautions, but I was quite certain I wouldn't need a code word because Brian wasn't going to do anything that would require me to call for reinforcements.

In fact, if I thought about it—which I'd been steadfastly refusing to do all day—the thing I was most in danger of was learning something about Sam, or his past, that I didn't want to know.

"Poodle," I muttered as I pulled off the King Street exit. Knowing Aunt Peg, she was already sitting by the phone, awaiting my call.

I turned onto Brian's road and pulled over onto the wide, grassy shoulder. All sorts of phone numbers are programmed into my cell phone, but not my home number since I can't be in two places at once. Carefully, I picked out the digits by the light of the dashboard.

Aunt Peg answered right away. "Melanie?"

"It's me. I'm going to put the phone in my pocket. Tell me if you can hear—"

Behind me, a police car came screaming up the darkened road. Its lights were flashing; the siren, on. I heard Aunt Peg squawk and lifted the phone to my ear.

"I heard *that*," she said. "What was it?"

"Police car."

I frowned, watching as the squad car's brake lights, then signal light, flashed on. Quickly I shifted into gear and pulled back onto the road. It looked as though the blue-and-white police car had turned into Brian's driveway.

"Melanie! What's going on?"

"I don't know yet. Give me a minute."

Gravel swished beneath the wheels of the Volvo as I careened past Brian's mailbox. The squad car I'd seen had joined another, already pulled up in front of the house. Their headlights lit a gruesome scene.

A body was lying crumpled in the driveway. A dark puddle that looked like blood, seeped out from beneath it. The body was on its stomach, face turned away; but I recognized the blue polo shirt and linen slacks, the topsiders on the splayed feet.

I'd seen those clothes earlier in the day, and Brian Endicott had been wearing them.

❧❖ *Twenty-six* ❖❧

"Melanie, what's happening? Are you all right?"

I'd forgotten all about the phone. I was still holding it to my ear.

"I'm okay, Aunt Peg."

"You're not in any danger? Do you want me to call the police?"

"No." I gazed at the scene, feeling helpless and sad. "The police are already here."

"What are they doing?" Her voice was insistent. "Are you at Brian's house? What's going on?"

"I think there's been another murder." Judging by the way nobody was rushing around trying to help Brian, that seemed like a pretty safe assumption. "It looks like Brian's dead."

"He can't be dead," Peg cried. "He was supposed to meet you at eight."

As if the two things were mutually exclusive. I heard her gasp softly and realized that the same thought had just occurred to both of us.

"The murderer was just here," I said, blowing out a long breath. "I must have just missed him."

"Melanie, turn your car around and come home this minute!"

"Too late."

At first the three officers on the scene had been too busy to notice me. Now they did. One left the others and strode purposefully in my direction.

"What do you mean it's too late?" Aunt Peg demanded.

"I'm hanging up now. One of the policemen wants to talk to me. I'll be home as soon as I can, okay?" I pressed the end button before she had a chance to protest, then rolled down my window.

As he approached, the officer stepped carefully out of the glare of my headlights. He took a moment to pull out a pen and jot down my license plate number before walking around the side of the car. He had short hair, smooth cheeks, and a direct gaze. The name tag on his dark blue uniform read, OFFICER TANDY.

"Ma'am," he said, leaning down to look in the window. "Do you mind telling me what you're doing here?"

"I had an appointment with . . ." I waved unhappily toward the body in the driveway. Even though I knew it had to be Brian, I had a hard time admitting it, even to myself. I swallowed hard and started over. "I was coming to see Brian Endicott. We were supposed to meet at eight."

Officer Tandy stared at me for what seemed like a very long time, then glanced back over his shoulder. "I'd think it would be hard to tell from here. What makes you so sure that's Mr. Endicott?"

"I recognized the clothes," I said. "I saw Brian earlier

today, and that's how he was dressed. That is him, isn't it?"

Tandy nodded. "The housekeeper heard the gunshots and called nine-one-one. She's already identified the deceased." He gestured toward the side of the driveway. "Detective Walden is on his way, I'm sure he'll want to talk to you. If you could just wait here in your car for a few minutes?"

Like I had nothing better to do.

I pulled over and turned off the engine. Officer Tandy was already walking away. I called after him. "Do you mind if I go inside and see about Brian's dogs?"

He stopped and turned. "I'd rather you stay where you are. Someone will be along to talk to you shortly."

What Officer Tandy's idea of shortly meant, and mine, were two vastly different things. I sat in my car and watched the crime-scene unit arrive and stake out its turf. More cars arrived. Official looking people began to mill around. Purchase is a quiet town; it doesn't see many murders. The Harrison police were out in full force.

While I waited, I called Aunt Peg and gave her an update, which contained no new information except for the fact that I apparently wasn't going to be home anytime soon. I listened to what I thought at first was the rumble of distant thunder, then gradually came to realize was the sound of Brian's dogs. The Saint Bernards, in their kennel behind the house, were filling the night with sound.

My fanciful side imagined them mourning their master's death. Then practicality kicked in. More likely, they were simply protesting all the unusual activity on their property.

More time passed. I wondered what Brian had been

planning to tell me about Sam. I wondered whether o
not I'd have believed him. All in all, it was not the mos
productive way to spend an hour and a half.

Eventually someone remembered my presence. B
then, I'd gotten out of the Volvo and was sitting on th
hood, watching the activity. If it hadn't concerned some
one I'd known, I might have found it fascinating.

Detective Walden seemed young for his job. His fac
didn't yet have the drawn, weary look I'd grown accus
tomed to seeing on men whose careers exposed them t
too many things they'd rather not think about. He care
fully looked me up and down as he approached, probabl
storing away an impression for future dissection.

"Detective Walden, Harrison police," he said, offerin
a hand. "Officer Tandy didn't get your name."

"Melanie Travis." I shook his hand and released it
"Don't go too hard on him. He did take down my plat
number."

He started to smile, then seemed to think better of it
"I hear you knew Mr. Endicott. You were supposed t
meet him here tonight?"

I explained the somewhat convoluted nature of ou
relationship, going into enough detail to have Walde
nodding with impatience.

"You need to know this," I said, when he tried to hurr
me along. "Because Sheila Vaughn, my fiancé's ex-wif
and Brian's business partner, died a week ago."

"How?"

"She was murdered. The state police in Somers ar
looking into it."

"State police?" He looked down and made a note
"Where did she die?"

"North Salem. Detective Holloway is investigating."

"I'll get in touch with him. What else can you tell me?"

Lots, I thought. It was just a matter of getting my facts in order. I kept talking, and Detective Walden kept taking notes. Occasionally he'd interject a comment or a question, but mostly he just let me ramble on. By the time I was done, he'd filled half a dozen pages in his small notebook.

"By the way," he asked at the end, "where were you earlier tonight, before coming here?"

"At home. With my aunt, my son, and a very pregnant Poodle. When I left them, I came straight here, and I'm a pretty fast driver, so I doubt there's any time unaccounted for. Feel free to check with my aunt." I gave him Peg's name and phone number. "She'll be really curious about what happened. I'm sure she'd love to hear from you."

Walden's eyes narrowed at that, and I doubted he'd be calling to check up on me. Probably just as well, for his sake.

"What about Brian's dogs?" I asked, when he was done.

"What about them?"

"He has a number of Saint Bernards here. Both in the house and the kennel out back."

"Is that what I've been hearing?" Walden's head craned around. "I wondered what that noise was."

"There are a couple of Pugs, too. Is there somebody here to take care of them?"

"The housekeeper's inside, I spoke to her earlier. She's upset, but managing. You might want to check with her tomorrow about making some arrangements."

"I could talk to her now—"

"Sorry." Walden was firm. "The house is off-limits for the time being."

I guessed that meant it was time to go. He didn't have to tell me twice. Checking my watch, I saw that it was nearly ten-thirty.

Davey had been in bed for more than an hour. Aunt Peg was probably drinking a cup of tea and reading a mystery novel, with Faith curled up at her feet.

Real life. Normal life. I couldn't wait to get back to it.

I woke up Saturday morning with the nagging feeling that I'd overlooked something. Something important, something I should have paid attention to. Showering, dressing, fixing breakfast, I assessed the various aspects of my life.

Faith, on day sixty-one, appeared calm and was eating normally. Aunt Peg had volunteered to check on Brian's dogs and see if anything needed to be done. By my reckoning, that would serve the dual purpose of satisfying her need to know what was going on, while conveniently keeping her out of my hair. Davey, running around in his bathing suit before I'd even gotten up, was angling for an afternoon at the beach. With any luck, Sam would be home by dinnertime.

As far as I could tell, everything was under control.

In my experience, that usually means it's time for all hell to break loose.

Nevertheless, in honor of the beautiful July day, I shrugged off my worries, packed a picnic lunch, and dug out a beach pass I'd pilfered from Aunt Peg earlier in the season. Davey got his swim and Faith enjoyed a long walk around Todd's Point. Just after four, we arrived

ome to a blinking light on the answering machine. As
sual.

Aunt Peg had called to say that she'd made arrange-
ents with the local Saint Bernard club to find temporary
oster care for all of Brian's Saints, except Boris. That big
og, plus the Pugs, were still in the house, where Brian's
ousekeeper was fussing over them like the orphans she
onsidered them to be.

By the way, Aunt Peg asked tartly before hanging up,
hy wasn't I at home minding my pregnant Standard
oodle? I considered calling to defend myself, but the
econd message put that thought right out of my head.

It was from Sam. He'd landed at Kennedy Airport and
ould be arriving within the hour.

"Yippee!" cried Davey.

My sentiments exactly.

There was just enough time to get most of the day's
ccumulation of sand off of Davey and to mix Faith a
inner, which she sniffed politely but didn't eat, before
e doorbell rang. Sam has a key. I hoped he hadn't lost
. It only took me half a minute to reach the front hall,
ut by the time I got there, Davey and Tar were already
olling around on the floor.

Sam was standing just outside on the step. For some
explicable reason, he seemed to be hesitating before
ntering. Then he saw me and smiled.

He looked tired, and sad, and somehow older than
e had only a week earlier. But Lord above, he looked
onderful to me. And in that moment when his eyes
ound mine and some of his weariness seemed to fall
way, the events of the last seven days began to feel, if
ot all right, at least infinitely more bearable.

Without even thinking, I began to run. I raced down

the hallway and didn't stop until my arms were tigh
around Sam's body and my face was pressed against hi
chest, absorbing his warmth, his scent, and all the comfor
that had lately been missing from my life.

His hand came up, fingers tangling in my hair as h
held me in place. Sam felt the tiny tremors that ripple
through me and soothed them away just by being there
For a long time, neither one of us said anything. Word
would have been superfluous to the connection we wer
somehow re-forming after what seemed like an eternit
apart.

Finally, I was the one to step away. Even then, Sam
didn't let go. He let his hand slide across my shoulde
and down my arm, grasping my hand and squeezing
solidly.

"It's good to be home," he said.

"It's about time you got back," Davey said. "You
should see how good I can dribble now."

"Well," I corrected automatically. "How well you ca
dribble."

"Really well," my son added for emphasis. "Want t
see?"

"Maybe in a few minutes." Sam glanced past us, look
ing around the living room and hall. "Where's Faith
Don't tell me I missed the big event?"

"No, not yet," I told him. "I put her out in the backyar
just before you got here. Poor thing, she's probably goin
crazy trying to get in and join all the excitement. Davey
would you go open the back door?"

"Sure." My son scrambled to his feet. "Come on, Tar!

"There's something I have to tell you," I said as soon a
Davey was out of earshot. "More bad news, I'm afraid.

Sam's expression sobered. "About Brian? I heard. It'

amazing how quickly the dog world grapevine travels. Someone called Sheila's parents because of the magazine connection. Like me, they hadn't seen Brian for years, but it was hard for them anyway, coming on top of everything else."

"How about you?" I asked as we walked into the living room. "How are you doing?"

"Better. A little." Sam sighed, shook his head. "It was good that I went to Illinois. Good for me, and for Sheila's family. I don't think any of us will ever understand what happened, but it helped us all to face it together."

"I'm glad. I've been worried about you."

"I've been worried about you, too." As we sat down on the couch, he gathered me closer to him. "What was I thinking? Asking you to look into things and then leaving town as if you were just supposed to handle everything on your own. I'm really sorry—"

"Mom? Sam?" Davey came tearing down the hallway and skidded around the doorway into the living room. "Where are you guys? Something's wrong with Faith."

"What is it?" I asked. "What's she doing?"

Before he could answer, the three of us were already hurrying toward the back door.

"She's walking in circles and making funny noises. And when Tar and I went outside to get her, she didn't want to pay any attention to us. I think she's sick!"

Beside me, Sam was smiling. His grin was infectious, and I laughed as I reached down and gave Davey a hug. "Don't worry, honey. Faith isn't sick. That's perfectly normal at a time like this. She's having her puppies."

⌒❀ *Twenty-seven* ❀⌒

We found Faith in a corner of the backyard, peeing.

Sam gazed at her with an experienced eye. "She's feeling contractions but doesn't understand what they are. That's why she thinks she has to go."

I went immediately to Faith, intent on getting her inside and upstairs to the whelping box. Sam began a hasty search of the small yard. By the time the Poodle and I reached the steps, he'd caught up.

"What were you looking for?"

"Just making sure she didn't already deliver any puppies. First time mothers sometimes get confused. She might have pushed out a puppy and not realized what it was. I didn't see anything, though."

My cheeks turned bright pink. "This is all my fault. I should have been watching her more closely."

"You didn't know it was time," Sam said sensibly. "Did her temperature drop?"

"I don't know. I was supposed to be taking it twice a day, but last night . . ."

"Something else came up," Sam finished for me, both

of us aware of Davey's presence as our procession made
its way to my bedroom. "Under the circumstances, I can
see how you might have been distracted."

When we reached the upstairs hallway, Faith pulled
away from me and trotted on ahead. I was afraid she
might dive under my bed or tunnel into the closet, but
for once she seemed to find the whelping box a welcoming sight. The Poodle hopped over the low side, turned
several quick circles, and lay down heavily. Quickly, Sam
shut the bedroom door, leaving Tar outside in the
hallway.

He and I crossed the room and sat down on the floor
beside the box. Davey climbed on the bed to watch.

"The contractions are getting stronger," said Sam. "It
won't be long now."

I hung over the side of the box and cradled Faith's
head in my palm. I wondered if she was feeling nervous.
I knew I was. I'd watched Aunt Peg whelp a litter once,
but that had been different. That time, it hadn't been
my pet who'd been doing the delivering, and my tiny,
helpless puppies who were about to be born.

"I can't believe it's happening," I said. "I'm not ready
yet."

"Of course you are." Sam looked at the supplies that
had been piled beside the whelping box for the last week,
as per Aunt Peg's instructions. "Trust me, nobody is
readier than this. You've got everything you need right
here. Davey, do you want to help?"

"Sure!" He slid down off the bed. "What can I do?"

Sam picked up a small carton, which had a heating
pad fitted into its bottom. He flipped the switch on and
turned the setting to low. "This is very important. You're
going to be in charge of this box."

Davey looked disappointed. "It's empty."

"Now maybe, but it won't be for long. Sometimes the puppies come one right after the other, and sometimes there's a long wait in between. When Faith has time between births, she'll want to have her puppies in the whelping box with her.

"But when things are moving really fast, she'll have other things to think about besides the puppies that have already been born. She might even injure one accidentally as she moves around having contractions. So what we'll do then is take the puppies and put them in this box, where they can stay warm and dry until she's ready for them again."

"Won't Faith mind if we take her puppies away?" Davey asked.

"We won't take them far. She'll be able to see and hear and smell them. And if it looks like she's upset, all we have to do is pick up the carton and put it in the whelping box with her."

In the five minutes we'd been in the bedroom, Faith had gotten up and lain back down several times. She'd dug into the waterproof pads that lined the floor of the box and turned around to gaze quizzically at her sides. When I placed my hands on her flanks, I could feel the contractions ripple through her. She lay back down and began to push.

"I think one's coming," I said in a hushed tone.

Sam reached in the box and moved Faith's tail out of the way. "I see the sac."

Faith strained briefly and I heard a sudden whooshing sound. The puppy, encased in its slippery membrane, came sliding out onto the pad. I could see its wet, rounded head. Its tiny feet were moving. Immediately, I reached for it.

Sam caught my hand. "Give her a moment. Let's see what she does."

"Aunt Peg said I have to be sure to get the sac off right away so the puppy can start breathing."

"Faith knows that instinctively. Give her another few seconds, then we'll step in."

I needn't have worried. Sam was right. After casting a startled glance at the wet bundle that had somehow arrived in the vicinity of her hind legs, instinct kicked in and Faith went to work.

She broke the sac that surrounded the puppy and began to lick vigorously. The puppy made a soft mewling sound, using its tiny paws to bat at her nose as her long pink tongue rolled it from side to side.

"Are you sure she's not being too rough?"

"No, that's good for him. It helps get the fluid out of his lungs and get the breathing started. In a minute she'll chew through the umbilical cord."

"Yuck," Davey said eloquently.

"Yuck?" I glanced at my son. "You get a chance to witness the miracle of birth and that's all you have to say? Yuck?"

"It's a mess in there," Davey said in his own defense. "The puppy's all wet, and it doesn't even look like a real dog. And what's all the green stuff anyway?"

"Believe me," Sam laughed, "you don't want to know." He shifted his gaze to Faith. "Uh-oh."

"What?" I cried. "What?"

"Nothing's wrong," Sam said quickly. "It's just that there's another puppy coming right away. That's normal in the beginning. It just means that we have to move a little faster."

Sam picked up the puppy, wrapped it in a small towel, and placed it in my hands. "Make sure he's totally dry, then he can go on the warm pad in Davey's box."

Faith started to protest as Sam lifted the puppy away, then another strong contraction claimed her attention. As she stood up and circled the box, Sam deftly slid out the soiled pad, leaving a clean one in its place. A moment later, while I was busy stuffing the old pad into a garbage bag, another puppy slid into the world. Sam caught it in a towel. Faith hadn't bothered to lie back down.

"Oops," I said, reaching too late for the slippery bundle. "Good thing you're here."

"I love having puppies." Sam broke the sac with his fingers before lowering the new arrival gently to the floor of the box. "I wouldn't have missed this for the world." He looked over his shoulder at Davey. "How's number one coming?"

"Good." Davey said importantly. "He keeps moving around the box. I think he's hungry."

"He is. And he's going to eat in just a minute, as soon as number two is dry. Now that the first two are here, we should get a break." Sam turned the new baby over. "A boy and a girl, so far. Who's got names picked out?"

Davey and I looked at each other blankly. His fingers stroked the boy puppy in the box. "Since he's the first, I think his name should be Adam."

"Good idea," I agreed. "That would make her Eve."

"A biblical litter?" Sam looked skeptical.

"Sure," I said blithely, though the idea had only just occurred to me. "What else would you expect from a Poodle whose name is Faith?"

Sam started to laugh, saw I was serious, and tried to cover his amusement by clearing his throat. It didn't work.

"What's so funny?" I demanded.

"You may call her Faith, but that's not her full name."

"No, of course not. Aunt Peg named her before she gave her to me. Her name is Cedar Crest Leap of Faith."

"Leap of Faith," Sam repeated. "Peg didn't name her that because she was feeling religious. That's what she thought she was making in letting a bitch as good as this go to a novice like you."

I frowned, feeling distinctly grumpy. Aunt Peg might have mentioned something about that at the time. But that had been nearly two years ago. In the meantime I'd managed to put the implied insult out of my mind.

"On the other hand," Sam aimed for a conciliatory tone, "look how well things turned out. I'd say you've justified Peg's faith, and more."

He leaned toward me over the side of the box and Davey groaned. "If you two start kissing, who's going to take care of the puppies?"

He had a point.

Carefully, I lifted the first puppy off the heating pad and put him back with Faith. She sniffed him all over, checking him as thoroughly as if they'd been separated for a matter of hours rather than minutes. Apparently satisfied with what she found, she nudged both puppies back toward her flank. Within moments, each had found a milk-filled nipple and were sucking blissfully.

Watching the puppies nurse, their small tongues latched tightly around the teats, their tiny paws kneading Faith's belly in rhythm to help bring down the milk, filled me with a sense of well-being. Stealing a glance at Sam in the quiet room, I could see that the simple domestic scene was having the same effect on him. For this one short moment, all was right with the world.

"Now what?" Davey demanded, shattering the illusion of tranquillity. He scooted over beside me. "How come you guys are just sitting there? When is Faith going to have more puppies?"

"When she's ready," I said. "This is her production, not ours. We're just here to help things along if she needs it."

"Well, hurry up and help then." Spoiled by video games, my son had been expecting thrill-a-minute action. "How come it takes so long?"

Sam straightened and leaned in for a closer look. "You're about to get your wish," he told Davey. Adam and Eve had finished nursing and were sleeping in the bottom of the box. He scooped them up and set them on the heating pad. "Here comes another puppy."

Forty-five minutes later, Faith's litter had doubled in size, with two more girl puppies joining the boy and girl we already had. Davey, who'd been informed that there would likely be another break in the action, had gone off in search of a Bible. With six-year-old determination, he'd decided that he didn't want just any names for these puppies, he wanted the best names. And that meant making an informed choice.

The fact that his reading skills weren't yet of Bible caliber probably meant that he'd be gone a while. Add that to the excited yips I'd heard from Tar when Davey had opened the bedroom door, and I figured he'd have plenty to keep him busy. Which would give Sam and me a chance to talk.

"I feel like I've been away forever," Sam said, when

all four puppies were warm and dry, and had had their first meal.

"Me too. I've been busy." Starting with the first trip I'd made to the magazine office on Monday, I related the week's events in detail.

Sam had already met many of the people I spoke of. Marlon Dickie was a new name, as was Alida Trent, although he'd heard of her dogs. Sam knew who Kenny Boyle was, and frowned darkly through my recitation of Bertie and my visit to the handler's kennel. Judging by the expression on Sam's face, I suspected that someday soon Kenny would be offering to make restitution for Bertie's ruined items.

"It sounds like you've rounded up a fair number of suspects," he said, leaning back against the bed. "Any idea who might have done it?"

"No. That's the problem. I've spoken to lots of people who had reasons for wanting Sheila out of the way, but none of them seem compelling to me. Except maybe for Brian, and now it looks like he's the one person who couldn't have done it."

Sam thought about that for a minute. "When I came in, you seemed surprised that I'd heard about Brian's murder. How did you find out so quickly?"

Uh oh, I thought. I'd been hoping he wouldn't wonder about that. Because lately I'd begun to feel that going to see Brian the night before had been a betrayal, both of Sam and of the trust we had in one another.

Technically I hadn't done anything behind Sam's back; at least that's what I kept telling myself. But it felt like I had. Brian had offered to tell me things about Sam which he claimed Sam didn't want me to know, and I'd gone running to find out what they were.

So what did that say about me? And about my belief in the relationship that Sam and I shared?

"I was there," I said slowly. "I got to Brian's house right after he was murdered."

Shock froze Sam's expression. Concern quickly followed. "What do you mean you were there? What were you doing there?"

"I'd seen Brian earlier in the day at his office. He said he had things to tell me. Things he wanted privacy to discuss. He asked me to meet him at his house last night."

"And you went?" He sounded angry. Even Faith, totally absorbed in her new brood, looked up and tilted her head at his tone. "After everything I've told you about Brian—"

"Yes, I went." My voice lifted too. "I had to go. Because what I know about Brian and Sheila, and the life you led before you met me, could pretty much fit in a thimble. Brian said he had things to tell me. I wanted to hear what they were."

"Things about me."

"Yes."

Sam sighed. "I don't know what Brian intended to tell you. I do know that whatever it was, was as likely to be a lie as the truth. He always had a way of shaping reality to suit his own purposes. Damn it, Melanie, I can't believe you would have been so desperate for information that you would have turned to him instead of coming to me."

I could see the pain in Sam's eyes. It didn't stop me from saying what I felt needed to be said. "I *have* come to you, Sam. There are things you don't talk about, questions you don't answer.

"Whenever I ask about Sheila and Brian and what went on among the three of you, you just shrug it off as if it didn't matter. Well it does matter, it matters to me. And you won't talk about it."

Wouldn't you know it, Faith chose that moment to start having contractions again. Despite the hurtful things I'd said, Sam and I still made a great team. Within minutes, another boy had been added to the litter.

Sam didn't say a thing until the fifth puppy was dry and nursing. Following his lead, I was silent as well. I'd had my say. Now it was his turn.

"I can take a pretty good guess what Brian would have told you," Sam said finally. "He would have wanted to strike out at me, and if hurting you would have accomplished that, he'd have done so without hesitating. I imagine he'd have warned you against marrying me."

"For what reason?"

"Brian would have said that I still cared for Sheila. That she was the love of my life, and I'd never gotten over her."

I felt a pain in my chest. My heart, constricting with sudden apprehension. "And would he have been wrong?"

I wanted reassurance. Sam looked annoyed.

"Of course," he said, his voice clipped, curt. "Do you have to ask?"

Yes, I thought. I did.

"Talk to me," I said. "Make me understand. Because no matter how hard I try, I still don't get it. What was so awful that happened between you and Brian to make you still despise each other?

"Yes, Sheila came between you. Both of you loved her, both of you lost her. But that was years ago. How come neither one of you ever got over it?"

Sam sucked in a deep breath and slowly let it out. He

was stalling. That was all right. Faith was resting quietly
again, and I could afford to wait.

The puppies had finished eating and dropped off to
sleep before Sam spoke again. "The animosity you saw
between Brian and me wasn't about Sheila," he said.
"Not after all this time."

I should have felt better. Maybe I would have, if I
hadn't still been confused. "What else was there?"

"Anger," Sam said slowly. "Guilt. Betrayal of a friend's
trust. Remember when I told you about the video game
that Brian stole and patented under his own name?"

"Island of Mutant Terror," I said. "The one that made
him millions."

Sam nodded. "I was the friend. That was my game.
Those were my millions. All those years ago, I took Sheila
from him, and he took that from me."

❧❀ Twenty-eight ❀❧

I felt like I'd been suckerpunched. I knew zip about video games, but I understood the concept of millions readily enough. I stared at Sam in shock.

"You designed Island of Mutant Terror?"

"Yes."

"But you didn't take it to market."

"It wasn't ready yet. There were still a few bugs I was working out. Back then, it was just an intellectual exercise, something to play around with when business school got to seem too much like real life."

I'd never thought of Sam as naive, but I hadn't known him a dozen years earlier. He'd been much younger then, with so many of the events that would shape his life yet to happen. "So it didn't occur to you to protect your creation."

He shook his head. "None of us realized that the game had the potential to become a best-seller. When you're living on peanut butter and jelly sandwiches, you don't think in terms of striking it rich overnight. Not unless you're standing in line to buy a lottery ticket."

I cast a quick glance at Faith. She was snoozing in the box, curled contentedly around her litter. "You might not have realized what you had, but what about Brian? It sounds like he must have had a pretty good idea."

"Maybe," Sam said thoughtfully. "I've wondered about that over the years. And to tell you the truth, I'm not sure. Sheila and I had just gotten together, so I had other things on my mind. I'd pretty much shoved the video game onto a back burner.

"I guess that gave Brian the opportunity he was looking for. I don't think he was hoping to make a fortune; I think he just wanted to hit back at me any way he could."

"Okay, I can see that." I trailed a finger over the nearest puppy. It felt warm and pudgy beneath my hand, just the way it was supposed to. "But I don't understand why you didn't go after him. Why didn't you sue or something? Wouldn't your other friends have supported your claim?"

"Probably. If I'd felt like dragging them into it, which I didn't. Remember, I had no idea how successful the game would become. None of us did. And besides, there was an element of guilt there on my part as well.

"There's an unwritten rule: you don't steal your best friend's girlfriend. And I'd broken it. Maybe I felt like I deserved to have him come back at me. Or maybe I just figured we'd made a fair exchange."

Millions of dollars versus a life with Sheila?

Don't even go there, I thought.

In the box beside us, Faith stirred uncomfortably. Contractions were starting again. I reached in and stroked the side of her face. Tipping her head, the Poodle leaned into the caress.

"You're doing great," I whispered. Mindful of the puppies beside her, Faith's tail wagged gently.

Since litters are delivered from back to front, with those nearest the end of the birth canal being born first, this puppy had the entire length of Faith's body to travel, and was a long time in coming. Faith pushed; Sam encouraged; I worried. I also had a few minutes to think.

By the time Faith pushed out the sixth puppy, something troubling had occurred to me. "Sam, where were you Friday evening?" I asked as we dried off the new girl and got her set up for a meal.

"At Sheila's parents' house. It was my last night, and we had dinner together. After that, Sheila's brother and I drove back to his house—it was Sheila's when she lived out there, but she sublet it to him when she came East—to pick up some papers I was going to need."

"So you were with other people all night?"

Sam saw where I was headed. "You're thinking I might need an alibi, aren't you?"

"Could be. Probably no one has a stronger motive for killing Brian than you do."

"Don't worry. Sheila's brother is pretty active in local politics, and he's friends with half the Evanston police force. I'm sure he'll back me up."

"Good." I offered Faith a sip of cool water. She lapped from the small bowl politely, then lay back down on her side.

"How do we know when she's done?" I asked. "Six puppies seems like a nice size litter. How do we know if there are more coming?"

"We don't. The best thing to do is just watch and wait."

Glancing at the clock by my bed, I was surprised to see how late it had gotten. I slipped out of the room and

went to find Davey and Tar. Both were sound asleep o
the couch. I put the puppy out in the backyard, the
carried Davey upstairs, changed him into pajamas, an
put him into bed.

"Did Faith have more puppies?" he asked sleepil
clutching the covers to his chin.

"Two more," I whispered. "You can see them in th
morning."

"Is she going to sleep on my bed?"

"Not tonight. How about Tar? Would you like him t
stay with you?"

Davey nodded, and drifted off. I went downstairs, le
Sam's puppy in, then warmed up some boiled chicke
I'd prepared for Faith earlier. With six hungry mouth
to feed, she was going to need plenty of sustenance.

By the time I got back to my bedroom, Sam and Faith
were snoozing, too. I paused in the doorway and smiled
Though there was a bed right beside him, Sam ha
stretched out on the floor. One arm cradled his head
the other reached up and dangled over the side of th
whelping box, resting gently on Faith's side. If she stirre
to signal another puppy on the way, he'd know about i

I took a pillow from the bed and placed it under hi
head. Sam opened one eye, looking just as sweetl
drowsy as my son had. He'd had a long week.

"Go back to sleep," I said, lifting his arm out of th
whelping box and placing it in a more comfortable posi
tion. "I'll take the first watch."

Sam nodded, sighing into his pillow. "Wake me up i
you need me."

"I will," I promised.

Hours passed. All around me the house was silent.
hand-fed Faith her chicken. I admired her beautiful new

litter. I gazed at the man lying on the floor next to them.
And through it all, I thought about how lucky I was.

Please God, I prayed, if this is all I ever have, I'll be
happy for the rest of my life. Just please don't let me
screw it up.

No more puppies arrived. Faith woke up diligently
every few hours to feed her litter. I kept watch, drifting
happily, feeling more at peace than I had in days. As the
first soft streaks of dawn lightened the window, I put
my head down on Sam's shoulder and fell asleep, too.

I awoke to the nudge of a none-too-gentle foot and the
sound of Aunt Peg's voice ringing in my ears.

"Six gorgeous puppies," she was saying as she leaned
over the box and praised Faith's efforts. "Aren't you a
wonderful girl?" Her gaze swung briefly my way. "I
hope you didn't sleep through the whole thing."

"Six puppies?" I sat up and registered surprise. "When
did that happen?"

"Knock it off, both of you," Sam said, grinning. Considering that he'd spent the night on the floor, he looked
remarkably cheery.

Slowly I pushed myself to my feet. "Faith must need
to go out."

"Mo-oom!" Davey's voice crescendoed in disgust. He
was sitting behind me on the bed. "We've already done
that. Sam and I have been up for *hours*. Faith and Tar
have already had breakfast, too."

Oh. "What about you?"

"I had shortbread cookies and milk," Davey said
smugly. "Sam said I could."

"You snooze, you lose," Sam informed me.

"I wouldn't mind having a few cookies myself," said

Aunt Peg. She sat down on the floor beside the whelping box and upended a canvas bag she'd brought with her. Half a dozen bottles of brightly colored nail polish spilled out onto the rug.

"Are you going to paint their toenails?" Davey giggled. I was glad he'd asked. It saved me from having to do it.

"Not their toenails, their backs." Peg unscrewed the nearest bottle, labeled Sonic Blue. "This used to be much harder back in the days when nail polish only came in red, pink, and taupe. Now look at all the choices. I was able to bring a color for each puppy."

I waited for more of an explanation. It didn't come. Instead, Peg reached in the box, picked up the nearest puppy and dabbed a big blue spot on the shiny black hair in front of his tail.

"Aunt Peg," I said, "what are you doing?"

"Making identifying marks. How else do you expect to be able to tell them apart? Six newborn puppies, all pure black. Even I think they look alike, and I've been doing this for years. You haven't got a prayer."

That was reassuring.

"Why do I need to tell them apart? I thought Faith took care of everything for the first few weeks."

"She does, but you still want to stay on top of things. Suppose you notice that five puppies are eating, but one is sleeping. You think, all right, maybe she's not hungry. But you wouldn't want her to miss two meals in a row, so you file that thought away: be sure that Pink eats next time around. See how that works?"

I nodded and yawned. On a full night's sleep, I could have probably figured that out for myself.

"Can I help?" asked Davey.

"Of course you can." Peg opened another bottle.

"Come sit by me. You and I are going to be in charge of the puppies for a while. We might even name them all. Meanwhile, Melanie's going to take a shower and wake up, and Sam's going to go pay some attention to his own puppy, who's feeling quite neglected at the moment."

Aunt Peg was in an organizing mode. Sam and I knew better than to argue. We simply went and did as we'd been instructed.

By the time I'd stood under the hot spray of the shower, washed my hair, and brushed my teeth, I was just about revived. Peeking into my bedroom, I heard Peg and Davey arguing over the merits of the name Ezekiel and decided to leave them to it. I found Sam in the kitchen, sitting at the table, papers spread out all around him. Tar was lying at his feet, gnawing happily on one of Faith's rawhide bones.

I opened the refrigerator, got out a cup of black cherry yogurt, stirred it up, then went to see what Sam was doing.

"Don't ever let anyone try to convince you that you want to be executor of their estate," he grumbled as I sat down. "You don't."

"Big job?"

"Enormous. Picture every little detail of your life as a loose end that has to be tied up by somebody. In this case, me."

"Funny that after all these years, Sheila still named you executor," I said idly.

"There's nothing funny about it," Sam muttered. "She probably did it for revenge. Somewhere, she's having a good laugh at my expense, watching me pay her tab at the beauty salon and decide whether or not to cut off the electricity at her house."

"Speaking of the house," I said. "There's something you need to know."

Sam wasn't going to like what I had to say, and we knew each other well enough that he picked up that from my tone. He shuffled the papers into a hasty pile, pushed them aside, and gave me his full attention. "Shoot."

"Have you seen the lease?"

"Not yet." He inclined his head toward an accordion file on the floor beneath the table. "It's probably in there. Sheila's brother, Pete, said that's where she kept all her important papers. I just hadn't gotten that far yet. Since the rent was paid through the end of the month, I figured it wasn't a priority."

"I was at Sheila's house on Friday. Remember I told you I went there with Tim?"

"Right."

"Chuck Andrews was there, too. Tim had called him to come and let us in. Chuck said something about looking for new tenants, and Tim told him not to bother because Brian had cosigned Sheila's lease and was planning to take it over."

Sam's brow creased as he frowned. "Why would Brian want a little house in North Salem. . . ?" His voice trailed away. That wasn't the question he should have been asking. Like me, it had just taken him an extra beat to realize it.

"Wait a minute," he said. "Sheila leased that house last winter. Since she was bringing the Pugs with her, she had to have everything in place before she arrived. She told me she came East for a temporary job assignment and because . . ." Once again, he didn't finish his thought.

"Because you were here," I said. "That's what she told Aunt Peg, too."

"She never said a word about Brian. The first time I knew they'd gotten back together was when we had dinner at her house. I just assumed they'd run into each other at a dog show and gotten the idea to work together." Sam paused, looking nonplussed. "Are you telling me that they'd planned all that in advance?"

"It looks that way."

Much as I hated the idea that Sheila had moved East with the intention of stealing my fiancé, I realized this was worse. She'd lied to all of us. More importantly, she'd lied to Sam.

Though he'd rejected Sheila's advances, I knew that Sam had been flattered, and maybe even a little bit intrigued by her attention. So how must he be feeling now with the knowledge that Sheila's attempt to rekindle their love had only been Plan A; that she'd begun her quest with a backup option already in place?

"If what Tim said is true, then Sheila and Brian were in touch before she came here," I said softly.

"It's easy enough to check." Sam reached down for the folder. "Pete said I'd have everything I needed right here."

He thumbed through several sleeves, pulling out papers and glancing at them, then shoving them back. It didn't take him long to find what he was looking for. Sam drew out a sheaf of stapled, typewritten pages and put it on the table. As I leaned over his shoulder, he flipped quickly to the last page.

Below Sheila's signature, was another: Brian Endicott.

"Damn," I said, as Sam slumped back in his chair. Sheila'd been two-timing everyone. Now I really was glad she was dead.

I'd hoped Sam would react with anger, but it was clear

he hadn't gotten that far. For the moment, he just looked sad and disillusioned.

I got up, tossed my empty yogurt container in the garbage, got a couple of mugs out of the cabinet, and poured us each some coffee. Lost in thought, Sam barely seemed to notice when I set his cup down on the table. He nodded his thanks, but didn't look up.

Give me some room, his expression said; so I did. I opened the dishwasher and began unloading clean plates. Upstairs, I heard Davey give a delighted squeal. I wondered if that meant we were going to be raising a puppy named Ezekiel.

Listening to my son's laugh, it occurred to me that I still hadn't solved the problem of the lunchtime bully. The older Davey became, the more I realized that a mother's relationship with her son was a complex bond, fraught with issues that needed to be negotiated with care. Was I protecting Davey too much, or not enough? Should I have stepped back and let him work out the problem himself, or swooped down and knocked the obstacle from his path? Clearly, what I needed was a man's input.

I glanced over. If Sam had looked like his thoughts were even in the same time zone as mine, I might have asked him. Instead, I finished putting away the dishes and walked back over to the table. The lease was resting where Sam had dropped it. Idly, I picked up the papers and began to read.

Davey's problem wasn't the only one I was having a hard time figuring out. It still didn't make sense to me that Brian would have cosigned a lease for a house in North Salem; nor that he would have wanted to assume responsibility for the rental after Sheila's death. I skimmed down the first page, stopped at the bottom, then read the last paragraph again.

My breath caught. Mothers and sons and their complicated relationships, indeed. Suddenly, it was all right in front of me.

"Sam," I said. "Listen to this. I think I know who killed Sheila and Brian."

❧❀ *Twenty-nine* ❀❧

"What are you talking about?" Sam reached for the papers.

"Look at the asking price on the house." I pointed to a figure near the bottom of the page. "This wasn't just a lease, it was a lease with option to buy. And look at the price Sheila had an option at."

He found the number I was referring to. "Two hundred thousand? Maybe it's a little low for the area but it's not totally out of line. The house is small and it's in terrible shape. Nobody had done any repairs on it in years—"

"The house isn't important," I broke in impatiently. "You're right, it's nothing, but the land it sits on must be worth a fortune. Remember how much room there was in the backyard? Sheila told me Mrs. Andrews had eight acres.

"That house predates all the others around it. When the neighborhood began to get built up, Mrs. Andrews must have held on to her land. Any developer would be thrilled to get his hands on it. They'd tear down the house and make three or four building lots in its stead. At today's prices, each lot would be worth the price Sheila was supposed to pay for the whole package."

"So Sheila got a terrific deal." Sam didn't sound entirely convinced. "I imagine that's why she took the option in the first place."

"Which she got from an old woman who'd lived in her house forever and probably thought two hundred thousand sounded like a lot of money." I was speaking faster as the pieces fell into place. "Remember Chuck saying that his mother wasn't very sharp anymore? When she left the house, she went into a nursing home. I bet she had no idea how those property values had soared."

I paced across the room, stepping over Tar and around Sam's chair. It might have been exultation that kept me on my feet, but it felt more like relief. Finally, a pattern was beginning to emerge.

"Chuck didn't find out that Sheila had rented the house from his mother until after everything was already signed. By then, it was too late for him to have any input. How much do you want to bet he's Mrs. Andrews's heir?"

"The man who kept telling us the house was his," Sam said thoughtfully.

"Exactly. Picture this: Chuck's mother is old and growing frail, and he's just found out that she's all but given away a major part of his inheritance. I can see how that might make a man angry enough to do something desperate.

"And here's something else," I added. "Go back to the beginning, the first thing we noticed. Sheila's dogs were outside, which meant she was home when the killer arrived. Sheila knew Chuck, he'd been fixing all sorts of things for her lately. Of course she would have let him in. She wouldn't have thought twice about it."

"Keep talking," said Sam. "This is beginning to make sense."

"Of course it makes sense. Your problem is that you haven't been here all week, you haven't met everyone who's involved. But I have. And the prospect of losing all that money gives Chuck a stronger motive than anyone else."

"Except maybe Brian," Sam pointed out.

"Brian didn't need the money enough to kill for it. But Chuck's situation is totally different." With satisfaction, I realized what it was I'd overlooked earlier. "And now that I think about it, he was pretty upset when Tim told him that Brian's name was on Sheila's lease, too."

"The two of them talked on Friday morning?" Sam asked, checking to see if he had the sequence right.

"Right. Chuck said something about trying to find a copy of the lease so he could see for himself. And Friday night, Brian was dead."

"We need to tell the police about this." Sam got up and walked over to the phone. "Detective Holloway gave me his card. Let's see if I can get through on a Sunday."

I followed him across the room. "If not, we can try Detective Walden in Harrison. He's the one who's looking into Brian's murder."

Our timing couldn't have been worse. Predictably, neither man was working on Sunday morning. Both police departments offered to pass along messages, however, and Sam and I took turns telling our story. Twice we were told to expect a return call, probably sometime that afternoon.

We'd accomplished something, but it wasn't enough for Sam. "I'm not going to sit here all day and wait," he said irritably. "I feel like that's all I've been doing ever since Sheila died. Waiting to find out what went wrong. Waiting for the funeral. Waiting to feel normal again. I've got to *do* something."

I was game. "What do you want to do?"

He thought for a minute. "I think I'll drive up to North Salem."

"You're not going after Chuck."

Sam snorted. "Give me some credit. I have no intention of tipping our hand. I'd much rather leave the next step up to the police and have it done right."

Thank God for a man with common sense. "Agreed. So why are we going to North Salem?"

Sam shook his head. "You're not going. I am. It will give me something useful to do. Now that I'm executor of Sheila's estate, I have to sort through every scrap of paper in that house from the electric bill to the warranty on her car. I may as well go and pick it all up."

"Chuck changed the locks," I said. "You won't be able to get in."

"That house was falling down around Sheila's ears. If there's even one window with a lock that holds, I'd be surprised. Don't worry, I'll get in."

As he spoke, Sam was already stuffing papers back into the folder. A sense of purpose, all out of proportion to the errand he'd proposed, seemed to galvanize his actions.

What was the rush? I wondered. Why did he need to go up there right now?

Tension hummed in the air. Or maybe it was my imagination. But once again, we seemed to have fallen out of sync. The unity that had come so easily to us that I'd almost taken it for granted was unraveling strand by strand, and nothing I did seemed to stop it.

"I want to come with you," I said.

"There's no need," Sam countered quickly. "Stay here and keep an eye on Faith and the puppies."

"Aunt Peg can do that."

"Melanie—"

The more he protested, the more determined I became to have my way. "I'm coming."

Sam didn't look happy. "All right then, let's go."

I ran upstairs. Since Aunt Peg, Davey, and Faith had six delightful, day-old puppies to keep them entertained, they barely spared me a glance when I told them that Sam and I were going out for a couple of hours.

"We'll take Tar with us," I told Aunt Peg. "Can you stay with Davey?"

"I don't see why not. Besides, it may take me that long to convince him that we don't want a puppy named Nebekenezer."

I flew back down the stairs and found Sam already loading Tar into the back of the Blazer. I grabbed up my purse and joined him in front. I'd barely shut my door before the car was moving. No use speculating whether he'd have left without me.

An uncomfortable silence lasted almost five miles. Even if I'd wanted to end it, I had no idea how. This chore Sam had been determined to do seemed precipitous, to say the least. Was he really in such a hurry to pick up Sheila's things? I wondered. Or was he just in a hurry to get away from me?

Finally, Sam spoke. "I was lying," he said.

I turned slowly in my seat. I'd been staring so hard

out the window that my eyes burned. Still, I was amazed how calm my voice sounded. "About what?"

"You must think I'm crazy for taking off like that. Who knows? Maybe I am. The worst part is, I'm not sure I even know anymore. I've been thinking about what you said last night. About how I wasn't talking, wasn't telling you things you needed to know. Maybe I figured you were better off not knowing . . ."

I swallowed hard and held my gaze steady. Dread welled up inside me. I knew with certainty that I didn't want to have this conversation. And I was just as certain that we had to have it.

"Tell me what's going on," I said quietly. "Whatever you're thinking, whatever you're feeling, even if it hurts, I'd rather know. I don't want secrets between us. I had that kind of marriage before. I don't want it again."

Sam's hands gripped the steering wheel, fingers clenched as if he meant to squeeze it into submission. His eyes never left the road. "If anyone had asked me a month ago to define how I felt about Sheila, I would have said she was someone from my past, nothing more. And yet now that she's gone, I find there was more."

My lower lip was trembling. I nipped it with my teeth and tried to hold it still. It didn't seem to help. Now my throat was fluttering.

"I guess it's because I always thought there'd be time. An opportunity for Sheila and me to sort out what we had and where we went wrong. It's not that I ever thought we'd get back together. Or that I even wanted it to happen. All these years we've been apart, getting back with Sheila was the farthest thing from my mind."

Right. That's why he'd repeated the thought three times.

Ever since Sheila's arrival in the spring, I'd sensed a gap opening up between Sam and me. Maybe I'd been naive, but I'd believed in our relationship. I'd thought it was strong enough to hold us together.

Now I realized how badly I'd been deluding myself. It wasn't a fissure that had come between us, it was an ever-widening gulf. And while I was reaching desperately across the expanse, Sam was looking the other way, off into some distant future that only he could see.

He seemed to be waiting for me to say something, but I couldn't. Words were wholly inadequate to express what I was feeling.

"Please try to understand," said Sam. "For the first time in my life, I have no idea what to do next. There are so many regrets, so many things I should have done differently. Now I'll never have the chance."

Pain and frustration dulled Sam's tone, even as it seemed to sharpen the blade that was turning inside me. Despite the fact that we were discussing a woman he'd loved and lost, part of me still yearned to reach out and soothe him. How dumb was that?

Better than the alternative, I realized. My own feelings were too raw. It was much easier to deal with his hurt than my own.

"There was no way you could have known what would happen," I said.

"Maybe not, but I feel like I should have. Sheila and I were together at such a formative time in my life. In many ways, who I was with her shaped the man I became. And yet, when it all fell apart we were so angry with each other that I wasn't able to see that. I certainly wasn't ever able to tell her."

"I'm sure she realized," I said softly. "She must have

known how much she meant to you or she wouldn't have followed you here."

Sam sucked in a breath. "Me and Brian," he said after a moment. His voice held a bitterness it hadn't earlier. "I can't believe she never told me they were still in touch. What an opportunity this must have been for her to play us off against each other. I wonder if Brian realized what she was up to."

"Probably. He seemed to have a pretty clear idea where Sheila was coming from."

Sam glanced over, waiting for me to point out that he hadn't. It was much too late for recriminations like that. I let the silence linger.

"Anyway," Sam said after a minute, "I'm not sure this makes any sense but I feel like I need to go back to where Sheila was, one last time. Maybe I need to touch some of her things. Maybe I need to wallow in a few memories. Who knows if it will help? All I do know is that I've run out of other ideas."

He reached across the seat, took my hand in his and squeezed it gently. "I'm sorry, Melanie. I know that's not what you wanted to hear. I realize how you felt about Sheila, that's why I didn't want you to come with me. I didn't want to hurt you any more than I already have—"

Abruptly Sam stopped speaking.

We'd rounded the corner onto Sheila's road, and I looked up to see what had caught his attention. Midway down the road, behind a stand of trees, a thick plume of dark smoke rose in the air.

Sam's foot bore down hard on the gas pedal, and the Blazer shot forward. By the time we reached Sheila's driveway, flames were visible through the trees. The Blazer bounced from rut to rut, but neither of us cared.

Smoke grew thicker as we burst out of the trees and into the yard. Fire was shooting out of Sheila's open front door. I was already reaching for the cell phone in the tray. An anguished cry was torn from deep within Sam's heart.

"Nooo!" he roared.

≈❀ Thirty ❀≈

The Blazer was still rolling when Sam jumped out. He ran toward the house. For several panicked seconds, I couldn't seem to move. Then a jolt of adrenaline shot through me. I scrambled out of the car and raced after him.

"Stop!" I yelled, grabbing Sam's shoulder and spinning him around just as he reached the front steps. "You can't go in there!"

Bright orange flames licked at the dry wood of the porch. The front door was open, and I could see that the interior of the small house was already engulfed. Smoke floated lazily along the eaves, creeping through every crack in the roofline. The old house was going up faster than a stack of dry newspapers.

"I have to get—"

"No you don't, damn it!" I was screaming so loudly my throat hurt. Inhaling a lungful of smoke didn't help. "There's nothing left in there. Everything's gone."

Sam looked around wildly. A hose was coiled on the ground beside the detached garage. As he ran to get it,

I dialed nine-one-one. The operator took my information calmly and told me to remain on the line.

I would have, except that when I turned back to see what was keeping Sam, I dropped the phone.

He was bent over a spigot that was attached to the garage. Old and rusty from lack of use, it turned only grudgingly. Oblivious to anything else, Sam swore and wrestled with it. Behind him, no more than half a dozen feet away, stood Chuck. He was cradling an ax in his hands.

"Sam!"

Even over the roar of the fire, he must have heard the panic in my voice. Sam stood up, spun around, and took in the situation in a glance.

"The house is going to burn," Chuck said. He shifted the weight of the ax from one hand to the other. "Nothing's going to stop it. Do you hear me?"

"I hear you." Sam lifted his hands and stepped slowly away from the garage. "It's going to burn. Fine by me."

He took several steps in my direction.

"Stop right there," Chuck ordered. "Let me think about what to do."

I cast a quick glance at Sam. I had no idea how he could look so calm when I was shaking. All at once I knew how he'd felt those times when I'd been in danger. Right now, I wished he were anywhere else but where he was; standing within striking distance of the sharp blade of a murderer's ax.

"Take your time," I said to Chuck. "Think all you want. Are you the one who set the fire?"

He didn't answer, but I kept talking anyway. "It looks like you did a good job. A few minutes more and there'll be nothing left of that house but embers."

"That's right," Chuck spat out. "Maybe then everyone will go away and leave us alone."

"Us?" asked Sam. Thwarted in his attempt to reach me, he was edging back toward the hose. "Who's us?"

"My mom and me. This is our land. It's been our land for decades. People have no right to come along and take advantage of an old lady."

"People like who?" I asked. I stepped toward the house, deliberately drawing Chuck's attention away from Sam and back to me. Heat from the fire poured over me like a molten wave. My hair lifted and crackled with it. "People like Sheila? Is that who you're talking about?"

"Big-city lady coming around here with her big-city ideas. She conned my mother good. Got her to sign a contract that gave away the house that I grew up in."

"The house that should have gone to you when your mother died," I prompted.

"Damn right," Chuck snapped. "I told her we were going to have to renegotiate the terms, but Sheila just laughed and said it was a done deal."

I didn't dare look at Sam. I hoped to hell he knew what he was doing. In his place, I'd have been moving away from the man with the ax. Sam was going the other way. I had to keep Chuck focused on me.

"Is that why you killed her?" I asked.

Chuck growled. That was the only word for it. The guttural sound was filled with pent-up rage and frustration. "It isn't right to take advantage of an old lady," he repeated stubbornly. "It isn't fair. Don't know what everyone wanted this house for anyway. It never was much."

He glanced past me at the blazing structure and spat.

"Pretty soon it won't be anything at all. Then everyone will just go away and leave me be."

"That's not going to happen," I said. "It's too late."

Chuck had started to look for Sam, but I'd made him mad, and his eyes came back to me. His glare was dark and menacing.

I strained my ears, listening for the sound of sirens. I'd called for help; what was taking so long?

"What do you mean it's too late?" he demanded.

I wondered if I should bring up the murder again. Under the circumstances, it didn't seem like the wisest course of action. I tried another tack.

"Your mother signed a contract. Even though Sheila and Brian are dead, it's still legally binding. Their heirs are going to inherit the option on this house."

"What house?" Chuck laughed harshly, but he was beginning to look concerned.

"On the land, then. That's what this is all about, isn't it?"

"My land!" Chuck screamed, swinging the ax to make his point. "This is *my* land!"

Sam made his move.

He swooped down and snatched up the hose, turning the nozzle on full blast. A jet of water shot out, catching Chuck square in the face. It wasn't enough to knock him down, but it was enough to blind him. The ax fell to the ground as his hands reached up reflexively to cover his eyes.

Sam and I both ran forward at the same time. He grabbed Chuck. I went for the ax, scooping it up off the ground and throwing it as far as I could.

Chuck screamed in outrage. Blinking, sputtering, he struck out blindly. His first blow glanced off Sam's shoulder. Sam ducked a second jab, then landed one of his own.

His fist connected solidly with Chuck's jaw. Chuck's head snapped back; his eyes fluttered shut. He dropped to the ground at my feet.

Coughing in the smoke, I bent at the waist and fought to catch my breath. "Nice job," I said.

Sam grinned. I suspected his knuckles hurt like hell.

I found a length of rope in the garage. As Sam bound Chuck's hands behind his back, the roof of the house collapsed. A rush of hot air billowed over us. Sparks and debris showered the lawn.

Finally, I heard the sound of sirens in the distance.

It was about damn time.

The firemen arrived too late to do anything but ensure that the fire didn't spread to the detached garage or surrounding trees. They did give Chuck an odd look. By the time they had the blaze under control, he'd woken up and was sitting, trussed and angry, on the ground beside the Blazer.

"Your arsonist," Sam said tersely.

I was keeping close, just in case. Sam looked as though he wouldn't mind taking another shot at the man who had killed his ex-wife.

That comment got the fire chief on the line to the state police. We were told that Detective Holloway was on his way. Hoping to tie things up in a neater bow, I called the Harrison Police Department and requested Detective Walden's presence, too.

It took half the afternoon, but by the time we were done, Chuck was being held for setting the fire and murder charges were pending. It helped that the police had found a rifle in Chuck's truck, which was parked behind the garage. The rifle matched the caliber of weapon used to kill Brian, and they had every hope that the bullets would match as well.

Sam and I dragged ourselves back to Stamford by late afternoon. Faith and the puppies were thriving. Davey and Peg had been to the supermarket and were in the midst of preparing dinner.

I was delighted by the prospect of being waited on for a change, but Sam begged off. He'd been away from home more than a week, he said. It was time he got back up to Redding and started getting his life put back in order.

Until very recently, I'd thought that Sam's life was here with Davey and me. I didn't voice that sentiment aloud, however, and Sam didn't think of it on his own. He and Tar left shortly thereafter.

Aunt Peg looked surprised by Sam's decision, but remained uncharacteristically silent on the subject. Over dinner, she chattered determinedly about all sorts of other things, including her plan for solving the problem of Randy Bowers, the camp bully.

"I've spoken to his mother," she announced. "I'm going to train their dog."

"Aunt Peg, what are you talking about?"

"Randy has a Wheaten Terrier. I've been to see it, and the poor thing is every bit as wild as its owner. It's quite obvious both dog and child have a lack of discipline in their lives. Randy's mother thought the idea of obedience training was simply wonderful."

"What do you mean you've been to see their dog? How did you manage that?"

"I called Mrs. Bowers on the phone. I told her she'd

won a free course at my obedience school for her Wheaten Terrier."

"Aunt Peg, you don't have an obedience school."

She frowned. "Melanie, don't be such a pill."

Pardon me for pointing out the obvious.

"And of course," Aunt Peg continued blithely, "one can't train a dog without training its owner. I'm starting the lessons Monday at the Bowers's house, and I suspect we'll be seeing a change in young Randy's deportment very shortly."

One problem solved. At that point, I was savoring any victories I could get.

Because although I'd managed to figure out who killed Sheila and Brian, it didn't feel as though I'd gained very much. By the end of the week, the dog show grapevine was buzzing with the news that *Woof!* was ceasing publication. The magazine hadn't been on the verge of bankruptcy as Marlon had predicted, but the loss of both copublishers proved to be an insurmountable blow.

The issue that would have carried Alida Trent's story never made it into print, so whether or not Aubrey would have killed the article became a moot point. Last I heard, Aubrey had moved on to bigger and better things by joining the staff of the American Kennel Club. I hoped they never made her a rep because if I saw her at a dog show, I was planning to run the other way.

Sam was in for a shock when Brian's will was read. It turned out that his old friend had bequeathed to him all rights, royalties, and revenues associated with the video game, Island of Mutant Terror. At least lottery winners know they've bought a ticket. Sam had had no way to prepare for this.

His first thought was to decline the bequest. His second:

to give the whole thing to charity. Brian's lawyer, perhaps seeing Sam as a new and potentially wealthy client, counseled him to think carefully about both decisions.

"There's no reason to be hasty," he said. "Sit on the decision. Take six months off. Let the rest of your life get back to normal, and then see how you feel."

Unfortunately for me, Sam took the man's advice to heart. He came to see me one sunny summer afternoon and blew my world to pieces.

"I need to get away," Sam said. "It isn't you, it's everything else. I just have to be alone for a while. Now more than ever, I need to figure out what the rest of my life is going to be about."

I sat beside him, looked into his eyes, and gave no indication that my heart was shearing in half.

"It won't be forever," said Sam. "I'll be back, I promise."

"I love you," I said. I knew the words weren't enough to hold him. Still, I couldn't keep myself from saying them.

"I love you, too. And I love Davey. You're my family, and this doesn't change that."

But it did, of course, whether Sam wanted to see it or not. Holding my breath, holding back tears, I watched the man of my dreams walk out of my life.

Later, I made up a story for Davey about a journey Sam needed to take, a trip that he'd be returning from soon. There was nothing I could do for my son but put the best spin on the situation and hope to hell that I wasn't lying.

My days were full; Aunt Peg and Davey and six, adorable, chubby black puppies saw to that. Little by little, the emptiness that had at first seemed all encompassing, began to recede. I still ached; I still grieved; but I found I was able to remember the good times, too.

I thought about a man who'd loved two women and left them both. And I wondered if one day his heart would bring him back.

Please turn the page for
an exciting sneak peek at
Lauren Berenson's
ONCE BITTEN
Now on sale!

For years I've resisted carrying a cell phone. Even now I do so only grudgingly, and mostly for the sake of security. But I have to admit there are times when having instant access to the rest of the world comes in very handy.

Back in the car, I dialed up Frank, told him I was only about twenty minutes away, and asked if he still had custody of my missing relatives.

"Sure do." He sounded happy enough about the arrangement. "Want to talk to them?"

Without waiting for an answer, my brother put Bob on. "It's about time you tracked us down," he said. "Didn't you find my note?"

"Yes, that's why I'm calling "

"Come on over. The game's great. So's the pizza."

With incentives like those, who could resist?

"And your Aunt Peg is on her way."

That got my attention. "Why?"

"Who knows?" Bob asked blithely. "Peg dances to her

own tune. I think this whole wedding thing is making her nervous."

Not Aunt Peg. Solving murders didn't make her nervous. Whelping premature puppies didn't make her nervous. Showing at Westminster didn't make her nervous. I doubted that something as simple as a family wedding could give her the jitters.

"I'm on my way," I said. "Do I need to stop and pick anything up?"

Bob repeated the question to the others and came back with a shopping list that included beer, bean dip and duct tape. Something about an indoor football toss gone awry.

The twenty minutes expanded to forty-five. By the time I reached Frank's apartment in Cos Cob, Aunt Peg's minivan was already parked on the street out front.

Frank lives on the first floor of a remodeled Victorian house. What was originally a large one-family home now holds three smaller apartments, with the house's elderly owner living upstairs. Being young and spry and usually short of cash, my brother pays for part of his rent by doing chores mowing the lawn, painting, and carrying porch furniture up and down from the basement as the seasons change.

Once he and Bertie were married, however, Frank would be moving to her place in Wilton. There was no way she could bring the kennel-full of dogs that comprised her livelihood here.

"Hey, good to see you!" Frank opened the door, threw an arm around my shoulder, and pulled me close for a hug.

The spontaneous gesture of affection felt good. And I was in no position to take such things for granted. Not too long ago, my brother and I seemed to be continually at loggerheads. Our parents had died eight years earlier, and though we'd both been nominal adults by then, I'd found myself having to step into the role of responsible big sister all too often as Frank wandered aimlessly from one escapade to the next.

Recently, however, everything had changed. Frank had opened his own business, finally finding something he was good at and could actually make a living doing. And Bertie had come into his life.

What had happened next was a revelation. My little brother was in love: joyously, dizzily, head over heels in love. Watching him tumble for the statuesque redhead had been delightful; seeing him now try to live up to the good qualities she saw in him, an unexpected pleasure.

Though I'd been the one to introduce them, I'd never expected them to form a permanent bond. Never had I been so pleased to be taken by surprise.

Frank used the arm he had around my shoulder to pull me inside, grocery bags bumping against my legs as he nudged the door shut behind us.

"Nacho chips!" Davey cried, eyeing the bags greedily.

"Hello to you, too." I leaned down and swiped a kiss across my son's forehead, earning myself a glare filled with all the injured dignity a seven-year-old boy could muster.

Bob and Davey were sitting on the couch facing the TV. Aunt Peg had commandeered the only chair in the room, and it, too, was angled to face the screen.

Eve was snuggled in Davey's lap, but Faith had gotten up to greet me at the door. I reached down to stroke the soft skin beneath the Poodle's chin. She was probably happier than my relatives were to see me. Never let anyone tell you that dogs aren't a blessing.

I shifted the bags to one hand so I could give Faith a better scratch. "Aunt Peg, I didn't know you liked football."

"Let's just say I'm flexible. When in Rome . . ."

Which begged the question of what she was doing in Rome. Or in Cos Cob, as the case may be.

"Let me just put this stuff away," I said, heading for the kitchen. "I'll be right back."

The phone rang as I was pouring the bean dip into a bowl. I picked up and found myself talking to Bertie, calling to check in with Frank before she left a dog show in New Jersey for the two-hour ride home. Most people have weekends off. Not professional handlers. That's when they do the majority of their work.

"Melanie, good," she said, when she realized who she had on the line. "I needed to talk to you anyway. Have you found out anything about Sara?"

"Not much." I gave her a quick run-through of the day's events. "But I did come up with a couple of odd things. First of all, Titus."

"What about him?"

"Remember those big bowls of food and water we saw in Sara's cottage? Apparently they were meant for him. Sara left the dog behind and it looks as though that stuff was supposed to tide him over."

"That makes no sense. Titus went everywhere with Sara. If she had left of her own accord, she'd have taken him with her. And if she didn't, when did she have the chance to fill those bowls?"

"The whole thing is pretty strange," I said. "According

to Delilah, someone from her kennel found Titus wandering around the grounds at the beginning of the week."

"And she still didn't think that meant something was wrong?" Bertie sounded outraged.

"Apparently not. Delilah said that Sara makes a habit of running when life gets tough." Leaning against the counter, I fished a chip out of the bag and ran it through the dip. "Which leads me to my next point. Everyone I've spoken to has mentioned that Sara goes through a lot of boyfriends. That once she gets a guy, she loses interest pretty quickly. I'm wondering if she might have dumped someone who took things a little too personally."

"It's possible," Bertie mused. "But since we don't know who she was seeing . . ."

"You said she was with your cousin Josh last summer."

"Right."

"I was thinking I ought to talk to him. He might know who was next in line, and from there I could trace things up to the present."

"It's worth a try," Bertie agreed. "Let me call Josh and I'll have him get back to you."

"Great. Last thing: Debra Silver said that Sara was trying to get a referral for a lawyer. Do you have any idea what that was about?"

"A lawyer?" Bertie sounded surprised. "No. None. Grant's a lawyer. At least he used to be. I don't think he practices anymore, but if she'd had a problem, I would think Sara would have talked to him."

"According to Debra, she was looking for outside help. Not that it looks as though she found any. Do you think Sara might have run away because she felt threatened by someone?"

"I wish I knew. At least if she ran away, it means she's okay. But if that's the case, why hasn't she called anyone? Her note said she'd be in touch."

"It also said that you weren't supposed to believe everything you heard about her," I pointed out.

"So what have we heard?" Bertie sounded frustrated. "Hardly anything we didn't know already. This whole mess is driving me crazy, Melanie, and time is passing. This wedding's going to happen in some shape or form whether I'm ready or not. Do you suppose you could do me a favor?"

"Probably." When it comes to my family, I never commit without first hearing what's involved.

"Would you possibly have time to stop by a place called Pansy's Flowers? It's in Stamford, so it shouldn't be too far out of your way. Sara told me she thought they'd be the best place for what I wanted. She'd already contacted them about the kinds of bouquets and arrangements we'd need, and they were going to get back to her with prices. Of course, now I'm sure they're wondering whatever happened to us. Could you pick up a price list and let them know that we're still interested in their services?"

"Sure." That didn't sound too hard. "I can probably do it Monday after school."

"Thanks. You're such a help. That makes one less thing to worry about. Is Frank around?"

"Watching football in the other room. I'll go get him."

While Frank talked to Bertie, I grabbed a few moments alone with Aunt Peg. Like Bertie, she wanted to know how things were progressing. "There's something that occurred to me after we spoke yesterday," she said. "That note that Sara left for Bertie didn't make a whole lot of sense."

I nodded and snagged another nacho chip. After a moment, Aunt Peg followed suit.

"Sara said she thought she could count on Bertie, which, under the circumstances, seems backwards. Count on Bertie to do what? Sara was the one who was supposed to be helping Bertie, not the other way around."

"I know."

"Maybe she meant that as kind of a nudge. Maybe Delilah is right and Sara did run away. For whatever reason, she couldn't take Titus with her, but she was hoping Bertie would go to her house and find him."

"Why?"

Aunt Peg aimed a withering look in my direction. "Am I supposed to know everything?"

"Why not? It would certainly make my life easier."

She slid another chip through the bean dip. "All I'm trying to do is broaden your thinking."

"Aunt Peg, I don't need any more questions."

"Maybe you do. Maybe you're not asking the right questions, have you ever thought of that?"

Always.

But that was going to have to be tomorrow's problem. Now I was tired of tracking down answers that only seemed to lead to more puzzles. It was Saturday night, and I was declaring myself off-duty. I popped the top on a can of beer, picked up the chips and dip, and went out to the living room to join my family.

The next morning I was planning to sleep late. I was determined to sleep late. Come on, it was Sunday. My last chance for a whole week.

The telephone woke me up just before seven.

I heard the ringing in my sleep. For an addled moment, it seemed to be part of my dream. Then the dream vanished and I thought I'd set my alarm by mistake. By the third ring, after swatting the clock to no avail, I had one eye open and Eve was dancing on the bed.

I groaned, rolled over, and picked up the receiver.

"Hi, Mel, it's me."

Bob? What could he possibly want at this hour? He'd been up just as late as I had the night before; our family gathering lasting through an impromptu dinner, followed by a killer game of team scrabble that had my ex and my aunt at each other's throats. Not that this was anything new.

Davey had been asleep on the couch by the time I'd loaded the two Poodles in the Volvo for the trip home. Bob had picked up his son and carried him outside, laying him gently on the back seat and tucking his jacket snugly around the small sleeping form.

When I'd thanked him for his help, Bob had offered to accompany me home. If I wanted.

It wasn't hard to see that he'd been disappointed when I shook my head. Now, a scant eight hours later, here he was again. If he said something suggestive about my being in bed, I was going to hang up on him.

"You there, Mel?" Bob asked. "Are you awake?"

"Not really." I hiked myself up on one elbow and debated how many seconds I could afford to waste before Eve lost control of her small puppy bladder on my comforter.

"You haven't seen today's paper?"

"Until the phone rang, Bob, today hadn't even started for me yet. Damn! Wait! Wait! Hold on!"

Dashing from side to side across the bed, Eve had that frantic look puppies get when they sense that a mistake is about to become inevitable. I threw back the covers, scooped her up, ran downstairs, and put her out the back door. Looking vastly relieved, the Poodle squatted at the bottom of the steps.

I hurried over to the counter and picked up the phone. "Still there?"

"I'm here." Bob didn't sound happy. "What the hell happened? Is everything okay? Do you need me to come over?"

"Everything's fine," I assured him. Awakened by our hasty descent, Faith came trotting into the kitchen. I opened the door again and she joined Eve in the backyard. "Eve needed to go outside. She's still a baby and her housebreaking isn't perfect yet."

"Thank God." Bob exhaled. "I thought something was really wrong."

Waiting for the Poodles to finish outside, I pulled out a kitchen chair and sat. "Why would you think that?"

"There's a story on the front page of today's newspaper. You know that woman you and Bertie have been looking for? She seems to have turned up dead."

* * *

Shock bounced me up off the chair. Carrying the phone, I ran out to the front hall. "Bob, what are you talking about? What newspaper are you looking at? How did you know about Sara?"

Cradling the receiver between cheek and shoulder, I fumbled with the lock on the front door.

"It's called . . ." Pages flipped. "The *Greenwich Time*.

Frank gets it delivered. It was outside the door this morning."

As if I cared where he'd gotten the paper from. Details! I wanted details.

The dead bolt slid free. I yanked open the door and ran outside. Frigid November air knifed right through my flannel pajamas. Bare feet freezing, I hopped from one to the other on the concrete step and scanned the yard. My paper boy has an erratic arm. Some mornings we're lucky he doesn't break a window.

The Sunday newspaper, rolled up in its plastic sack, was out by the sidewalk. I didn't get the same paper as Frank, but if there was a story, the *Advocate* would have it, too. Still carrying the phone, I skipped down the steps and ran across the dry winter grass. Good thing it hadn't snowed recently.

"Bertie's been talking about Sara all week," Bob was saying. "Frank filled me in on the details. Anyway, it looks like there was a house fire last night. Do you want me to read you the story?"

"No." I reached down, grabbed the paper, and raced back inside. I could only hope it was early enough on a Sunday morning that none of my neighbors had been watching. There are days when it seems like the show going on at my house is better than cable. "In a minute, I'll have it here. House fire? What house fire? Where was Sara?"

"New Canaan, it says. Some big estate."

Shivering, I shut the front door behind me and ran back to the kitchen, where the Poodles were now waiting outside that door. The Three Stooges probably deal with crisis better.

"You mean that whole huge house burned down?"

"No, not the big place. A guest cottage."

I yanked open the back door. The two dogs raced up the stairs, happily anticipating their peanut butter biscuits. What choice did I have but to go to the pantry? On top of that, my feet were still freezing. At this rate, I'd never get the paper opened.

"The cottage burned down?"

"Almost a complete loss. According to the article, it wasn't wired to any sort of smoke detection system, and nobody noticed the flames right away. By the time the fire department arrived, the place was already engulfed. The roof caved in as the first fire trucks were arriving. They never even had a chance to go inside. All they could do at that point was put the fire out."

"But Sara?" Now my teeth were chattering. Delayed reaction, probably. "What does it say about Sara?"

I heard the sound of more pages being turned, as I pulled a couple of large dog biscuits out of the box.

"Here it is." Bob skimmed through the details. "Charred remains discovered by a closet in the bedroom . . . no immediate identification possible . . . medical examiner believes it to be the body of a young woman.

"But listen to this. Here's how it ends.

> *Resident of the cottage, Sara Bentley, could not be reached for comment. According to her parents, on whose estate the house is located, Ms. Bentley's whereabouts are unknown."*

"Damn," I said, sinking down into a chair.

All at once, I was simply too heavy, too filled with the weight of the bad news, to stand. Despite Bertie's fears,

I'd held onto the hope that Sara would turn up. Now it looked as though I'd been wrong.

"Mel, are you there?"

"I'm here," I sighed.

"Don't go anywhere. I'm coming over."

It was surely a sign of how deflated I felt that I didn't even have the energy to argue. Instead, I called Aunt Peg. She's an early riser. I wondered if she'd gotten around to opening up her paper yet.

While the phone rang, I slid the plastic sleeve off my copy of the *Stamford Advocate* and spread the newspaper out on the kitchen table. There isn't a lot of crime in lower Fairfield County. Like the Greenwich paper, the *Advocate* had carried the New Canaan fire as front-page news.

I was scanning the article when Aunt Peg picked up on the fifth ring. It didn't contain any more facts than Frank had already given me.

"Melanie!" Aunt Peg sounded out of breath. "What's the matter?"

Despite the fact that I had other things to worry about, I was still piqued. "How did you know it was me?"

"Nobody calls at seven A.M. unless there's a problem." Her inference was clear: obviously nobody had as many problems as I did.

"I guess you haven't looked at today's paper yet."

"It's still out by the mailbox. Shall I go get it?"

"No, I can read you what's in front of me. Sara Bentley's cottage burned to the ground last night and the body of a young woman was found inside."

"Sara?" Peg gasped.

"It says that the body was badly burned and the police haven't been able to make an identification yet. They're seeking dental records from the owner of the cottage."

"Poor Delilah," Peg said softly. "I'll have to call her and see if there's anything I can do. Have you spoken to Bertie?"

"No, she's showing this weekend. I'm sure she left hours ago. I'll talk to her tonight. I wonder . . ." I stared down at the paper, drumming my fingers on the page.

"What?"

"Where had Sara been for the last week and why did she suddenly decide to come back? And why on the night that the cottage burned down?"

"Maybe she had something to do with the fire," said Peg, voicing my thoughts aloud. "Does it say what started it?"

"No." I read the official wording. "Cause of the blaze has yet to be determined. That could mean anything."

"Including that the fire marshall knows what happened but they just haven't released their findings yet." Aunt Peg paused. "Here's a gruesome thought."

"What?"

"What if Sara didn't return to her cottage last night? What if she's been dead since she disappeared and the murderer brought her body back?"

"Oh, Lord." It was definitely too early in the morning for me to deal with possibilities like that.